Praise for *Turtles All the Way Down*

"A thoughtful look at mental illness and a debilitating obsessive-compulsive disorder that doesn't ask but *makes* you feel the constant struggles of its main character.... Green expertly communicates the confusion and pain of Aza's invasive thoughts, the way they spin out of control and their inescapable hold on her. But there's also a neat depth to the way *Turtles* explores the definition of happy endings, whether love is a tragedy or a failure, and a universal lesson for us all: 'You work with what you have.'" —*USA Today*

"An existential teenage scream.... Aza's story accordingly feels real, and exhausting, and authentic." —Vox

"Compassionate and compelling."
—*Southern Living*, Best Books of the Year

"Each year, more young people are diagnosed with anxiety, depression and other mental health disorders. Having someone like Green speaking so publicly and writing so well about these problems is a real gift." —*Chicago Tribune*

"Green does more than write about; he endeavours to write inside, making explicit attempts to describe the non-sensorial and inexplicable nature of the spiral. He brings readers on the terrifying slide down with Aza, to a place even scarier than rock bottom because it's both unknowable and undefinable... John Green hasn't created a book as much as he's created a place—a place to have your most indefinable and grotesque thoughts articulated, to ponder the disconnected reality you experience when you can't actually remember how you got to school or work, to acknowledge the times when your body feels like a disgusting cage, even as it does the vital work to keep you alive. No matter where you are on the spiral—and we're all somewhere—Green's novel makes the trip, either up or down, a less solitary experience." —*Globe and Mail*

"A powerful tale for teens (and adults) about anxiety, love and friendship." —*Los Angeles Times*

"A new modern classic." —*Guardian*

"[Green's] descriptions are visceral, emotional, and difficult to read at times, because they are raw and unflinching in the face of the realities of mental illness. *Turtles* is a moving treatise on the many ways mental health can affect our lives, and a loving reminder that it's possible to have a happy, successful life with mental illness." —Bustle

"John Green novels are filled with quiet moments that tap into the universal feelings that both young and older readers alike experience: navigating friendships, fear of loss, the magic of falling in love. Those quintessential John Green moments are still featured in *Turtles*, but now John Green takes those meditations and turns them inward. Aza is not striving to find and love someone else. She's striving to find and love herself.... Even during its most painful moments, there is tenderness that radiates out of *Turtles All the Way Down*.... *Turtles* delivers a lesson that we so desperately need right now: Yes, it is okay not to be okay." —Mashable

"Funny, clever, and populated with endearing characters."

—*Entertainment Weekly*

"An unflinching look at mental illness." —*Seattle Times*

"With *Turtles All the Way Down*, John Green has crafted a dynamic novel that is deeply honest, sometimes painful, and always thoughtful, delivered with the characteristic charm the author is known for. . . . Many adults reading it will find themselves wishing they'd had a book like this as a kid."

—AV Club, Best Books of the Year

★ "Superb. . . . Green, a master of deeply felt material, handles all of this with aplomb. With its attention to ideas and trademark introspection, it's a challenging but richly rewarding read."

—*Booklist*

★ "[A] heartbreaker, full of intelligent questions. It's also a very writerly book, as Aza frames a lot of the questions she asks herself in literary terms. Am I a fiction? Who is in charge of my story? Why do we describe pain with the language of metaphor? . . . In an age where troubling events happen almost weekly, this deeply empathetic novel about learning to live with demons and love one's imperfect self is timely and important." —*Publishers Weekly*

★ "[Aza's] tough, brutally honest first-person narrative will leave teens battered and raw but will also show them that, with love, everything is possible. . . . A deeply resonant and powerful novel that will inform and enlighten readers even as it breaks their hearts. A must-buy." —*SLJ*

ALSO BY JOHN GREEN:

Looking for Alaska

An Abundance of Katherines

Paper Towns

Will Grayson, Will Grayson
WITH DAVID LEVITHAN

The Fault in Our Stars

TURTLES ALL THE WAY DOWN

TURTLES ALL THE WAY DOWN

JOHN GREEN

PENGUIN BOOKS

PENGUIN BOOKS
An imprint of Penguin Random House LLC, New York

First published in the United States of America by Dutton Books,
an imprint of Penguin Random House LLC, 2017
Published by Penguin Books, an imprint of Penguin Random House LLC, 2019

Visit us online at penguinrandomhouse.com

CIP Data is available

Penguin Books ISBN 9780525555377

Printed in the United States of America

Edited by Julie Strauss-Gabel
Design by Anna Booth
Text set in Adobe Caslon Pro

20th Printing

To Henry and Alice

Man can do what he wills,
but he cannot will what he wills.

—ARTHUR SCHOPENHAUER

ONE

AT THE TIME I FIRST REALIZED I might be fictional, my weekdays were spent at a publicly funded institution on the north side of Indianapolis called White River High School, where I was required to eat lunch at a particular time—between 12:37 P.M. and 1:14 P.M.—by forces so much larger than myself that I couldn't even begin to identify them. If those forces had given me a different lunch period, or if the tablemates who helped author my fate had chosen a different topic of conversation that September day, I would've met a different end—or at least a different middle. But I was beginning to learn that your life is a story told about you, not one that you tell.

Of course, you pretend to be the author. You have to. You

think, *I now choose to go to lunch*, when that monotone beep rings from on high at 12:37. But really, the bell decides. You think you're the painter, but you're the canvas.

Hundreds of voices were shouting over one another in the cafeteria, so that the conversation became mere sound, the rushing of a river over rocks. And as I sat beneath fluorescent cylinders spewing aggressively artificial light, I thought about how we all believed ourselves to be the hero of some personal epic, when in fact we were basically identical organisms colonizing a vast and windowless room that smelled of Lysol and lard.

I was eating a peanut butter and honey sandwich and drinking a Dr Pepper. To be honest, I find the whole process of masticating plants and animals and then shoving them down my esophagus kind of disgusting, so I was trying not to think about the fact that I was eating, which is a form of thinking about it.

Across the table from me, Mychal Turner was scribbling in a yellow-paper notebook. Our lunch table was like a long-running play on Broadway: The cast changed over the years, but the roles never did. Mychal was The Artsy One. He was talking with Daisy Ramirez, who'd played the role of my Best and Most Fearless Friend since elementary school, but I couldn't follow their conversation over the noise of all the others.

What was my part in this play? The Sidekick. I was

Daisy's Friend, or Ms. Holmes's Daughter. I was somebody's something.

I felt my stomach begin to work on the sandwich, and even over everybody's talking, I could *hear* it digesting, all the bacteria chewing the slime of peanut butter—the students inside of me eating at my internal cafeteria. A shiver convulsed through me.

"Didn't you go to camp with him?" Daisy asked me.

"With who?"

"Davis Pickett," she said.

"Yeah," I said. "Why?"

"Aren't you listening?" Daisy asked. *I am listening*, I thought, *to the cacophony of my digestive tract*. Of course I'd long known that I was playing host to a massive collection of parasitic organisms, but I didn't much like being reminded of it. By cell count, humans are approximately 50 percent microbial, meaning that about half of the cells that make you up are not yours at all. There are something like a thousand times more microbes living in my particular biome than there are human beings on earth, and it often seems like I can *feel* them living and breeding and dying in and on me. I wiped my sweaty palms on my jeans and tried to control my breathing. Admittedly, I have some anxiety problems, but I would argue it isn't irrational to be concerned about the fact that you are a skin-encased bacterial colony.

Mychal said, "His dad was about to be arrested for bribery

or something, but the night before the raid he disappeared. There's a hundred-thousand-dollar reward out for him."

"And you know his kid," Daisy said.

"*Knew* him," I answered.

I watched Daisy attack her school-provided rectangular pizza and green beans with a fork. She kept glancing up at me, her eyes widening as if to say, *Well?* I could tell she wanted me to ask her about something, but I couldn't tell what, because my stomach wouldn't shut up, which was forcing me deep inside a worry that I'd somehow contracted a parasitic infection.

I could half hear Mychal telling Daisy about his new art project, in which he was using Photoshop to average the faces of a hundred people named Mychal, and the average of their faces would be this new, one-hundred-and-first Mychal, which was an interesting idea, and I wanted to listen, but the cafeteria was so loud, and I couldn't stop wondering whether there was something wrong with the microbial balance of power inside me.

Excessive abdominal noise is an uncommon, but not unprecedented, presenting symptom of infection with the bacteria *Clostridium difficile*, which can be fatal. I pulled out my phone and searched "human microbiome" to reread Wikipedia's introduction to the trillions of microorganisms currently inside me. I clicked over to the article about *C. diff*, scrolling to the part about how most *C. diff* infections occur in hospitals. I scrolled down farther to a list of symptoms, none of which I had, except for the excessive abdominal noises, although I knew from previous searches that the Cleveland Clinic had reported the case of one person who'd died of *C. diff* after presenting at the hospital with only abdominal pain and fever. I reminded myself that I didn't have a fever, and my self replied: *You don't have a fever YET*.

At the cafeteria, where a shrinking slice of my consciousness still resided, Daisy was telling Mychal that his averaging project shouldn't be about people named Mychal but about imprisoned men who'd later been exonerated. "It'll be easier, anyway," she said, "because they all have mug shots taken from the same angle, and then it's not just about names but about race and class and mass incarceration," and Mychal was like, "You're a genius, Daisy," and she said, "You sound surprised," and meanwhile I was thinking that if half the cells inside of you are not you, doesn't that challenge the whole notion of *me* as a singular pronoun, let alone as the author of my fate? And I fell pretty far down that recursive wormhole until it transported me completely out of the White River High School cafeteria into some non-sensorial place only properly crazy people get to visit.

Ever since I was little, I've pressed my right thumbnail into the finger pad of my middle finger, and so now there's this weird callus over my fingerprint. After so many years of doing this, I can open up a crack in the skin really easily, so I cover it up with a Band-Aid to try to prevent infection. But sometimes I get worried that there already is an infection, and so I need to drain it, and the only way to do that is to reopen the wound and press out any blood that will come. Once I start thinking about splitting the skin apart, I literally cannot not do it. I apologize for the double negative, but it's a real double negative of a situation, a bind from which negating the negation is truly the only escape. So anyway, I started to want to feel my thumbnail biting into the skin of my finger pad, and I knew that resistance was more or less futile, so beneath the cafeteria table, I slipped the Band-Aid off my finger and dug my thumbnail into the callused skin until I felt the crack open.

"Holmesy," Daisy said. I looked up at her. "We're almost through lunch and you haven't even mentioned my hair." She shook out her hair, with so-red-they-were-pink highlights. Right. She'd dyed her hair.

I swum up out of the depths and said, "It's bold."

"I know, right? It says, 'Ladies and gentlemen and also people who do not identify as ladies or gentlemen, Daisy Ramirez won't break her promises, but she will break your heart.'" Daisy's self-proclaimed life motto was "Break Hearts, Not Promises." She kept threatening to get it tattooed on her ankle when she turned eighteen. Daisy turned back to Mychal, and I to my thoughts. The stomach grumbling had grown, if anything, louder. I felt like I might vomit. For someone who actively dislikes bodily fluids, I throw up quite a lot.

"Holmesy, you okay?" Daisy asked. I nodded. Sometimes I wondered why she liked me, or at least tolerated me. Why any of them did. Even I found myself annoying.

I could feel sweat sprouting from my forehead, and once I begin to sweat, it's impossible to stop. I'll keep sweating for hours, and not just my face or my armpits. My neck sweats. My boobs sweat. My calves sweat. Maybe I did have a fever.

Beneath the table, I slid the old Band-Aid into my pocket and, without looking, pulled out a new one, unwrapped it, and then glanced down to apply it to my finger. All the while, I was breathing in through my nose and out through my mouth, in the manner advised by Dr. Karen Singh, exhaling at a pace "that would make a candle flicker but not go out. Imagine that candle, Aza, flickering from your breath but still there, always there." So I tried that, but the thought spiral kept tightening anyway. I could hear Dr. Singh saying I shouldn't get out my phone, that I mustn't look up the same questions over and over, but I got it out anyway, and reread the "Human Microbiota" Wikipedia article.

The thing about a spiral is, if you follow it inward, it never actually ends. It just keeps tightening, infinitely.

I sealed the Ziploc bag around the last quarter of my sandwich, got up, and tossed it into an overfilled trash can. I heard a voice from behind me. "How concerned should I be that you haven't said more than two words in a row all day?"

"Thought spiral," I mumbled in reply. Daisy had known me since we were six, long enough to get it.

"I figured. Sorry, man. Let's hang out today."

This girl Molly walked up to us, smiling, and said, "Uh, Daisy, just FYI, your Kool-Aid dye job is staining your shirt."

Daisy looked down at her shoulders, and indeed, her striped top had turned pink in spots. She flinched for a second, then straightened her spine. "Yeah, it's part of the look, Molly. Stained shirts are huge in Paris right now." She turned away from Molly and said, "Right, so we'll go to your house and watch *Star Wars: Rebels*." Daisy was really into Star Wars—and not just the movies, but also the books and the animated shows and the kids' show where they're all made out of Lego. Like, she wrote fan fiction about Chewbacca's love life. "And we will improve your mood until you are able to say three or even four words in a row; sound good?"

"Sounds good."

"And then you can take me to work. Sorry, but I need a ride."

"Okay." I wanted to say more, but the thoughts kept coming, unbidden and unwanted. If I'd been the author, I would've stopped thinking about my microbiome. I would've told Daisy how much I liked her idea for Mychal's art project, and I would've told her that I did remember Davis Pickett, that I remembered being eleven and carrying a vague but constant fear. I would've told her that I remembered once at camp lying next to Davis on the edge of a dock, our legs dangling over, our backs against the rough-hewn planks of wood, staring together up at a cloudless summer sky. I would've told her that Davis and I never talked much, or even looked at each other, but it didn't matter, because we were looking at the same sky together, which is maybe more intimate than eye contact anyway. Anybody can look at you. It's quite rare to find someone who sees the same world you see.

TWO

THE FEAR HAD MOSTLY SWEATED OUT OF ME, but as I walked from the cafeteria to history class, I couldn't stop myself from taking out my phone and rereading the horror story that is the "Human Microbiota" Wikipedia article. I was reading and walking when I heard my mother shout at me through her open classroom door. She was seated behind her metal desk, leaning over a book. Mom was a math teacher, but reading was her great love.

"No phones in the hallway, Aza!" I put my phone away and went into her classroom. There were four minutes remaining in my lunch period, which was the perfect length for a Mom conversation. She looked up and must've seen something in my eyes. "You okay?"

"Yeah," I said.

"You're not anxious?" she asked. At some point, Dr. Singh had told Mom not to ask if I was feeling anxious, so she'd stopped phrasing it as a direct question.

"I'm fine."

"You've been taking your meds," she said. Again, not a direct question.

"Yeah," I said, which was broadly true. I'd had a bit of a crack-up my freshman year, after which I was prescribed a circular white pill to be taken once daily. I took it, on average, maybe thrice weekly.

"You look . . ." *Sweaty*, is what I knew she meant.

"Who decides when the bells ring?" I asked. "Like, the school bells?"

"You know what, I have no idea. I suppose that's decided by someone on the superintendent's staff."

"Like, why are lunch periods thirty-seven minutes long instead of fifty? Or twenty-two? Or whatever?"

"Your brain seems like a very intense place," Mom answered.

"It's just weird, how this is decided by someone I don't know and then I have to live by it. Like, I live on someone else's schedule. And I've never even met them."

"Yes, well, in that respect and many others, American high schools do rather resemble prisons."

My eyes widened. "Oh my God, Mom, you're so right. The metal detectors. The cinder-block walls."

"They're both overcrowded and underfunded," Mom

said. "And both have bells that ring to tell you when to move."

"And you don't get to choose when you eat lunch," I said. "And prisons have power-thirsty, corrupt guards, just like schools have teachers."

She shot me a look, but then started laughing. "You headed straight home after school?"

"Yeah, then I gotta take Daisy to work."

Mom nodded. "Sometimes I miss you being a little kid, but then I remember Chuck E. Cheese."

"She's just trying to save money for college."

My mom glanced back down at her book. "You know, if we lived in Europe, college wouldn't cost much." I braced myself for Mom's cost-of-college rant. "There are free universities in Brazil. Most of Europe. China. But here they want to charge you *twenty-five thousand dollars a year*, for in-state tuition. I just finished paying off my loans a few years ago, and soon we'll have to take out ones for you."

"I'm only a junior. I've got plenty of time to win the lottery. And if that doesn't work out, I'll just pay for school by selling meth."

She smiled wanly. Mom really worried about paying for me to go to school. "You sure you're okay?" she asked.

I nodded as the bell sounded from on high, sending me to history.

By the time I made it to my car after school, Daisy was already in the passenger seat. She'd changed out of the stained shirt she'd been wearing into her red Chuck E. Cheese polo, and was sitting with her backpack in her lap, drinking a container of school milk. Daisy was the only person I'd trusted with a key to Harold. Mom didn't even have her own Harold key, but Daisy did.

"Please do not drink non-clear liquids in Harold," I told her.

"Milk is a clear liquid," she said.

"Lies," I answered, and before we set off, I drove Harold over to the front entrance and waited while Daisy threw away her milk.

Maybe you've been in love. I mean real love, the kind my grandmother used to describe by quoting the apostle Paul's First Letter to the Corinthians, the love that is kind and patient, that does not envy or boast, that beareth all things and believeth all things and endureth all things. I don't like to throw the L-word around; it's too good and rare a feeling to cheapen with overuse. You can live a good life without ever knowing real love, of the Corinthians variety, but I was fortunate to have found it with Harold.

He was a sixteen-year-old Toyota Corolla with a paint color called Mystic Teal Mica and an engine that clanked in a steady rhythm like the beating of his immaculate metallic heart. Harold had been my dad's car—in fact, Dad had named him Harold. Mom never sold him, so he stayed in the garage for eight years, until my sixteenth birthday.

Getting Harold's engine running after so long took all of the four hundred dollars I'd saved over the course of my life—allowances, change ferreted away when Mom sent me down the street to buy something at the Circle K, summer work at Subway, Christmas gifts from my grandparents—so, in a way, Harold was the culmination of my whole being, at least financially speaking. And I loved him. I dreamed about him quite a lot. He had an exceptionally spacious trunk, a custom-installed, huge white steering wheel, and a backseat bench clad in pebble-beige leather. He accelerated with the gentle serenity of the Buddhist Zen master who knows nothing really needs to be done quickly, and his brakes whined like metal machine music, and I loved him.

However, Harold did not have Bluetooth connectivity, or for that matter a CD player, meaning that while in Harold's company, one had three choices: 1. Drive in silence; 2. Listen to the radio; or 3. Listen to Side B of my dad's cassette of Missy Elliott's excellent album *So Addictive*, which—because it would not eject from the cassette player—I'd already heard hundreds of times in my life.

And in the end, Harold's imperfect audio system happened to be the last note in the melody of coincidences that changed my life.

Daisy and I were scanning stations in search of a song by a particular brilliant and underappreciated boy band when we landed upon a news story. "—Indianapolis-based Pickett Engineering, a construction firm employing more than ten thousand people worldwide, today—" I moved my hand toward the scan button, but Daisy pushed it away.

"This is what I was telling you about!" she said as the radio continued, "—one-hundred-thousand-dollar reward for information leading to the whereabouts of company CEO Russell Pickett. Pickett, who disappeared the night before a police raid on his home related to a fraud and bribery investigation, was last seen at his riverside compound on September eighth. Anyone with information regarding his whereabouts is encouraged to call the Indianapolis Police Department."

"A hundred thousand dollars," Daisy said. "And *you know his kid.*"

"Knew," I said. For two summers, after fifth and sixth grades, Davis and I had gone to Sad Camp together, which is what we'd called Camp Spero, this place down in Brown County for kids with dead parents.

Aside from hanging out together at Sad Camp, Davis and I would also sometimes see each other during the school year, because he lived just down the river from me, but on the opposite bank. Mom and I lived on the side that sometimes flooded. The Picketts lived on the side with the stone-gabled walls that forced the rising water in our direction.

"He probably wouldn't even remember me."

"Everyone remembers you, Holmesy," she said.

"That's not—"

"It's not a value judgment. I'm not saying you're good or generous or kind or whatever. I'm just saying you're *memorable*."

"I haven't seen him in years," I said. But of course you don't forget playdates at a mansion that contains a golf course, a pool with an island, and five waterslides. Davis was the closest thing to a proper celebrity I'd ever encountered.

"A hundred thousand dollars," Daisy said again. We pulled onto I-465, the beltway that circumscribes Indianapolis. "I'm fixing Skee-Ball machines for eight forty an hour and there's a hundred grand waiting for us."

"I wouldn't say *waiting for us*. Anyway, I have to read about the effects of smallpox on indigenous populations tonight, so I can't really solve The Case of the Fugitive Billionaire." I eased Harold up to highway speed. I never drove him faster than the speed limit. I loved him too much.

"Well, you know him better than I do, so to quote the infallible boys in the world's greatest pop group, 'You're the One,'" which was this super-cheesy song I was way too old to love, but loved nonetheless.

"I want to disagree with you, but that is such a great song."

"You're. The. One. 'You're the one that I choose. The one I'll never lose. You're my forever. My stars. My sky. My air. It's you.'"

We laughed, and I changed the radio station and thought it was over, but then Daisy started reading me an *Indianapolis Star* story from her phone. "'Russell Pickett, the controversial CEO and founder of Pickett Engineering, wasn't home when a search warrant was served by the Indianapolis police Friday morning, and he hasn't been home since. Pickett's lawyer, Simon Morris, says he has no information about Pickett's whereabouts, and in a press conference today, Detective Dwight Allen said that no activity on Pickett's credit cards or bank accounts has been noted since the evening before the raid.' Blah-blah-blah . . . 'Allen also asserted that aside from a camera at the front gate, there were no surveillance cameras on the property. A copy of a police report obtained by the *Star* says that Pickett was last seen Thursday evening by his sons, Davis and Noah.' Blah-blah-blah . . . 'estate just north of Thirty-Eighth Street, lots of lawsuits, supports the zoo,' blah-blah-blah . . . 'call the police if you know anything,' blah-blah-blah. Wait, how are there no security cameras? What kind of billionaire doesn't have security cameras?"

"The kind who doesn't want his shady business recorded," I said. As we drove, I kept turning the story over in my head. I knew some edge of it was jagged, but I couldn't figure out which one, until I snagged a memory of eerie green coyotes with white eyes. "Wait, there was a camera. Not a security one, but Davis and his brother had a motion-capture camera in the woods by the river. It had, like, night vision, and it would snap a picture whenever something walked past—deer or coyotes or whatever."

"Holmesy," she said. "We have a lead."

"And because of the camera at the front gate, he couldn't have just driven off," I said. "So either he climbs over his own wall, or else he walks through the woods down to the river and leaves from there, right?"

"Yes . . ."

"So he could've tripped that camera. I mean, it's been a few years since I was there; maybe it's gone."

"And maybe it's not!" Daisy said.

"Yeah. Maybe it's not."

"Exit here," she said suddenly, and I did. I knew it was the wrong exit, but I took it anyway, and without Daisy even telling me to, I got in the right lane to drive back into the city, toward my house. Toward Davis's house.

Daisy took out her phone and raised it to her ear. "Hey, Eric. It's Daisy. Listen, I'm really sorry, but I've got the stomach flu. Could be norovirus."

". . ."

"Yeah, no problem. Sorry again." She hung up, put her phone in her bag, and said, "If you even *imply* diarrhea, they tell you to stay home because they're so scared of outbreaks. Right, okay, we're doing this. You still got that canoe?"

THREE

YEARS BEFORE, Mom and I had sometimes paddled down the White River, past Davis's house to the park behind the art museum. We'd beach the canoe and walk around for a bit, then paddle back home against the lazy current. But I hadn't been down to the water in years. The White River is beautiful in the abstract—blue herons and geese and deer and all that stuff—but the actual water itself smells like human sewage. Actually, it doesn't smell *like* human sewage; it smells *of* human sewage, because whenever it rains, the sewers overflow and the collective waste of Central Indiana dumps directly into the river.

We pulled into my driveway. I got out, walked to the garage door, squatted down, wriggled my fingers under the door, and then lifted it up. I got back into the car and parked, while Daisy kept telling me we were going to be rich.

The garage door exertion had gotten me sweating a bit, so when I got inside I headed straight for my room and turned on the window AC unit, sat cross-legged on my bed, and let the cold air blow against my back. My room was a cluttered mess, with dirty clothes everywhere and a spill of papers—worksheets, old tests, college pamphlets Mom brought home—that covered my desk and also sort of spread out along the floor. Daisy stood in the doorway. "You got any clothes around here that would fit me?" she asked. "I feel like you shouldn't meet a billionaire in a Chuck E. Cheese uniform, or in a shirt stained pink by your hair, which are my only outfits at the moment."

Daisy was about my mom's size, so we decided to raid her closet, and as we tried to find the least Momish top and jeans combo available, Daisy talked. She talked a lot. "I've got a theory about uniforms. I think they design them so that you become, like, a nonperson, so that you're not Daisy Ramirez, a Human Being, but instead a thing that brings people pizza and exchanges their tickets for plastic dinosaurs. It's like the uniform is designed to *hide me*."

"Yeah," I said.

"Fucking systemic oppression," Daisy mumbled, and then pulled a hideous purple blouse out of the closet. "Your mom dresses like a ninth-grade math teacher."

"Well, she is a ninth-grade math teacher."

"That's no excuse."

"Maybe a dress?" I held up a calf-length black dress with pink paisleys. Just awful.

"I think I'm gonna roll with the uniform," she said.

"Yeah."

I heard Mom drive up, and even though she wouldn't mind us borrowing clothes, I felt a jolt of nervousness. Daisy saw it and took me by the wrist. We snuck out to the backyard before Mom made it inside, and then picked our way through a little bramble of honeysuckle bushes at the edge of the yard.

It turned out we *did* still have that canoe, overturned and full of dead spiders. Daisy flipped it over, then wrenched the paddles and two once-orange life jackets from the ivy that had grown over them. She swept out the canoe by hand, tossed the paddles and the life jackets into it, and dragged the canoe toward the riverbank. Daisy was short and didn't look fit, but she was super strong.

"The White River is so dirty," I said.

"Holmesy, you're being irrational. Help me with this thing."

I grabbed the back part of the canoe. "It's like fifty percent urine. And that's the good half."

"You're the one," she said again, then heaved the canoe over the riverbank into the water. She jumped down the bank onto a little peninsula of mud, wrapped a too-small life vest around her neck, and climbed into the front of the canoe.

I followed her, settled into the rear seat, and then used the paddle to push us out into the river. It had been a long time since I'd steered a canoe, but the water was low, and the river was so wide I didn't have to do much. Daisy looked back at me and smiled with her mouth closed. Being on the river made me feel little again.

As kids, Daisy and I had played all up and down the riverbank when the water was low like this. We played a game called "river kids," imagining we lived alone on the river, scavenging for our livelihood and hiding from the adults who wanted to put us in an orphanage. I remembered Daisy throwing daddy longlegs at me because she knew I hated them, and I'd scream and run away, flailing my arms but not actually scared, because back then all emotions felt like play, like I was experimenting with feeling rather than stuck with it. True terror isn't being scared; it's not having a choice in the matter.

"You know this river is the only reason Indianapolis even exists?" Daisy said. She turned around in the canoe to face me. "So, like, Indiana had just become a state, and they wanted to build a new city for the state capital, so everybody's debating where it should be. The obvious compromise is to put it in the middle. So these dudes are looking at a map of their new state and they notice there is a river right here, smack in the center of the state, and they're like—boom—perfect place for our capital, because it's 1819 or whatever, and you need water to be a real city for shipping and stuff.

"So they announce, we're gonna build a new city! On a river! And we're gonna be clever and call it Indiana-*polis*! And it's only after they make the announcement that they notice the White River is, like, six inches deep, and you can't float a kayak down it, let alone a steamship. For a while, Indianapolis was the largest city in the world not on a navigable waterway."

"How do you even know that?" I asked.

"My dad's a big history nerd." Right then her phone started ringing. "Holy shit. I just conjured him." She held the phone up to her ear. "Hey, Papa. . . . Um, yeah, of course. . . . No, he won't mind. . . . Cool, yeah, be home at six." She slid her phone back into her pocket and turned around to me, squinting into the sunlight. "He was asking if I could switch shifts to watch Elena because Mom got extra hours, *and* I didn't have to lie about already not being at work, *and* now my dad thinks I care about my sister. Holmesy, everything's working out. Our destiny is coming into focus. We are about to live the American Dream, which is, of course, to benefit from someone else's misfortune."

I laughed, and my laughter seemed freakishly loud as it echoed across the deserted river. On a half-submerged tree near the river's bank, a softshell turtle noticed us and plopped into the water. The river was lousy with turtles.

After the first bend in the river, we passed a shallow island made of millions of white pebbles. A blue heron stood perched on an old bleached tire, and when she saw us she spread her wings and flew away, more pterodactyl than bird. The island forced us into a narrow channel on the east side of the river, and we floated underneath sycamore trees leaning out over the water in search of more sunlight.

Most of the trees were covered in leaves, some streaked with pink in the first hints of autumn. But we passed under one dead tree, leafless but still standing, and I looked up through its branches, which intersected to fracture the cloudless blue sky into all kinds of irregular polygons.

I still have my dad's phone. I keep it and a charging cord hidden in Harold's trunk next to the spare tire. A ton of the pictures on his phone were of leafless branches dividing up the sky, like the view I had as we floated under that sycamore. I always wondered what he saw in that, in the split-apart sky.

Anyway, it really was a beautiful day—golden sunshine bearing down on us with just enough heat. I'm not much of an outside cat, so I rarely have occasion to consider the weather, but in Indianapolis we get eight to ten properly beautiful days a year, and this was one of them. I hardly had to paddle at all as the river bent to the west. The water crinkled with sunlight. A pair of wood ducks noticed us and took off, their wings flapping desperately.

At last, we came to the bit of land that as kids we'd named Pirates Island. It was a real river island, not like the pebble beach we'd paddled past earlier. Pirates Island had thickets of honeysuckle and tall trees with trunks gnarled from the yearly spring floods. Because the river has so much agricultural runoff, there were crops, too: Little tomato and soybean plants sprang up everywhere, well fertilized by all the sewage.

I steered the canoe onto the algae-soaked beach and we got out to walk around. Something about the river had made Daisy and me quiet, almost unaware of each other, and we wandered in different directions.

I'd spent part of my eleventh birthday here. Mom had made a treasure map, and after cake at home, Daisy and Mom and I got into the canoe and paddled down to Pirates Island. We dug with spades at the base of a tree and found a little chest full of chocolate coins wrapped in gold foil. Davis had met us down there, with his little brother, Noah. I remembered digging until my spade hit the plastic of the treasure chest, and allowing myself to feel like it was real treasure, even though I knew it wasn't. I was so good at being a kid, and so terrible at being whatever I was now.

I walked along the whole edge of the island until I found Daisy sitting on an uprooted barkless tree that had beached here as some flood receded. I sat down next to her and looked into the little pool below our feet, where crawfish were darting around. The pool seemed to be shrinking—it had been a drier summer than usual, and hotter.

"Remember that birthday party you had here?" she asked.

"Yeah," I said. At the party, Davis had briefly lost this Iron Man action figure he always had with him. He'd had it for so long that all the decals had been rubbed away; it was just a red torso and yellow limbs. He'd really freaked out when he lost it, I remembered, but then my mom found it.

"You okay, Holmesy?"

"Yeah."

"Can you say anything other than yeah?"

"Yeah," I said, and smiled a little.

We sat for a while, and then stood up together without speaking and waded through the knee-deep water until we got to the river's edge. Why didn't it bother me to slosh through the filthy water of the White River when hours earlier I'd found it intolerable to hear my stomach rumble? I wish I knew.

A chain-link fence held in the boulders that formed the floodwall, and I climbed it, then reached down to help Daisy. We crawled up the riverbank and found ourselves in a forest of sycamore and maple trees. In the distance, I could see the manicured lawns of Pickett's golf course, and beyond that the glass-and-steel Pickett mansion, which had been designed by some famous architect.

We wandered around for a while as I tried to get my bearings, and then I heard Daisy whisper, "*Holmesy*." I picked my way through the woods toward her. She'd found the night-vision camera, mounted to a tree, about four feet off the ground. It was a black circle, maybe an inch in diameter—the kind of thing you'd never notice in a forest unless you knew to look for it.

I opened up my phone and connected to the night-vision camera, which wasn't password protected. In seconds, photos started downloading to my phone. I deleted the first two, which the camera had taken of us, and swiped past a dozen more from the past week—deer and coyotes and raccoons and possums, all of them either daytime shots or green silhouettes with bright white eyes.

"Don't want to alarm you, but there's a golf cart headed in our vague direction," Daisy said quietly. I looked up. The cart was still a ways away. I swiped through more pictures until I got back to September 9th, and there, yes, in shades of green I could see the back of a stocky man wearing a striped nightshirt. Time stamp 1:01:03 A.M. I screenshotted it.

"Dude's definitely spotted us," Daisy said nervously.

I glanced up again and mumbled, "I'm hurrying." I'd swiped to see the previous picture, but it was taking forever to load. I heard Daisy run off, but I stayed, waiting for the photograph. It was odd, for me to be the calm one while feeling Daisy's nerves jangling. But the things that make other people nervous have never scared me. I'm not afraid of men in golf carts or horror movies or roller coasters. I didn't know precisely what I *was* afraid of, but it wasn't this. The image revealed itself in slow motion, one line of pixels at a time. Coyote. I glanced up, saw the man in the golf cart seeing me, and I bolted.

I wove back toward the river, scrambled down the riverbank wall, and found Daisy standing above my overturned canoe, holding a large jagged rock high above her head.

"What the hell are you doing?" I asked.

"Whoever that guy is, he definitely saw you," she said, "so I'm making an excuse for you."

"What?"

"We've got no choice but to damsel-in-distress this situation, Holmesy," she said, and then brought the rock down with all her force onto the hull of the canoe, splintering the green paint and revealing the fiberglass below. She flipped the canoe back over; it immediately started taking on water. "Okay, now I'm gonna hide and you're gonna talk to whoever is coming in that golf cart."

"What? No. No way."

"A distressed damsel has no companions," she said.

"No. Way."

And then a voice called out from atop the gabled wall. "You all right down there?" I looked up and saw a skinny old man with deep lines in his face, wearing a black suit and white shirt.

"Our canoe," Daisy said. "It has a hole in it. We're actually friends with Davis Pickett. Doesn't he live here?"

"I'm Lyle," the man said. "Security. I can get you home."

FOUR

LYLE USHERED US INTO HIS GOLF CART and then drove us down a narrow asphalt path along the golf course, past a big log cabin with a wooden sign out front identifying it as THE COTTAGE.

I hadn't visited the Pickett estate in many years, and it had grown even more majestic. The sand traps of the golf course were newly raked. The cart path we drove on had no cracks or bumps. Newly planted maple trees lined the path. But mostly I just saw endless grass, weedless, freshly mown into a diamond pattern. The Pickett estate was silent, sterile, and endless—like a newly built housing subdivision before actual people move into it. I loved it.

As we drove, Daisy struck up a wholly unsubtle conversation. "So you head up security here?"

"I *am* security here," he answered.

"How long have you worked for Mr. Pickett?"

"Long enough to know you're not friends with Davis," he answered.

Daisy, who lacked the capacity to experience embarrassment, was not discouraged. "Holmesy here is the friend. Were you working the day Pickett disappeared?"

"Mr. Pickett doesn't like staff on the property after dark or before dawn," he answered.

"How many staff are there exactly?"

Lyle stopped the golf cart. "Y'all best know Davis, or else I'm taking you downtown and having you booked for trespassing."

We rounded a corner and I saw the pool complex, a shimmering blue expanse with the same island I remembered from my childhood, except now it was covered by a glass-plated geodesic dome. The waterslides—cylinders that curved and wove around one another—were still there, too, but they were dry.

On a patio beside the pool were a dozen teak lounge chairs, each with a white towel laid out atop the cushions. We drove halfway around the pool to another patio, where Davis Pickett was reclining on a lounger. He was wearing his school polo shirt and khaki pants, holding a book at an angle to block the sun as he read.

When he heard the cart, he sat up and looked over at us.

He had skinny, sunburned legs and knobby knees. He wore plastic-rimmed glasses and an Indiana Pacers hat.

"Aza Holmes?" he asked.

He stood up. The sun was behind him, so I could hardly see his face. I got out of the golf cart and walked over to him.

"Hi," I said. I didn't know if I should hug him, and he didn't seem to know if he should hug me, so we just sort of stood there not touching, which to be honest is my preferred form of greeting.

"To what do I owe the pleasure?" he asked, his voice flat, neutral, unreadable.

Daisy walked up behind me and held out her hand, then shook Davis's forcefully. "Daisy Ramirez, Holmesy's best friend. We had a canoe puncture."

"We hit a rock and landed on Pirates Island," I said.

"You know these people?" Lyle asked.

"Yeah, it's fine, thanks, Lyle. Can I get you guys anything? Water? Dr Pepper?"

"Dr Pepper?" I said, a bit confused.

"Wasn't that your favorite soda?"

I just blinked at him for a second and then said, "Um, yeah. I'll have a Dr Pepper."

"Lyle, can we get three Dr Peppers?"

"Sure thing, boss," Lyle answered, and took off on the golf cart.

Daisy's glance at me said, *I told you he'd remember*, and then she wandered off. Davis didn't seem to notice. There was something sweetly shy about the way he looked at me, glancing at, and then away from, my face, his brown eyes bigger than life through his glasses. His eyes, his nose, his mouth—all his facial features were a bit too big for him, like they'd grown up but his face was still a kid's.

"I'm not sure what to say," he said. "I'm . . . not good at chitchat."

"Try saying what you're thinking," I said. "That's something I never ever do."

He smiled a little and then shrugged. "Okay. I'm thinking, *I wish she wasn't after the reward.*"

"What reward?" I asked, unconvincingly.

Davis sat down on one of the teak loungers, and I sat across from him. He leaned forward, bony elbows on bony knees. "I thought of you a couple weeks ago," he said. "Right when he disappeared, I kept hearing his name on the news, and they would say his full name—Russell Davis Pickett—and I kept thinking, you know, that's my name; and it was just so weird, to hear the newscasters say, 'Russell Davis Pickett has been reported missing.' Because I was right here."

"And that made you think of me?"

"Yeah, I don't know. I remember you telling me—like, I asked about your name once and you said that your mom named you Aza because she wanted you to have your own name, a sound you could make your own."

"It was my dad, actually." I could remember Dad talking

to me about my name, telling me, *It spans the whole alphabet, because we wanted you to know you can be anything.* "Whereas, your dad . . ." I said.

"Right, made me a junior. Resigned me to juniority."

"Well, you're not your name," I said.

"Of course I am. I can't not be Davis Pickett. Can't not be my father's son."

"I guess," I said.

"And I can't not be an orphan."

"I'm sorry."

His tired eyes met mine. "A lot of old friends have been in touch the last few days, and I'm not an idiot. I know why. But I don't know where my dad is."

"The truth is—" I said, and then stopped as a shadow flashed over us. I turned around. Daisy was standing over me.

"The truth is," she said, "we were listening to the radio, heard a news report about your father, and then Holmesy here told me she had a crush on you when you were kids."

"Daisy," I sputtered.

"And I was, like, let's go see him, I bet it's true love. So we arranged for a shipwreck, and then you remembered she likes Dr Pepper, and IT *IS* TRUE LOVE. It's just like *The Tempest*, and okay, I'm going to leave you now so you can live happily ever after." And her shadow was gone, replaced by the golden light of the sun.

"Is that—really?" Davis asked.

"Well, I don't think it's exactly like *The Tempest*," I said. But I couldn't stand to tell him the truth. Anyway, it wasn't a lie. Not all the way. "I mean, we were just kids."

After a minute, he said, "You almost don't even look like the same person."

"What?"

"Like, you were this scrawny little lightning bolt, and now you're . . ."

"What?"

"Different. Grown up." My stomach was kind of churning, but I couldn't tell why. I never understood my body—was it scared or excited?

Davis was looking past me at the stand of trees along the river's edge. "I really am sorry about your dad," I said.

He shrugged. "My dad's a huge shitbag. He skipped town before getting arrested because he's a coward." I didn't know how to answer that. The way people talked about fathers could almost make you glad not to have one. "I really don't know where he is, Aza. And if anyone does know, they're not gonna say anything, because he can pay them a lot more than the reward. I mean, a hundred thousand dollars? A hundred thousand dollars isn't a lot of money." I just stared at him. "Sorry," he said. "That probably sounded dickish."

"Probably?"

"Right, yeah," he said. "I just mean . . . he'll get away with it. He always gets away with it."

I was starting to respond when I heard Daisy return. She

had a guy with her—tall, broad-shouldered, wearing matching khaki shorts and a polo shirt. "We are going to meet a tuatara," Daisy said excitedly.

Davis got up and said, "Aza, this is Malik Moore, our zoologist." He said "our zoologist" as if they were normal words to say in the course of everyday conversation, as if most people who reached a certain standing in life acquired a zoologist.

I stood up and shook Malik's hand. "I take care of the tuatara," he explained. Everyone seemed to assume I knew what the hell a tuatara was. Malik walked over to the edge of the pool, knelt down, lifted a door hidden in the patio's tile, and pressed a button. A reticulated chrome walkway emerged from the pool's edge and arched over the water to reach the island. Daisy grabbed my arm and whispered, "Is this real life?" and then the zoologist waved his hand dramatically, gesturing for us to walk across the bridge.

He followed behind us, across the metal bridge to the geodesic dome. Malik swiped a card near the glass door. I heard a seal break, and then the door opened. I stepped in and was suddenly in a tropical climate at least twenty degrees warmer and considerably more humid than the actual outdoors.

Daisy and I stayed near the entryway while Malik darted around and finally emerged with a large lizard, maybe two feet long and three inches tall. Its dragon-like tail wrapped around Malik's arm.

"You can pet her," Malik said, and Daisy did, but I could

see scratch marks on Malik's hand indicating that it didn't always like being petted, so when he turned it toward me, I said, "I don't really like lizards."

He then explained to me in rather excruciating detail that Tua (it had a name) was not a lizard at all, but a genetically distinct creature that dated back to the Mesozoic Era 200 million years ago, and that it was basically a living dinosaur, and that tuatara can live to be at least 150 years old, and that the plural of tuatara is tuatara, and that they are the only extant species from the order Rhynchocephalia, and that they were endangered in their native New Zealand, and that he'd written his PhD thesis on tuatara molecular evolution rates, and on and on until the door opened again, and Lyle said, "Dr Peppers, boss." I took them and handed one to Davis and one to Daisy.

"You sure you don't want to pet her?" Malik asked.

"I'm also afraid of dinosaurs," I explained.

"Holmesy has most of the major fears," Daisy said as she petted Tua. "Anyway, we should get going. I've got some babysitting duties to attend to."

"I'll give you a ride home," said Davis.

Davis said he needed to stop by the house, and I was going to wait for him outside, but Daisy shoved me forward so hard I found myself walking alongside him.

Davis pulled open the front door, a massive pane of glass at least ten feet high, and we walked into an enormous marble-floored room. To my left, Noah Pickett lay on a couch, playing a space combat video game on a huge screen. "Noah," Davis said, "you remember Aza Holmes?"

"'Sup," he said, without turning away from the game.

Davis darted up a flight of floating marble stairs, leaving me alone with Noah—or so I thought—until a woman I hadn't seen called out, "That's a real Picasso." She was dressed all in white, slicing berries in the gleaming white kitchen.

"Oh, wow," I said, following her eyes to the painting in question. A man made of wavy lines rode atop a horse made of wavy lines.

"It's like working in a museum," she said. I looked at her and thought about Daisy's observation about uniforms.

"Yeah, it's a beautiful house," I said.

"They have a Rauschenberg, too," she said, "upstairs." I nodded, although I didn't know who that was. Mychal would, probably. "You can go and see." She gestured toward the stairs, so I walked up, but didn't pause to examine the assemblage of recycled trash at the top of the staircase. Instead, I took a quick look inside the first open door I came to. It seemed to be Davis's room, immaculately clean, lines still in the carpet from a vacuum cleaner. King-size bed with lots of pillows, and a navy-blue comforter. In a corner of the room, by a wall of windows, a telescope, pointed up toward the sky. Pictures on his desk of his family—all from years ago, when he was little. Framed concert posters on one wall—the Beatles, Thelonious Monk, Otis Redding, Leonard Cohen, Billie Holiday. A bookshelf packed with hardcover books, with an entire shelf of comics in plastic sleeves. And on his bedside table, next to a stack of books, the Iron Man.

I picked it up, turned it over in my hands. The plastic was cracked on the back of one leg, revealing a hollow space, but the arms and legs still turned.

"Careful," he said from behind me. "You're holding the only physical item I actually love."

I put the Iron Man down and spun around. "Sorry," I said.

"Iron Man and I have been through some serious shit together," he said.

"I have to tell you a secret," I said. "I've always thought Iron Man was kind of the worst."

Davis smiled. "Well, it was fun while it lasted, Aza, but our friendship has come to an end." I laughed and followed him down the stairs. "Rosa, can you stay until I get back?"

"Yes, of course," she said. "I've left you some chicken chili and salad for dinner in the fridge."

"Thanks," Davis said. "Noah, my man, I'll be back in twenty minutes, cool?"

"Cool," Noah said, still in outer space.

As we walked toward Davis's Cadillac Escalade, which Daisy was leaning against, I asked, "Was that your housekeeper?"

"She's the house manager. Has been since I was born. She's like what we have now instead of a parent, kinda."

"But she doesn't live with you?"

"No, she leaves every day at six, so not *that* much like a parent." Davis unlocked the doors. Daisy got in the backseat and told me to take shotgun. As I walked around the front of the car, I noticed Lyle standing next to his golf cart. He was talking to a man raking up the first fallen leaves of autumn, but staring at Davis and me.

"Just gonna drop these two off," Davis told him.

"Be safe, boss," Lyle answered.

Once the car doors were closed, he said, "Everyone is always watching me. It's exhausting."

"I'm sorry," I said.

Davis opened his mouth as if to speak, seemed to think better of it, and then, a moment later, continued. "Like, you know how in middle school or whatever you feel like everyone is looking at you all the time and secretly talking about you? It's like that middle-school feeling, only people really *are* looking at me and whispering about me."

"Maybe they think you know where your dad is," Daisy said.

"Well, I don't. And I don't want to." He said it firmly, unshakably.

"Why not?" Daisy asked.

I was watching Davis as he spoke, and I saw something in his face flicker without quite going out. "At this point, the best thing my dad can do for Noah and me is stay gone. It's not like he ever took care of us anyway."

Although only the river separated us, it was a ten-minute, winding drive back to my house because there's only one bridge in my neighborhood. We were quiet except for my occasional directions. When we at last pulled into my driveway, I asked for his phone and typed my number into it. Daisy got out without saying good-bye, and I was about to do the same, but when I gave him his phone back, Davis took my right hand and turned it over, palm up. "I remember this," he said, and I followed his eyes down to the Band-Aid covering my fingertip. I pulled my hand away and closed my fingers into a fist.

"Does it hurt?" he asked.

For some reason, I wanted to tell him the truth. "Whether it hurts is kind of irrelevant."

"That's a pretty good life motto," he said.

I smiled. "Yeah, I don't know. Okay, I should go."

Right before I closed the door, he said, "It's good to see you, Aza."

"Yeah," I said. "You too."

FIVE

AS DAISY AND I DROVE toward her apartment in Harold's warm embrace, she wouldn't shut up about the crush she was certain I had. "Holmesy, you're aglow. You're luminous. You're beaming."

"I'm not."

"You *are*."

"I honestly can't even tell if he's cute."

"He's in that vast boy middle," she said. "Like, good-looking enough that I'm willing to be won over. The whole problem with boys is that ninety-nine percent of them are, like, okay. If you could dress and hygiene them properly, and make them stand up straight and listen to you and not be dumbasses, they'd be totally acceptable."

"I'm really not looking to date anyone." I know people often say that when secretly looking for a romantic partner, but I meant it. I definitely felt attracted to some people, and I liked the idea of being with someone, but the actual mechanics of it didn't much suit my talents. Like, parts of typical romantic relationships that made me anxious included 1. Kissing; 2. Having to say the right things to avoid hurt feelings; 3. Saying more wrong things while trying to apologize; 4. Being at a movie theater together and feeling obligated to hold hands even after your hands become sweaty and the sweat starts mixing together; and 5. The part where they say, "What are you thinking about?" And they want you to be, like, "I'm thinking about you, darling," but you're actually thinking about how cows literally could not survive if it weren't for the bacteria in their guts, and how that sort of means that cows do not exist as independent life-forms, but that's not really something you can say out loud, so you're ultimately forced to choose between lying and seeming weird.

"Well, *I* want to date someone," Daisy said. "I'd make a go at Little Orphan Billionaire myself, except he wouldn't stop looking at you. Hey, speaking of which, here's a fascinating piece of trivia: Guess who gets Pickett's billions if he dies?"

"Um, Davis and Noah?"

"No," Daisy said. "Guess again."

"The zoologist?"

"No."

"Just tell me."

"Guess."

"Fine. You."

"Alas, no, which is so unjust. I'm such a billionaire without the billions, Holmesy. I have the soul of a private jet owner, and the life of a public transportation rider. It's a real tragedy. But no, not me. Not Davis. Not the zoologist. The tuatara."

"Wait, what?"

"The tua-fucking-tara, Holmesy. Malik told me it was a matter of public record and it totally is. Listen." She held up her phone. "*Indianapolis Star* article from last year. 'Russell Pickett, the billionaire chairman and founder of Pickett Engineering, shocked the black-tie audience at last night's Indianapolis Prize by announcing that his entire estate would be left to his pet tuatara. Calling the creatures, which can live to more than one hundred and fifty years of age, "magical animals," Pickett said that he had created a foundation to study his tuatara and provide the best possible care for it. "Through investigating Tua's secrets," he said, referring to his pet by name, "humans will learn the key to longevity and better understand the evolution of life on earth." When asked by a *Star* reporter to confirm he planned to leave his entire estate to a trust benefitting a single animal, Pickett confirmed, "My wealth will benefit Tua and only Tua—until her death. After that, it will go to a trust to benefit all tuatara everywhere." A representative of Pickett Engineering said that Pickett's private affairs had no bearing on the direction of the company.' Nothing says fuck you to your kids quite like leaving your fortune to a lizard."

"Well, as you'll recall, it isn't a lizard," I pointed out.

"Holmesy, someday you're going to win the Nobel Prize for Being Incredibly Pedantic, and I'm going to be so proud of you."

"Thanks," I said. I pulled up outside of Daisy's apartment complex and parked Harold. "So, if Davis's dad died, he and his brother get *nothing*? Don't you at least have to pay for your kids to go to college or something?"

"Dunno," she said, "but it makes me think Davis really *would* turn his dad in if he knew where he was."

"Yeah," I said. "Someone has to know. He needed help, right? You can't just disappear."

"Right, but there's so many possible accomplices. Pickett has, like, thousands of employees. And who knows how many people working on that property. I mean, they have a *zoologist*."

"It would sort of suck, having all those people around your house all day. Like, people who aren't in your family just, like, constantly in your space."

"Indeed, Holmesy, however does one bear the pain of overenthusiastic servants?" I laughed, and Daisy clapped her hands and said, "Okay. My to-do list: Research wills. Get police report. Your to-do list: Fall for Davis, which you've already mostly done. Thanks for the ride; time to go pretend I love my sister." She grabbed her backpack, climbed out of Harold, and slammed his precious, fragile door behind her.

When I got home, I watched TV with Mom, but I couldn't stop thinking about Davis looking down at my finger, holding my hand in his.

I have these thoughts that Dr. Karen Singh calls "intrusives," but the first time she said it, I heard "invasives," which I like better, because, like invasive weeds, these thoughts seem to arrive at my biosphere from some faraway land, and then they spread out of control.

Supposedly everyone has them—you look out from over a bridge or whatever and it occurs to you out of nowhere that you could just jump. And then if you're most people, you think, *Well, that was a weird thought*, and move on with your life. But for some people, the invasive can kind of take over, crowding out all the other thoughts until it's the only one you're able to have, the thought you're perpetually either thinking or distracting yourself from.

You're watching TV with your mom—this show about time-traveling crime solvers—and you remember a boy holding your hand, looking at your finger, and then a thought occurs to you: *You should unwrap that Band-Aid and check to see if there is an infection.*

You don't actually want to do this; it's just an invasive. Everyone has them. But you can't shut yours up. Since you've had a reasonable amount of cognitive behavioral therapy, you tell yourself, *I am not my thoughts*, even though deep down you're not sure what exactly that makes you. Then you tell yourself to click a little x in the top corner of the thought to make it go away. And maybe it does for a moment; you're back in your house, on the couch, next to your mom, and then your brain says, *Well, but wait. What if your finger is infected? Why not just check? The cafeteria wasn't exactly the most sanitary place to reopen that wound. And then you were in the river.*

Now you're nervous, because you've previously attended this exact rodeo on thousands of occasions, and also because you want to choose the thoughts that are called yours. The river was filthy, after all. Had you gotten some river water on your hand? It wouldn't take much. *Time to unwrap the Band-Aid.* You tell yourself that you were careful not to touch the water, but your self replies, *But what if you touched something that touched the water*, and then you tell yourself that this wound is almost certainly not infected, but the distance you've created with the *almost* gets filled by the thought, *You need to check for infection; just check it so we can calm down*, and then fine, okay, you excuse yourself to the bathroom and slip off the Band-Aid to discover that there isn't blood, but there might be a bit of moisture on the bandage pad. You hold the Band-Aid up to the yellow light in the bathroom, and yes, that definitely looks like moisture.

Could be sweat, of course, but also might be water from the river, or worse still seropurulent drainage, a sure sign of infection, so you find the hand sanitizer in the medicine cabinet and squeeze some onto your fingertip, which burns like hell, and then you wash your hands thoroughly, singing your ABCs while you do to make sure you've scrubbed for the full twenty seconds recommended by the Centers for Disease Control, and then you carefully dry your hands with a towel. And then you dig your thumbnail all the way into the crack in the callus until it starts bleeding, and you squeeze the blood out for as long as it comes, and then you blot the wound dry with a tissue. You take a Band-Aid from inside your jeans pocket, where there is never a shortage of them, and you carefully reapply the bandage. You return to the couch to watch TV, and for a few or many minutes, you feel the shivering jolt of the tension easing, the relief of giving in to the lesser angels of your nature.

And then two or five or six hundred minutes pass before you start to wonder, *Wait, did I get all the pus out? Was there pus even or was that only sweat? If it was pus, you might need to drain the wound again.*

The spiral tightens, like that, forever.

SIX

AFTER SCHOOL THE NEXT DAY, I joined the swarm of people filing out through the overstuffed hallways of WRHS and made my way to Harold. I had to change the Band-Aid, which took a few minutes, but I preferred to let the traffic thin out a bit before driving home anyway. To kill time, I texted Daisy, asking her to meet me at Applebee's, our go-to restaurant for studying together.

She responded a few minutes later: *I have work until 8. Meet you after?*

Me: *Do you need a ride?*

Her: *Dad picked me up. He's taking me. Has Davis texted?*

Me: *No, should I text him?*

Her: *ABSOLUTELY NOT.*

Her: *Wait between 24 and 30 hours. Obviously. You're intrigued but not obsessed.*

Me: *Got it. I didn't know there were Texting Commandments.*

Her: *Well there are. We're almost there so I gotta go. First order of business, drawing straws to see who has to get in the Chuckie costume. Pray for me.*

Harold and I started our drive home, but then it occurred to me that I could go anywhere. Not *anywhere*, I guess, but nearly. I could drive to Ohio, if I wanted, or Kentucky, and still be home before curfew. Thanks to Harold, a couple hundred square miles of the American Midwest were mine for the taking. So instead of turning to go home, I kept driving north up Meridian Street until I merged onto I-465. I turned the radio up as a song I liked called "Can't Stop Thinking About You" came on, the bass sizzling in Harold's long-blown speakers, the lyrics stupid and silly and everything I needed.

Sometimes you happen across a brilliant run of radio songs, where each time one station goes to commercial, you scan to another that has just started to play a song you love but had almost forgotten about, a song you never would've picked but that turns out to be perfect for shouting along to. And so I drove along to one of those miraculous playlists, headed nowhere. I followed the highway east, and then south, then west, then north, and then east again, until I ended up at the same Meridian Street exit where I'd started.

The journey around Indianapolis cost about seven dollars in gas, and I knew it was wasteful, but I felt so much better after circling the city.

When I parked in the driveway to open up the garage door, I saw I had a series of texts from Daisy:

I just drew the short straw so I have to get inside the fricking Chuckie costume.

See you later if I survive.

If I die weep at my grave every day until a seedling appears in the dirt, then cry on it to make it grow until it becomes a beautiful tree whose roots surround my body.

They're making me go now they're taking away my phone REMEMBER ME HOLMESY.

Update: I survived. Getting a ride to Applebee's after work. See you.

In the living room, Mom was grading quizzes with her feet up on the coffee table. I sat down next to her, and without looking up, she said, "A Lyle from the Pickett estate brought over our canoe today, repaired. Said you and Daisy were paddling down the White River and hit a rock."

"Yeah," I said.

"You and Daisy," she said. "Paddling on the White River."

"Yeah," I said.

She looked up at last. "Seems like something you would only do if, say, you wanted to run into Davis Pickett."

I shrugged.

"Did it work?" she asked.

I shrugged again, but she kept looking at me until I gave in and spoke. "I was just thinking about him. Wanted an excuse to check on him, I guess."

"How is he doing, without his father?"

"I think he's okay," I said. "Most people don't seem to like their dads much."

She leaned into me, her shoulder against mine. I knew we were both thinking about my dad, but we had never been good at talking about him. "I wonder if you would have clashed with your father."

I didn't say anything.

"He would've understood you, that's for sure. He got your whys in a way I never could. But he was such a worrier, and you might have found that exhausting. I know I did, sometimes."

"You worry, too," I said.

"I suppose. Mostly about you."

"I don't mind worriers," I said. "Worrying is the correct worldview. Life is worrisome."

"You sound just like him." She smiled a little. "I still can't believe he left us." She said it like it was a decision, like he'd been mowing the lawn that day and thought, *I think I'll fall down dead now.*

I cooked dinner that night, a macaroni scramble with canned vegetables, boxed macaroni, and some proper cheddar cheese, and then we ate while watching a reality show about regular people trying to survive in the wild. My phone finally buzzed while Mom and I were doing the dishes—Daisy telling me she'd arrived at Applebee's—so I told Mom I'd be back by midnight and reunited with Harold, who was, as always, a pure delight.

Applebee's is a chain of mid-quality restaurants serving "American food," which essentially means that Everything Features Cheese. Last year, some kid had showed up on our doorstep and talked my mom into buying a huge coupon book to support his Boy Scout troop or something, and the book turned out to include sixty Applebee's coupons offering "Two burgers for $11." Daisy and I had been working our way through them ever since.

She was waiting for me at a booth, changed out of her work shirt and into a scoop-neck turquoise top, staring into the depths of her phone. Daisy didn't have a computer, so she did everything on her phone, from texting to writing fan fiction. She could type on it faster than I could on a regular keyboard.

"Have you ever gotten a dick pic?" she asked in lieu of saying hello.

"Um, I've seen one," I said, scooting into the bench across from her.

"Well, of course you've seen one, Holmesy. Christ, I'm not asking if you're a seventeenth-century nun. I mean have you ever received an unsolicited, no-context dick pic. Like, a dick pic as a form of introduction."

"Not really," I said.

"Look at this," she said, and handed me her phone.

"Yeah, that's a penis," I said, squinting and turning it slightly counterclockwise.

"Right, but can we talk about it for a minute?"

"Can we please not?" I dropped the phone as Holly, our server, appeared at the table. Holly was our server quite regularly, and she wasn't exactly a card-carrying member of the Daisy and Holmesy fan club, possibly on account of our coupon-driven Applebee's strategy and limited resources for tipping.

Daisy spoke up, as she always did. "Holly, have you ever received—"

"Nope," I said. "No no no." I looked up at Holly. "I'd just like a water with no food please, but around nine forty-five I'll take a veggie burger, no mayonnaise no condiments at all, just a veggie burger and bun in a to-go box please. With fries."

"And you'll have the Blazin' Texan burger?" Holly asked Daisy.

"With a glass of red wine, please."

Holly just stared at her.

"Fine. Water."

"I assume y'all have a coupon?" Holly asked.

"As it happens, we do," I said, and slid it across the table to her.

Holly had hardly turned away when Daisy started back up. "I mean, how am I supposed to react to a semi-erect penis as fan mail? Am I supposed to feel *intrigued*?"

"He probably thinks it'll end in marriage. You'll meet IRL and fall in love and someday tell your kids that it all started with a picture of a disembodied penis."

"It's just such an odd response to my fiction. Like, okay, follow the thread of thoughts with me: 'I really enjoyed this story about Rey and Chewbacca's romantic adventure scavenging a wrecked Tulgah spaceship on Endor in search of the famed Tulgah patience potion; as a thank-you, I believe I will send the author of that story a photograph of my dick.' How do you get from A to B, Holmesy?"

"Boys are gross," I said. "Everyone is gross. People and their gross bodies; it all makes me want to barf."

"Probably just some loser Kylo stan," she mumbled. I had no understanding of her fan-fiction language.

"*Please* can we talk about something else."

"Fine. During my break at work, I became an expert in

wills. So, get this: You can't actually leave any money to a nonhuman animal when you die, but you *can* leave all your money to a corporation that exists solely to benefit a nonhuman animal. Basically, the state of Indiana doesn't consider pets people, but it does consider corporations people. So Pickett's money would all go to a company that benefits the tuatara. And it turns out you don't have to leave your kids *anything* when you die. No matter how rich you are—not a house, not college money, nothing."

"What happens if their dad goes to prison?"

"They'd get a guardian. Maybe the house manager or a family member or something, and that person would get money to pay the kids' expenses. If finding fugitives doesn't work out for me as a career, I might get into guardianship of billionaire children.

"Okay, you start putting together background files on the case and the Pickett family. I'm gonna get the police report and also do my calc homework, because there are only so many hours in a day and I have to spend too many of them at Chuck E. Cheese."

"How are you going to get a copy of the police report, anyway?"

"Oh, you know. Wiles," she said.

I happened to be friends with Davis Pickett on Facebook, and while his profile was a long-abandoned ghost town, it did provide me with one of his usernames—dallgoodman, which led to an Instagram.

The Instagram contained no real pictures, only quotes rendered in typewritery fonts with soft-focused, crumpled-paper backgrounds. The first one, posted two years ago, was from Charlotte Brontë. "I care for myself. The more solitary, the more friendless, the more unsustained I am, the more I will respect myself."

The most recent quote was, "He who doesn't fear death dies only once," which I thought was maybe some veiled reference to his father, but I couldn't unpack it. (For the record, he who *does* fear death also dies only once, but whatever.)

Scrolling through the quotes, I noticed a few users who consistently liked Davis's posts, including one, anniebellcheers, whose feed was mostly cheerleading pictures until I scrolled back more than a year and found a series of pictures of her with Davis, featuring a lot of heart emojis.

Their relationship seemed to have started the summer between ninth and tenth grades and lasted a few months. Her Instagram profile had a link to her Twitter, where she was still following a user named nkogneato, which turned out to be Davis's Twitter handle—I knew because he'd posted a picture of his brother doing a cannonball into their pool.

The nkogneato username led me to a YouTube profile—the user seemed to like mostly basketball highlights and those really long videos where you watch someone play a video game—and then eventually, after scrolling through many pages of search results, to a blog.

At first, I couldn't tell for sure if the blog was Davis's. Each post began with a quote and then featured a short little paragraph that was never quite autobiographical enough to place him, like this one:

> "At some point in life the world's beauty becomes enough. You don't need to photograph, paint or even remember it. It is enough." —TONI MORRISON
>
> Last night I lay on the frozen ground, staring up at a clear sky only somewhat ruined by light pollution and the fog produced by my own breath—no telescope or anything, just me and the wide-open sky—and I kept thinking about how sky is a singular noun, as if it's one thing. But the sky isn't one thing. The sky is everything. And last night, it was enough.

I didn't know for sure that it was him until I started to notice that many of the quotes from his Instagram feed were also used in the blog, including the Charlotte Brontë one:

> "I care for myself. The more solitary, the more friendless, the more unsustained I am, the more I will respect myself." —CHARLOTTE BRONTË

At the end, when walking was work, we sat on a bench looking down at the river, which was running low, and she told me that beauty was mostly a matter of attention. "The river is beautiful because you are looking at it," she said.

Another, written the previous November, around the time he and anniebellcheers stopped replying to each other on Twitter:

"By convention hot, by convention cold, by convention color, but in reality atoms and void."

—DEMOCRITUS

When observation fails to align with a truth, what do you trust—your senses or your truth? The Greeks didn't even have a word for blue. The color didn't exist to them. Couldn't see it without a word for it.

I think about her all the time. My stomach flips when I see her. But is it love, or just something we don't have a word for?

The next one stopped me cold:

"The greatest weapon against stress is our ability to choose one thought over another." —WILLIAM JAMES

I don't know what superpower William James enjoyed,

> but I can no more choose my thoughts than choose
> my name.

The way he talked about thoughts was the way I experienced them—not as a choice but as a destiny. Not a catalog of my consciousness, but a refutation of it.

When I was little, I used to tell Mom about my invasives, and she would always say, "Just don't *think* about that stuff, Aza." But Davis got it. You can't choose. That's the problem.

The other interesting thing about Davis's online presence was that everything ceased the day his father went missing. He'd posted on the blog almost every day for more than two years, and then on the afternoon after his dad disappeared, he wrote:

> "Sleep tight, ya morons." —J. D. SALINGER
>
> I think this is good-bye, my friends, although, then
> again: No one ever says good-bye unless they want to
> see you again.

It made sense. People had probably started snooping around—I mean, if I could find his secret blog, I imagine the cops could, too. But I wondered whether Davis had really quit the internet entirely, or whether he'd just decamped to some farther shore.

I couldn't pick his trail back up, though. Instead, I got stuck searching his usernames and variants of them, and ended up meeting a lot of people who weren't *my* Davis Pickett—the fifty-three-year-old Dave Pickett who was a truck driver in Wisconsin; the Davis Pickett who'd died of ALS after years of posting short blog entries written with the help of eye-tracking software; a Twitter user named dallgoodman whose blog was nothing but vitriolic threats directed at members of Congress. I found a reddit account that commented on Butler basketball and so probably belonged to Davis, but that, too, had been silent since Pickett Sr.'s disappearance.

"I'm very close," Daisy said suddenly. "Very, very close. If only I were as good at life as I am at the internet." I looked up, returning to the sensorial plane of Applebee's. Daisy was tapping at her phone with one hand while holding her cup of water with the other. Everything was loud and bright. At the bar, people were shouting about some sports occurrence. "What've you got?" she asked me as she put down her water.

"Um, Davis had a girlfriend, but they broke up last November-ish. He has a blog, but hasn't updated anything since his dad disappeared. I don't know. In the blog, he seems . . . sweet, I guess."

"Well, I'm glad you've used your internet detective skills to determine that Davis is sweet. Holmesy, I love you, but find some info on the *case*."

So I did. The *Indianapolis Star* wrote about Russell Pickett a lot because his company was one of Indiana's biggest employers, but also because he was constantly getting sued. He had some huge real estate deal downtown that devolved into multiple lawsuits; his former executive assistant and Pickett Engineering's chief marketing officer had both sued him for sexual harassment; he'd been sued by a gardener on his estate for violating the Americans with Disabilities Act; the list went on and on.

In all those articles, the same lawyer was quoted—Simon Morris. Morris's website described his company as "a boutique law firm focusing on the comprehensive needs of high-net-worth individuals."

"Can I get a charge off your computer BTW?" She actually said the letters B-T-W, which I wanted to point out required more syllables than just saying "by the way," but she was clearly locked into something. Without ever taking her eyes from her phone, Daisy reached into her purse, pulled out a USB cable, and handed it to me. I plugged it into my laptop, and she just mumbled, "That's better, thanks; I'm really close here."

I noticed Holly had come with my to-go order. I cracked the plastic container and grabbed a couple fries before returning to my investigation of Pickett. I stumbled onto a website called Glassdoor, where current and former employees could review the company anonymously. Observations about Russell Pickett himself included:

> "The CEO is skeezy as hell."
>
> "Russell Pickett is a straight-up megalomaniac."
>
> "I'm not saying Pickett executives make you break the law, but we do frequently hear executives start sentences with 'I'm not saying you should break the law, but . . .'"

So that's the kind of guy Pickett was. And although he'd gotten around all the lawsuits by settling them, the criminal investigation wouldn't go away. From what I could gather, the company had bribed a bunch of state officials in exchange for contracts to build a better sewer overflow system in Indianapolis.

Fifteen years ago, the government had set aside all this money to clean up the White River by building more sewage retention pools and expanding this tunnel system that runs underneath downtown, diverting a creek called Pogue's Run. The idea was that within a decade, the sewers would stop dumping into the river every time it rained. Pickett Engineering had gotten the initial contract, but they'd never finished the work, and it had gone way over budget, so the government pulled the contract from Pickett's company and allowed anyone to bid on finishing the project.

And then, even though they'd done a terrible job the first time, Pickett Engineering won the new contract—apparently by bribing state officials. Two of Pickett's executives had already been arrested and were believed to be cooperating with the police. Pickett himself hadn't yet been charged, although an editorial in the paper from three days before his disappearance criticized the authorities: "The *Indianapolis Star* Has Enough Evidence to Indict Russell Pickett; Why Don't the Authorities?"

"Annnnddd it's happening. Okay. Hold on. Hold on. Just waiting for the zip to download, yes, and opening, and . . . oh, hell yes." Daisy finally looked up at me and smiled. Her front teeth were a little crooked, turning toward each other, and she was self-conscious about it, so she rarely smiled all the way. But now I could even see her gums. "Can I do the thing, like, at the end of *Scooby-Doo* and tell you how I did it?"

I nodded.

"So the first article about Pickett's disappearance refers to a police report obtained by the *Indianapolis Star*. That story was written by Sandra Oliveros, with additional reporting by this dude Adam Bitterley, which is a bummer of a last name, but anyway, he's clearly the junior guy on the story, and a quick google shows him to be a recent IU grad.

"So I made up an email address that looks almost exactly like Sandra Oliveros's and emailed Bitterley an order to send me a copy of the police report. And he replied, like, 'I can't; I don't have it on my home computer,' so I told him to go the hell into the office and email it to me, and he was like, 'It's Friday night,' and I was, like, 'I know it's Friday night, but the news doesn't stop breaking on the weekend; do your job, or I'll find someone else who will do it.' And then he went to the fucking office and emailed me scans of the fucking police report."

"Jesus."

"Welcome to the future, Holmesy. It's not about hacking computers anymore; it's about hacking human souls. The file is in your email." Sometimes I wondered if Daisy was my friend only because she needed a witness.

As the file downloaded, I glanced away from my screen, through the slits of the blinds to the parking lot outside. A streetlight was shining right at us, which made everything around it look pitch-black.

I was trying to shake off a thought, but as I opened the police report and began scanning through it, the thought grew.

"What?" Daisy asked.

"Nothing," I said, and tried again to swallow the thought. But I couldn't. "Just, won't he get in trouble? Like, when he goes into work on Monday, won't he ask his boss why she needed that file, and then won't she be, like, 'What file,' and then won't he get in trouble? Like, he could get fired."

Daisy just rolled her eyes, but I was in the spiral now, and I started to worry that Mr. Bitterley would figure out how to track down Daisy, that he would have her arrested, and maybe me, too, since I was probably an accomplice. We were just playing a silly game, but people go to prison all the time for lesser crimes. I imagined a news story—girl hackers obsessed with billionaire boy.

"He'll find us," I said after a while.

"Who?" she asked.

"The guy," I said. "Bitterley."

"No, he won't; I'm on public Wi-Fi in an Applebee's using an IP address that locates me in Belo Horizonte, Brazil. And if he does find me, I'll say you had no idea what I was doing, and I'll go to prison for you, and in thanks for my refusal to snitch, you'll get my face tattooed on your bicep. It'll be great."

"Daisy, be serious."

"I am being serious. Your skinny little bicep needs a tattoo of my face. Also, he's not going to get fired. He's not going to find us. At most, he will learn an important lesson about phishing in a way that's minimally harmful to his life and the company he works for. Calm down, all right? I gotta get back to this very important argument I'm having with a stranger on the internet about whether Chewbacca is a person."

Holly came by with the check, an unsubtle reminder that we'd overstayed our welcome. I put down the debit card Mom had given me—Daisy never had any money and my mom let me charge twenty-five dollars a week as long as I kept straight As. Beneath the table, I rubbed my thumb against the callus of my finger. I told myself that Daisy was probably right, that everything would probably be fine. Probably.

Daisy didn't look up from her phone, but said, "Seriously, Holmesy. I won't let anything happen. I promise."

"You can't control it, that's the thing," I said. "Life is not something you wield, you know?"

"Hell yes, it is," she mumbled, still sunk into her phone. "Ugh, God, now this guy is saying I write bestiality."

"Wait, what?"

"Because in my fic, Chewbacca and Rey were in love. He's saying it is—and I am quoting—'criminal' because it's inter-species romance. Not *sex*, even—I keep it rated Teen for the kids out there—just *love*."

"But Chewbacca isn't human," I said.

"It's not a question of whether Chewie was *human*, Holmesy; it's a question of whether he was a person." She was almost shouting. She took Star Wars stuff quite seriously. "And he was *obviously* a person. Like, what even makes you a person? He had a body and a soul and feelings, and he spoke a language, and he was an adult, and if he and Rey were in hot, hairy, communicative love, then let's just thank God that two consenting, sentient adults found each other in a dark and broken galaxy."

So often, nothing could deliver me from fear, but then sometimes, just listening to Daisy did the trick. She'd straightened something inside me, and I no longer felt like I was in a whirlpool or walking an ever-tightening spiral. I didn't need similes. I was located in my self again. "So he's a person because he's sentient?"

"Nobody complains about male humans hooking up with female Twi'leks! Because of course *men* can choose whatever they want to bone. But a human woman falling in love with a Wookiee, God forbid. I mean, I know I'm just feeding the trolls here, Holmesy, but I can't stand for it."

"I just mean, like, a baby isn't sentient, but a baby is still a person."

"Nobody is saying anything about babies, Holmesy. This is about one adult person who happened to be human falling in love with another adult person who happened to be a Wookiee."

"Can Rey even speak Wookiee?"

"You know, it's a little annoying that you don't read *my* fanfic, but what's really annoying is that you don't read *any* Chewie fanfic. If you did, you'd know that Wookiee was not a language, it was a species. There were at least three Wookiee languages. Rey learned Shyriiwook from Wookiees who came to Jakku, but she didn't usually speak it because Wookiees mostly understood Basic."

I was laughing. "And why are you using the past tense?"

"Because all of this happened a long time ago in a galaxy far, far away, Holmesy. You always use the past tense when talking about Star Wars. Duh."

"Wait, can humans speak Shyri—the Wookiee language?"

Daisy did a very passable Chewbacca impersonation in response, then translated herself. "That was me asking if you're gonna eat your fries." I passed the to-go carton across the table to her, and she took a handful, then made another Chewbacca noise with her mouth half full.

"What did that mean?" I asked her.

"It's been over twenty-four hours; time to text Davis."

"Wookiees have texting?"

"*Had* texting," she corrected me.

SEVEN

MONDAY MORNING, I drove Mom to school because her car was in the shop. I could feel the burning in my middle finger from the hand sanitizer I'd applied just before leaving, and so I was pressing the Band-Aid into my middle finger, simultaneously worsening and relieving the pain. I hadn't texted Davis over the weekend. I kept thinking about it, but the night at Applebee's passed, and then I'd started to feel nervous about it, like maybe it had been too long, and Daisy wasn't around to bully me into it because she was working all weekend.

Mom must've noticed the Band-Aid pressing, because she said, "You have an appointment with Dr. Singh tomorrow, don't you?"

"Yeah."

"What are your thoughts on the med situation?"

"It's okay, I guess," which wasn't quite the whole truth. For one thing, I wasn't convinced the circular white pill was doing anything when I did take it, and for another, I was not taking it quite as often as I was technically supposed to. Partly, I kept forgetting, but also there was something else I couldn't quite identify, some way-down fear that taking a pill to become myself was wrong.

"You there?" Mom asked.

"Yeah," I said. Enough of me—but only just enough—was still located inside Harold to hear her voice, to follow the well-worn path to school.

"Just be honest with Dr. Singh, okay? There's no need to suffer." Which I'd argue is just a fundamental misunderstanding of the human predicament, but okay.

I parked in the student parking lot, parted ways with Mom, and then lined up to walk through the metal detectors. Once declared weapon-free, I joined the flow of bodies filling the hallways like blood cells in a vein.

I made it to my locker a few minutes early and took a second to look up the reporter Daisy had phished, Adam Bitterley. He'd shared a link that morning to a new story he'd written about a school board voting to ban some book, so

I guessed he hadn't been fired. Daisy was right—nothing happened.

I was about to head toward class when Mychal jogged up to my locker and pulled me over to a bench. "How's it going, Aza?"

"Good," I said. I was thinking about how part of your self can be in a place while at the same time the most important parts are in a different place, a place that can't be accessed via your senses. Like, how I'd driven all the way to school without really being inside the car. I was trying to look at Mychal, trying to hear the clamor of the hallway, but I wasn't there, not really, not deep down.

"Um," he said. "So, listen, I don't want to mess up our friend group, because it's really great, but, this is awkward, but do you think, and seriously you can say no . . ." He trailed off, but I could see where he was going.

"I don't really think I can date anyone right now," I said. "I'm, like—"

He cut in. "Well, now it's super awkward. I was gonna ask if you think Daisy would go out with me, or if that's crazy. I mean, you're great, Aza . . ."

I knew Mychal well enough not to *actually* die of mortification, but only just. "Yes," I said. "Yes. That is a great idea. But you should just talk to her about it, not me. But yes. By all means, ask her out. I am embarrassed. This has been an embarrassment. You should ask out Daisy. I am going to stand up and exit the conversation now with whatever self-respect I still have."

"I'm really sorry," he said as I stood up and backed away. "I mean, you're beautiful, Aza. It's not that."

"No," I said. "No. Say nothing more. It's definitely my bad. I'm just . . . I'm gonna go now. Do ask out Daisy." Mercifully, a beep rang out from above, allowing me to scamper off to biology class. Our teacher was late, so everyone was talking. I hunched down in my seat and immediately texted Daisy.

Me: *I thought Mychal was asking me out so I tried to let him down easy but he was not asking me out. He was asking me if I would ask you out FOR HIM. Humiliation level—all-time high. But you should say yes. He's cute.*

Her: *Oh God. Panic. He looks like a giant baby.*

Me: *What?*

Her: *He looks like a giant baby. Molly Krauss said that once and I've never been able to unsee it. I can't hook up with a giant baby.*

Me: *Because of the shaved head?*

Her: *Because of the everything Holmesy. Because he looks exactly like a giant baby.*

Me: *He really doesn't.*

Her: *Next time you see him look at him and tell me he does not look like a giant baby. He looks exactly like if Drake and Beyoncé had a giant baby.*

Me: *That would be a hot giant baby.*

Her: *I'm saving that text in case I ever need to blackmail you. btw* HAVE YOU LOOKED AT THE POLICE REPORT?

Me: *Not really, have you?*

Her: *Yes, even though I had to close yesterday AND Saturday AND I had this calc stuff that is like reading Sanskrit AND I had to wear the Chuckie costume like twelve separate times. I didn't find any clues, but I did read the whole thing. Even though it's super boring. I really am the unsung hero of this investigation.*

Me: *I think you are fairly sung. I'll read it today I gotta go Ms. Park is looking at me weird.*

Throughout bio, each time Ms. Park turned to the blackboard, I read the missing persons report from my phone.

The report went on only for a few pages, and over the course of the school day, I was able to read all of it. The mp (missing person) was fifty-three, male, gray haired, blue eyed, with a tattoo reading *Nolite te bastardes carborundorum* ("Don't let the bastards get you down," apparently) on his left shoulder blade, three small surgical scars in his abdomen from a gallbladder removal, six feet in height, approximately 220 pounds, last seen wearing his standard sleeping attire: a horizontally striped navy-and-white nightshirt and light-blue boxer shorts. He was discovered missing at 5:35 A.M. when the police raided his house in connection with a corruption investigation.

The report was mostly "witness statements" from witnesses who had not witnessed anything. Nobody was there that night except Noah and Davis. The camera at the front entrance had captured two groundskeepers driving away at 5:40 P.M. Malik the Zoologist left that day at 5:52. Lyle left at 6:02, and Rosa at 6:04. So what Lyle told us about Pickett not having nighttime staff seemed true.

One page was devoted to Davis's witness summary:

> Rosa left pizza for us. Noah and I ate while playing a video game together. Dad came down for a few minutes and sat with us while he ate pizza, and then went back upstairs. There was nothing unusual. Most nights I only see Dad for a few minutes, or not at all. He didn't seem anxious. It was just a regular day. After Noah and I finished dinner, we put our dishes in the sink. I helped him with some homework and then read on the couch for school while he played a video game. I went upstairs

around 10, did some homework in my room, and looked at a couple stars with my telescope—Vega and Epsilon Lyrae. I went to bed around 11:00 P.M. Even looking back, there was nothing weird about that day.

[Witness also stated that he did not observe anything unusual via the telescope, adding, "My kind of telescope isn't for looking at the ground. You'd be seeing everything upside down and backward."]

Noah's statement came next:

I played Battlefront for a while with Davis. We had pizza for dinner. Dad was with us for a bit, talked about how the Cubs are doing. He told Davis he needed to do a better job of watching out for me, and then Davis was, like, I'm not his father. He and Dad were always sniping like that, though. Dad put a hand on my shoulder when he got up to leave, which felt a little weird. I could really feel him holding on to my shoulder. It almost hurt. Then he let go and headed upstairs. Davis helped me with my algebra homework and then I played Battlefront for another couple hours. I went upstairs around midnight and fell asleep. I didn't see Dad after he said good night.

There were also pictures—almost a hundred of them—of every room in the house.

Nothing appeared disrupted. In Pickett's office, I saw stacks of papers that seemed to have been left for an evening, not for a lifetime. A cell phone could be seen on his bedside table. The carpets were so clean I could see a single set of footprints leading to Pickett's desk, and a single set leading away from them. The closets were full of suits, dozens of them perfectly aligned from lightest gray to darkest black. A photograph of the kitchen sink showed three dirty dishes, each with little smudges of pizza grease and tomato sauce. To judge from the pictures, Pickett didn't seem to be missing so much as he seemed to have been raptured.

The report did not, however, contain any mention of the night-vision photograph, meaning we had something the cops didn't: a timeline.

After school, I got into Harold and screamed when Daisy suddenly appeared in the backseat. "Shit, you scared me."

"Sorry," she said. "I've been hiding, because Mychal and I are in the same history class, and I don't want to deal with it yet, and also I've got a bunch of comments to reply to. It's a hard life for a minor fan-fiction author. Did you notice anything in the police report?"

I was still catching my breath, but eventually said, "They seem to know slightly less than we do."

"Yeah," Daisy said. "Wait. Holmesy, that's it. That's it! They know slightly less than we do!"

"Um, so?"

"The reward is for 'information leading to the whereabouts of Russell Davis Pickett.' We may not know where he is, but we have information they don't that will help them find his whereabouts."

"Or not," I said.

"We should call. We should call and be, like, hypothetically, if we knew where Pickett was the night he disappeared, how much would that be worth? Maybe not the full hundred thousand, but *something*."

"Let me talk to Davis about it," I said. I worried about betraying him, even though I barely knew him.

"Break hearts, not promises, Holmesy."

"Just . . . I mean, who knows if they'd even give us money for that, you know? It's just a picture. You need a ride to work?"

"As it happens, I do."

While eating dinner with Mom in front of the TV that night, I kept thinking about the case. What if they did give us a reward? It *was* valuable information the police didn't have. Maybe Davis would hate me, if he ever found out, but why should I care what some kid from Sad Camp thought of me?

After a while, I begged homework and escaped to my room. I thought maybe I'd missed something from the police report, so I went through it again and was still reading when

Daisy called me. She started talking before I'd finished saying "Hi."

"I had a highly hypothetical conversation with the tip line, and they said that the reward is coming from the company, not the police, so it's up to the company to decide what is relevant, and that the reward would only be given out after they found Pickett. Our info is definitely relevant, but it's not like they'll find Pickett just with the night-vision picture, so we might have to split the reward with other people. Or if they never find him, we might not get it. Still, better than nothing."

"Or exactly equal to nothing, if they don't find him."

"Yeah, but it's evidence. We should at least get part of the reward."

"If they find him."

"Crook gets caught. We get paid. I don't see why you're waffling here, Holmesy."

Just then, my phone buzzed. "I have to go," I said, and hung up.

I'd gotten a text from Davis: *I used to think you should never be friends with anyone who just wants to be near your money or your access or whatever.*

I started typing a response, but then another text came in. *Like, never make a friend who doesn't like* YOU.

I started to type again, but saw the . . . that meant he was still typing, so I stopped and waited. *But maybe the money is just part of me. Maybe that's who I am.*

A moment later, he added: *What's the difference between who you are and what you have? Maybe nothing.*

At this point I don't care why someone likes me. I'm just so goddamned lonely. I know that's pathetic. But yeah.

I'm lying in a sand trap of my dad's golf course looking at the sky. I had kind of a shitty day. Sorry for all these texts.

I got under the covers and wrote him back. *Hi.*

Him: *I told you I was bad at chitchat. Right. That's how you start a conversation. Hi.*

Me: *You're not your money.*

Him: *Then what am I? What is anyone?*

Me: *I is the hardest word to define.*

Him: *Maybe you are what you can't not be.*

Me: *Maybe. How's the sky?*

Him: *Great. Huge. Amazing.*

Me: *I like being outside at night. It gives me this weird feeling, like I'm homesick but not for home. It's kind of a good feeling, though.*

Him: *I am drenched in that feeling at the moment. Are you outside?*

Me: *I'm in bed.*

Him: *Light pollution makes naked eye stargazing suck here, but I can see all eight stars in the Big Dipper right now, if you include Alcor.*

Me: *What was shitty about your day?*

I watched the . . . and waited. He wrote for a long time, and I imagined him typing and deleting, typing and deleting.

Him: *I'm all alone out here, I guess.*

Me: *What about Noah?*

Him: *He's all alone, too. That's the worst part. I don't know how to talk to him. I don't know how to make it stop hurting. He's not doing any homework. I can't even get him to take a shower regularly. Like, he's not a little kid. I can't MAKE him do stuff.*

Me: *If I knew something...like, something about your dad? And I told, would that make it better or worse?*

He was typing for a long time. *Much worse*, came the reply at last.

Me: *Why?*

Him: *Two reasons: If Noah can be eighteen or sixteen*

or even fourteen when he has to watch his father go to jail, that will be better than it happening when he's thirteen. Also, if Dad gets caught because he tries to contact us, that will be okay. But if he gets caught despite NOT reaching out to us, Noah will be completely crushed. He still thinks our dad loves us and all that.

For a moment, and only for a moment, I entertained the notion that Davis might've helped his father disappear. But I couldn't see Davis as his father's accomplice.

Me: *I'm sorry. I won't say anything. Don't worry.*

Him: *Today is our mom's birthday, but Noah barely knew her. It's all just so different for him.*

Me: *Sorry.*

Him: *And the thing is, when you lose someone, you realize you'll eventually lose everyone.*

Me: *True. And once you know that, you can never forget it.*

Him: *Clouds are blowing in. I should go to bed. Good night, Aza.*

Me: *Good night.*

I put the phone on my bedside table and pulled my blanket up over me, thinking about the big sky over Davis and the weight of the covers on me, thinking about his father and mine. Davis was right: Everybody disappears eventually.

EIGHT

DAISY WAS STANDING NEXT TO MY PARKING SPOT when Harold and I arrived at school the next morning. Summer doesn't last in Indianapolis, and even though it was still September, Daisy was underdressed for the weather in a short-sleeve top and skirt.

"I have a crisis," she announced once I was out of the car. As we walked through the parking lot, she explained. "So last night, Mychal called to ask me out, and I could've handled myself via text but you know I get nervous on the phone, plus I remain unsure Mychal can handle all . . . *this*," she said, gesturing vaguely at herself. "I am willing to give the giant baby a chance. But in a flustered moment, not wanting to commit to a full-on proper date, I may have suggested he and I go on a double date with you and Davis."

"You did not," I said.

"And then he was, like, 'Aza said she wasn't looking for a relationship,' and I was, like, 'Well, she already has a crush on this dude who goes to Aspen Hall,' and then he was, like, 'The billionaire's kid,' and I was, like, 'Yeah,' and then he was, like, 'I can't believe I got fake rejected by someone for a fake reason.' But anyway, on Friday night, you and me and Davis and a man-size baby are having a picnic."

"A picnic?"

"Yeah, it'll be great."

"I don't like eating outside," I said. "Why can't we just go to Applebee's and use two coupons instead of one?"

She stopped and turned to me. We were on the steps outside school, people all around us, and I worried we might get trampled, but Daisy had the ability to part seas. People made room for her. "Let me list my concerns here," she said. "One: I don't want to be alone with Mychal on our first and probably only date. Two: I have already told him you have a crush on a guy from Aspen Hall. I can't unsay that. Three: I have not actually made out with a human being in *months*. Four: Therefore, I am nervous about the whole thing and want my best friend there. You will note that nowhere in my top four concerns is whether we picnic, so if you want to move this mofo to Applebee's, that is A-OK by me."

I thought about it for a second. "I'll try," I said. So I texted Davis while waiting for the second bell to ring and commence biology.

Couple friends are getting dinner at Applebee's at 86th and Ditch on Friday. Are you free?

He wrote back immediately. *I am. Pick you up or meet you there?*

Meet us there. Does seven work?

Sure. See you then.

After school that day, I had an appointment with Dr. Singh in her windowless office in the immense Indiana University North Hospital up in Carmel. Mom offered to drive me, but I wanted some time alone with Harold.

The whole way up, I thought about what I'd say to Dr. Singh. I can't properly think and listen to the radio at the same time, so it was quiet in the car, except for the thumping rumble of Harold's mechanical heart. I wanted to tell her that I was getting better, because that was supposed to be the narrative of illness: It was a hurdle you jumped over, or a battle you won. Illness is a story told in the past tense.

"How are you?" she asked as I sat down. The walls in Dr. Singh's office were bare except for this one small picture of a fisherman standing on a beach with a net slung over his shoulder. It looked like stock photography, like the picture that came free with the frame. She didn't even have any diplomas up on the wall.

"I feel like I might not be driving the bus of my consciousness," I said.

"Not in control," she said.

"I guess."

Her legs were crossed, and her left foot was tapping the ground like it was trying to send a Morse code SOS. Dr. Karen Singh was in constant motion, like a badly drawn cartoon, but she had the single greatest resting poker face I'd ever seen. She never betrayed disgust or surprise. I remember when I told her that I sometimes imagine ripping my middle finger off and stomping on it, she said, "Because your pain has a locus there," and I said, "Maybe," and she shrugged and said, "That's not uncommon."

"Has there been an uptick in your rumination or intrusive thoughts?"

"I don't know. They continue to intrude."

"When did you put that Band-Aid on?"

"I don't know," I lied. She stared at me, unblinking. "After lunch."

"And with your fear of *C. diff*?"

"I don't know. Sometimes it happens."

"Do you feel that you're able to resist the—"

"No," I said. "I mean, I'm still crazy, if that's what you're asking. There has been no change on the being crazy front."

"I've noticed you use that word a lot, *crazy*. And you sound angry when you say it, almost like you're calling yourself a name."

"Well, everyone's crazy these days, Dr. Singh. Adolescent sanity is so twentieth century."

"It sounds to me like you're being cruel to yourself."

After a moment, I said, "How can you be anything to *your* self? I mean, if you can be something to your self, then your self isn't, like, singular."

"You're deflecting." I just stared at her. "You're right that self isn't simple, Aza. Maybe it's not even singular. Self is a plurality, but pluralities can also be integrated, right? Think of a rainbow. It's one arc of light, but also seven differently colored arcs of light."

"Okay, well, I feel more like seven things than one thing."

"Do you feel like your thought patterns are impeding your daily life?"

"Uh, *yeah*," I said.

"Can you give me an example?"

"I don't know, like, I'll be at the cafeteria and I'll start thinking about how, like, there are all these things living inside of me that eat my food for me, and how I sort of *am* them, in a way—like, I'm not a human person so much as this disgusting, teeming blob of bacteria, and there's not really any getting myself *clean*, you know, because the dirtiness goes all the way through me. Like, I can't find the deep down part of me that's pure or unsullied or whatever, the part of me where my soul is supposed to be. Which means that I have maybe, like, no more of a soul than the bacteria do."

"That's not uncommon," she said. Her catchphrase. Dr. Singh then asked if I was willing to try exposure response therapy again, which I'd done back when I first started seeing her. Basically I had to do stuff like touch my callused finger against a dirty surface and then not clean it or put a Band-Aid on. It had sort of worked for a while, but now all I could remember was how scared it had made me, and I couldn't bear the thought of being that scared again, so I just shook my head no at the mention of it. "Are you taking your Lexapro?" she asked.

"Yeah," I said. She just stared at me. "It freaks me out some to take it, so not every day."

"Freaks you out?"

"I don't know." She kept watching me, her foot tapping. The air felt dead in the room. "If taking a pill makes you different, like, if it changes the way-down you . . . that's just a screwed-up idea, you know? Who's deciding what me means—me or the employees of the factory that makes Lexapro? It's like I have this demon inside of me, and I want it gone, but the idea of removing it via pill is . . . I don't know . . . weird. But a lot of days I get over that, because I do really hate the demon."

"You often try to understand your experience through metaphor, Aza: It's like a demon inside of you; you'll call your consciousness a bus, or a prison cell, or a spiral, or a whirlpool, or a loop, or a—I think you once called it a scribbled circle, which I found interesting."

"Yeah," I said.

"One of the challenges with pain—physical or psychic—is that we can really only approach it through metaphor. It can't be represented the way a table or a body can. In some ways, pain is the opposite of language."

She turned to her computer, shook her mouse to wake it up, and then clicked an image on her desktop. "I want to share something Virginia Woolf wrote: 'English, which can express the thoughts of Hamlet and the tragedy of Lear, has no words for the shiver and the headache. . . . The merest schoolgirl, when she falls in love, has Shakespeare or Keats to speak her mind for her; but let a sufferer try to describe a pain in his head to a doctor and language at once runs dry.' And we're such language-based creatures that to some extent we cannot know what we cannot name. And so we assume it isn't real. We refer to it with catch-all terms, like *crazy* or *chronic pain*, terms that both ostracize and minimize. The term *chronic pain* captures nothing of the grinding, constant, ceaseless, inescapable hurt. And the term *crazy* arrives at us with none of the terror and worry you live with. Nor do either of those terms connote the courage people in such pains exemplify, which is why I'd ask you to frame your mental health around a word other than *crazy*."

"Yeah," I said.

"Can you say that? Can you say that you're courageous?"

I screwed up my face at her. "Don't make me do that therapy stuff," I said.

"That therapy stuff works."

"I am a brave warrior in my internal Battle of Valhalla," I deadpanned.

She almost smiled. "Let's talk about a plan to take that medication every single day," she said, and then proceeded to talk about mornings versus evenings, and how we could also try to get off the medication and try a different one, but that might be best attempted during a less stressful period, like summer vacation, and on and on.

Meanwhile, for some reason I felt a twinge in my stomach. Probably just nerves from listening to Dr. Singh talk about dosages. But that's also how *C. diff* starts—your stomach hurts because a few bad bacteria have managed to take hold in your small intestine, and then your gut ruptures and seventy-two hours later you're dead.

I needed to reread that case study of the woman who had no symptoms except a stomachache and turned out to have *C. diff*. Can't get out my phone right now, though—she'll get pissed off—but did that woman have some other symptom at least, or am I exactly like her? Another twinge. Did she have a fever? Couldn't remember. Shit. It's happening. You're sweating now. She can tell. Should you tell her? She's a doctor. Maybe you should tell her.

"My stomach hurts a little," I said.

"You don't have *C. diff*," she answered.

I nodded and swallowed, then said in a small voice, "I mean, you don't know that."

"Aza, are you having diarrhea?"

"No."

"Have you recently taken antibiotics?"

"No."

"Have you been hospitalized recently?"

"No."

"You don't have *C. diff.*"

I nodded, but she wasn't a gastroenterologist, and anyway, I literally knew more about *C. diff* than she did. Almost 30 percent of people who died of *C. diff* didn't acquire it in a hospital, and over 20 percent didn't have diarrhea. Dr. Singh returned to the medication conversation, and as I half listened, I started thinking I might throw up. My stomach really hurt now, like it was twisting in on itself, like the trillions of bacteria within me were making room for a new species in town, the one that would rip me apart from the inside out.

The sweat was pouring out of me. If I could just confirm that case study. Dr. Karen Singh saw what was happening.

"Should we try a breathing exercise?" And so we did, inhaling deeply and then exhaling as if to flicker the candle but not extinguish it.

She told me she wanted to see me in ten days. You can kind of measure how crazy you are based on how soon they want to see you back. Last year, for a while, I'd been at eight weeks. Now, less than two.

On the walk from her office to Harold, I looked up the case report. That woman, she did have a fever. I told myself to feel relieved, and maybe I did for a little while, but by the time I got home, I could hear the whisper starting up again, that something was definitely wrong with my stomach since the gnawing ache wouldn't go away.

I think, *You will never be free from this.*

I think, *You don't pick your thoughts.*

I think, *You are dying, and there are bugs inside of you that will eat through your skin.*

I think and I think and I think.

NINE

BUT I ALSO HAD A LIFE, a normal-ish life, which continued. For hours or days, the thoughts would leave me be, and I could remember something my mom told me once: Your now is not your forever. I went to class, got good grades, wrote papers, talked to Mom after lunch, ate dinner, watched television, read. I was not always stuck inside myself, or inside my selves. I wasn't *only* crazy.

On date night, I got home from school and spent a solid two hours getting dressed. It was a cloudless day in late September, cold enough to justify a coat, but warm enough that a sleeved dress with tights could be managed. Then again, that might seem like trying, and texting Daisy was no help because she responded she was going to wear an evening gown, and I couldn't totally tell if she was kidding.

In the end, I went for my favorite jeans and a hoodie over a lavender T-shirt Daisy had given me featuring Han Solo and Chewbacca in a fierce embrace.

I then spent another half hour applying and unapplying makeup. I'm not the sort of person who usually gets carried away with that stuff, but I was nervous, and sometimes makeup feels kind of like armor.

"Are you wearing eyeliner?" Mom asked when I emerged from my room. She was sorting through bills and had spread them out across the entire coffee table. The pen she held hovered over a checkbook.

"A little," I said. "Does it look weird?"

"Just different," Mom said, failing to disguise her disapproval. "Where are you headed?"

"Applebee's with Daisy and Davis and Mychal. Back by midnight."

"Is this for a date?"

"It's dinner," I said.

"Are you dating Davis Pickett?"

"We are both eating dinner at the same restaurant at the same time. It's not marriage."

She gestured at the spot next to her on the couch. "I'm supposed to be there at seven," I said. She pointed at the couch again. I sat down, and she put her arm around me.

"You don't talk much to your mother."

Dr. Singh told me once that if you have a perfectly tuned

guitar and a perfectly tuned violin in the same room, and you pluck the D string of the guitar, then all the way across the room, the D string on the violin will also vibrate. I could always feel my mother's vibrating strings. "I also don't talk much to other people."

"I want you to be careful about that Davis Pickett, okay? Wealth is careless—so around it, you must be careful."

"He's not wealth. He's a person."

"People can be careless, too." She squeezed me so tight it felt like she was pressing the breath out of me. "Just be careful."

I was the last to arrive, and the remaining space was next to Mychal, across from Davis, who was wearing a plaid button-down, nicely ironed, sleeves rolled up just so, exposing his forearms. I'm not sure why, but I've always been pretty keen on the male forearm.

"Cool shirt," Davis said.

"Birthday present from Daisy," I said.

"You know, some people think it's bestiality, for a Wookiee to love a human," Daisy said.

Mychal sighed. "Don't get her started on the whole Are-Wookiees-people thing."

"That's actually the most fascinating thing about Star Wars," said Davis.

Mychal groaned. "Oh God. It's happening." Daisy immediately launched into a defense of Wookiee-human love. "You know, for a moment in Star Wars Apocrypha, Han was actually *married* to a Wookiee, but does anyone freak out about that?" Davis was leaning forward, listening intently. He was smaller than Mychal, but he took up more room—Davis's gangly limbs occupied space like an army holds territory.

Davis and Daisy were chatting back and forth about the dehumanization of Clone troopers, and Mychal jumped in to explain that Daisy was actually kind of a famous writer of Star Wars fan fiction. Davis looked her username up on his phone and was impressed by the two thousand reads on her most recent story, and then they were all laughing about some Star Wars joke I couldn't quite follow.

"Waters for everyone," Daisy said when Holly arrived to take our drink order.

Davis turned to me and said, "They don't have Dr Pepper?"

"Soft drinks aren't covered by the coupon," Holly explained, monotone. "But also, no. We have Pepsi."

"Well, I think we can spring for a round of Pepsis," he said.

I realized in the silence that followed that I hadn't spoken since answering Davis's compliment about my shirt. Davis, Daisy, and Mychal eventually went back to talking about Star Wars and the size of the universe and traveling faster than light. "Star Wars is the American religion," Davis said at one point, and Mychal said, "I think religion is the American religion," and even though I laughed with them, it felt like I was watching the whole thing from somewhere else, like I was watching a movie about my life instead of living it.

After a while, I heard my name and snapped into my body, seated at Applebee's, my back against the green vinyl cushion, the smell of fried food, the din of conversation pressing in from all around me. "Holmesy has a Facebook," Daisy said, "but her last status update is from middle school." She shot me a look that I couldn't quite interpret, and then said, "Holmesy's like a grandmother when it comes to the internet." She paused again. "*Aren't you?*" she said pointedly, and then I realized at last she was trying to make room for me to talk.

"I use the internet. I just don't feel a need to, like, contribute to it."

"It does feel like the internet already contains plenty of information," Davis allowed.

"Wrong," Daisy said. "For instance, there is very little high-quality romantic Chewbacca fic on the internet, and I am just one person, who can only write so much. The world needs Holmesy's Wookiee love stories." There was a brief pause in the conversation. I felt my arms prickling with nervousness, sweat glands threatening to burst open. And then they went back to talking, the conversation shifting this way and that, everyone telling stories, talking over one another, laughing.

I tried to smile and shake my head at the right times, but I was always a moment behind the rest of them. They laughed because something was funny; I laughed because they had.

I didn't feel hungry, but when our food arrived I picked at my veggie burger with a knife and fork to make it look like I was eating more than I could actually stomach. Eating quieted the conversation for a while, until Holly dropped off the check, which I picked up.

Davis reached across the table and put his hand on top of mine. "Please," he said. "It is not an inconvenience to me." I let him take it.

"We should do something," Daisy said. I was ready to go home, eat something in private, and go to sleep. "Let's go to a movie or something."

"We can just watch one at my house," Davis said. "We get all the movies."

Mychal's head tilted. "What do you mean you 'get all the movies'?"

"I mean, we get all the movies that go to theaters. We have a screening room, and we . . . just pay for them or whatever. I actually don't know how it works."

"You mean, when a movie comes out in theaters, it . . . also comes out at your house?"

"Yeah," Davis said. "When I was a kid, we had to have a projectionist come out, but now it's all digital."

"Like, inside your house?" Mychal asked, still confused.

"Yeah, I'll show you," Davis said.

Daisy looked over at me. "You up for it, Holmesy?" I contracted my face into a smile and nodded.

I drove Harold to Davis's house; Daisy drove with Mychal in his parents' minivan, and Davis led in his Escalade. Our little caravan headed west on Eighty-Sixth Street to Michigan Road, and then followed it down past Walmart, past the pawnshops and payday loan outfits to the gates of Davis's estate across the road from the art museum. The Pickett estate wasn't in a nice neighborhood, exactly, but it was so gigantic that it functioned as a neighborhood unto itself.

The gate opened, and we followed Davis to a parking lot beside the glass mansion. The house looked even more amazing in the dark. Through the walls, I could see the whole kitchen suffused with gold light.

Mychal ran up to me as I exited Harold. "Do you know—oh my God, I've always wanted to see this house. This is Tu-Quyen Pham, you know."

"Who?"

"The architect," he said. "Tu-Quyen Pham. She's crazy famous. She's only designed three residences in the U.S. Oh my God, I can't believe I am seeing this."

We followed him into the house, and Mychal exclaimed a series of artist names. "Pettibon! Picasso! Oh my God, that's KERRY JAMES MARSHALL." I only knew who Picasso was.

"Yeah, I actually pressed Dad to buy that one," Davis said. "Couple years ago, he took me to an art fair in Miami Beach. I really love KJM's work." I noticed Noah was lying on the same couch, playing what appeared to be the same video game. "Noah, these are my friends. Friends, Noah."

"'Sup," Noah said.

"Is it okay if I just, like, walk around?" Mychal asked.

"Yeah, of course. Check out the Rauschenberg combine upstairs."

"No *way*," Mychal said, and charged up the stairs, Daisy trailing behind him.

I found myself pulled toward the painting that Mychal had called "Pettibon." It was a colorful spiral, or maybe a multicolored rose, or a whirlpool. By some trick of the curved lines, my eyes got lost in the painting so that I kept having to refocus on tiny individual pieces of it. It didn't feel like something I was looking at so much as something I was part of. I felt, and then dismissed, an urge to grab the painting off the wall and run away with it.

I jumped a little when Davis placed his hand on the small of my back. "Raymond Pettibon. He's most famous for his paintings of surfers, but I like his spirals. He was a punk musician before he became an artist. He was in Black Flag before it was Black Flag."

"I don't know what Black Flag is," I said.

He pulled out his phone and tapped around a bit, and then a screeching wave of sound, complete with a screaming, gravelly voice, filled the room from speakers above. "That's Black Flag," he said, then used his phone to stop the music. "Want to see the theater?"

I nodded, and he took me downstairs to the basement, except it wasn't *really* a basement because the ceilings were like fifteen feet high. We walked down the hallway to a bookshelf lined with hardcover books. "My dad's collection of first editions," he said. "We're not allowed to read any of them, of course. The oil from human hands damages them. But you can take out this one," he said, and pointed at a hardcover copy of *Tender Is the Night*.

I reached for it, and the moment my hand touched the spine, the bookshelf parted in the middle and opened inward to reveal the theater, which had six stadium-style rows of black leather seats. "By F. Scott Fitzgerald," Davis explained, "whose full name was Francis Scott *Key* Fitzgerald." I didn't say anything; I couldn't get over the size of the movie screen. "It's probably obvious how hard I'm trying to impress you," he said.

"Well, it's not working. I always hang out in mansions with hidden movie theaters."

"Want to watch something? Or we could go for a walk? There's something I want to show you outside."

"We shouldn't abandon Daisy and Mychal."

"I'll let them know." He fiddled around on his phone

for a second and then spoke into it. "We're going for a walk. Make yourselves at home. Theater's in the basement if you're interested."

A moment later, his voice began playing over the speakers, repeating what he'd just said. "I could've just texted her," I said.

"Yeah, but that wouldn't have been as awesome."

I zipped up my hoodie and followed Davis outside. We walked in silence down one of the asphalt golf paths, past the pool, which was lit from inside the water, slowly changing colors from red to orange to yellow to green. The light cast an eerie glow up onto the windows of the terrarium that reminded me of pictures of the northern lights.

We kept walking until we reached one of the oblong sand bunkers of the golf course. Davis lay down inside of it, his head resting on its grassy lip. I lay down next to him, our jackets touching without our skin touching. He pointed up at the sky and said, "So the light pollution is terrible, but the brightest star you see—there, see it?" I nodded. "That's not a star. That's Jupiter. But Jupiter is, like, depending on orbits and stuff, between three hundred sixty and six hundred seventy million miles away. Right now, it's around five hundred million miles, which is around forty-five light-minutes. You know what light-time is?"

"Kinda," I said.

"It means if we were traveling at the speed of light, it would take us forty-five minutes to get from Earth to Jupiter, so the Jupiter we're seeing right now is actually Jupiter forty-five minutes ago. But, like, just above the trees there, those five stars that kind of make a crooked *W*?"

"Yeah," I said.

"Right, that's Cassiopeia. And the crazy thing is, the star on the top, Caph—it's 55 light-years away. Then there's Shedar, which is 230 light-years away. And then Navi, which is 550 light-years away. It's not only that we aren't close to them; they aren't close to one another. For all we know, Navi blew up five hundred years ago."

"Wow," I said. "So, you're looking at the past."

"Yeah, exactly." I felt him fumbling for something—his phone, maybe—and then glanced down and realized he was trying to hold my hand. I took it. We were quiet beneath the old light above us. I was thinking about how the sky—at least this sky—wasn't actually black. The real darkness was in the trees, which could be seen only in silhouette. The trees were shadows of themselves against the rich silver-blue of the night sky.

I heard him turn his head toward me and could feel him looking at me. I wondered why I wanted him to kiss me, and how to know why you want to be with someone, how to disentangle the messy knots of wanting. And I wondered why I was scared to turn my head toward him.

Davis started talking about the stars again—as the night got darker, I could see more and more of them, faint and wobbly, just teetering on the edge of visibility—and he was telling me about light pollution and how I could see the stars moving if I waited long enough, and how some Greek philosopher thought the stars were pinpricks in a cosmic shroud. Then, after he fell quiet for a moment, he said, "You don't talk much, Aza."

"I'm never sure what to say."

He mimicked me from the day we'd met again by the pool. "Try saying what you're thinking. That's something I never ever do."

I told him the truth. "I'm thinking about mere organism stuff."

"What stuff?"

"I can't explain it," I said.

"Try me."

I looked over at him now. Everyone always celebrates the easy attractiveness of green or blue eyes, but there was a depth to Davis's brown eyes that you just don't get from lighter colors, and the way he looked at me made me feel like there was something worthwhile in the brown of my eyes, too.

"I guess I just don't like having to live inside of a body? If that makes sense. And I think maybe deep down I am just an instrument that exists to turn oxygen into carbon dioxide, just like merely an organism in this . . . vastness. And it's kind of terrifying to me that what I think of as, like, my quote unquote *self* isn't really under my control? Like, as I'm sure you've noticed, my hand is sweating right now, even though it's too cold for sweating, and I really hate that once I start sweating I can't stop, and then I can't think about anything else except for how I'm sweating. And if you can't pick what you do or think about, then maybe you aren't really real, you know? Maybe I'm just a lie that I'm whispering to myself."

"I can't tell that you're sweating at all, actually. But I bet that doesn't help."

"Yeah, it doesn't." I took my hand from his and wiped it on my jeans, then wiped my face with the sleeve of my hoodie. I disgusted myself. I was revolting, but I couldn't recoil from my self because I was stuck inside of it. I thought about how the smell of your sweat isn't from sweat itself, but from the bacteria that eat it.

I started telling Davis about this weird parasite, *Diplostomum pseudospathaceum*. It matures in the eyes of fish, but can only reproduce inside the stomach of a bird. Fish infected with immature parasites swim in deep water to make it harder for birds to spot, but then, once the parasite is ready to mate, the infected fish suddenly start swimming close to the surface. They start trying to get themselves eaten by a bird, basically, and eventually they succeed, and the parasite that was authoring the story all along ends up exactly where it needs to be: in the belly of a bird. The parasite breeds there, and then baby parasites get crapped out into the water by birds, whereupon they meet with a fish, and the cycle begins anew.

I was trying to explain to him why this freaked me out so much but not really succeeding, and I recognized that I'd pulled the conversation very far away from the point where we'd held hands and been close to kissing, that now I was talking about parasite-infected bird feces, which was more or less the opposite of romance, but I couldn't stop myself, because I wanted him to understand that I felt like the fish, like my whole story was written by someone else.

I even told him something I'd never actually said to Daisy or Dr. Singh or anybody—that the pressing of my thumbnail against my fingertip had started off as a way of convincing myself that I was real. As a kid, my mom had told me that if you pinch yourself and don't wake up, you can be sure that you're not dreaming; and so every time I thought maybe I wasn't real, I would dig my nail into my fingertip, and I would feel the pain, and for a second I'd think, *Of course I'm real.* But the fish can feel pain, is the thing. You can't *know* whether you're doing the bidding of some parasite, not really.

After I said all that, we were quiet for a long time, until finally he said, "My mom was in the hospital for, like, six months after her aneurysm. Did you know that?" I shook my head. "I guess she was kind of in a coma or whatever—like, she couldn't talk or anything, or feed herself, but sometimes if you put your hand in her hand, she would squeeze.

"Noah was too young to visit much, but I got to. Every single day after school, Rosa would take me to the hospital and I would lie in bed with her and we would watch *Teenage Mutant Ninja Turtles* on the TV in her room.

"Her eyes were open and everything, and she could breathe by herself, and I would lie there next to her and watch *TMNT*, and I would always have the Iron Man in my hand, my fingers squeezed into a fist around it, and I would put my fist in her hand and wait, and sometimes she would squeeze, her fist around my fist, and when it happened, it made me feel . . . I don't know . . . *loved*, I guess.

"Anyway, I remember once Dad came, and he stood against the wall at the edge of the room like she was contagious or something. At one point, she squeezed my hand, and I told him. I told him she was holding my hand, and he said, 'It's just a reflex,' and I said, 'She's holding my hand, Dad, look.' And he said, 'She's not in there, Davis. She's not in there anymore.'

"But that's not how it works, Aza. She was still real. She was still alive. She was as much a person as any other person; you're real, but not because of your body or because of your thoughts."

"Then what?" I said.

He sighed. "I don't know."

"Thanks for telling me that," I said. I'd turned to him and was looking at his face in profile. Sometimes, Davis looked like a boy—pale skin, acne on his chin. But now he looked handsome. The silence between us grew uncomfortable until eventually I asked him the stupidest question, because I actually wanted to know its answer. "What are *you* thinking?"

"I'm thinking it's too good to be true," he said.

"What is?"

"You."

"Oh." And then after a second, I added, "Nobody ever says anything is too bad to be true."

"I know you saw the picture. The night-vision picture." I didn't answer, so he continued. "That's the thing you know, that you want to tell the cops. Did they offer you a reward for it?"

"I'm not here looking for—" I said.

"But how can I ever know that, Aza? How will I ever know? With anyone? Did you give it to them yet?"

"No, we won't. Daisy wants to, but I won't let her. I promise."

"I can't know that," he said. "I keep trying to forget it, but I can't."

"I don't want the reward," I said, but even I didn't know if I meant it.

"Being vulnerable is asking to get used."

"That's true for anybody, though," I said. "It's not even

important. It's just a picture. It doesn't say anything about where he is."

"It gives them a time and a place. You're right, though. They won't find him. But they will ask me why I didn't turn over that picture. And they'll never believe me, because I don't have a good reason. It's just that I don't want to deal with kids at school while he's on trial. I don't want Noah to have to deal with that. I want . . . for everything to be like it was. And him gone is closer to that than him in jail. The truth is, he didn't tell me he was leaving. But if he had, I wouldn't have stopped him."

"Even if we gave them that picture, it's not like they're going to arrest you or anything."

Suddenly, Davis stood up and took off across the golf course. "This is a completely solvable problem," I heard him say to himself.

I followed him up the walkway to the cottage, and we went inside. It was a rustic cabin with wood paneling everywhere, high ceilings, and an astonishing variety of animal heads on the walls. A plaid, overstuffed couch and matching chairs formed a semicircle facing a massive fireplace.

Davis walked over to the bar area, opened the cabinet above the sink, pulled out a box of Honey Nut Cheerios, and started shaking out its contents. A few Cheerios poured out of the box into the sink, and then a bundle of bills banded with a strip of paper. I stepped forward and saw that the wrapping read "$10,000," which seemed impossible, because the stack was so small—a quarter-inch high at the most. Another stack came out of the Cheerios box, and then another. He reached up for a box of shredded wheat puffs and repeated the process. "What—what are you doing?"

As he grabbed a third box of cereal, he said, "My dad, he hides them everywhere. These stacks. I found one inside the living room couch the other day. He hides cash like alcoholics hide vodka bottles." Davis brushed some cereal dust off the hundred-dollar bills, stacked them next to the sink, and then grabbed them. The entire stack fit in one hand. "A hundred thousand dollars," he said, and offered it to me.

"No way, Davis. I can't—"

"Aza, the cops found, like, two million dollars executing their warrant, but I bet they didn't even get half of it. Everywhere I look, I find these stacks, okay? Not to sound out of touch, but for my dad, this is a goddamned rounding error. It's a reward for *not* sharing the picture. I'll have our lawyer call you. Simon Morris. He's nice, just a little lawyery."

"I'm not trying—"

"But I can't *know* that," he said. "Please, just—if you still call or text or whatever, I'll know it's not about the reward. And you will, too. That would be a nice thing to know—even if you don't call." He walked over to a closet, opened it, stuffed the money into a blue tote bag, and offered it to me.

He looked like a kid now—his watery brown eyes, the

fear and fatigue in his face, like a kid waking up from a nightmare or something. I took the bag.

"I'll call you," I said.

"We'll see."

I left the cabin calmly, then sprinted through the golf course, skirting the pool complex, and ran up to the mansion. I ran upstairs and walked along a hallway until I could hear Daisy talking behind a closed door. I opened it. Daisy and Mychal were kissing in a large four-poster bed.

"Um," I said.

"A bit of privacy, please?" Daisy asked.

I closed the door, muttering, "Well, but it isn't your house."

I didn't know where to go then. I walked back downstairs. Noah was on the couch watching TV. As I walked over to him, I noticed he was wearing actual pajamas—Captain America ones—even though he was thirteen. On his lap, there was a bowl of what appeared to be dry Lucky Charms. He took a handful and shoved them into his mouth. "'Sup," he said while chewing. His hair was greasy and matted to his forehead, and up close he looked pale, almost translucent.

"You doing okay, Noah?"

"Kickin' ass and takin' names," he said. He swallowed, and then said, "So, did you find anything yet?"

"Huh?"

"About Dad," he said. "Davis said you were after the reward. Did you find anything?"

"Not really."

"Can I send you something? I took all the notes off Dad's phone from iCloud. They might help you. Might be a clue or something. The last note, the one he wrote that night, was 'the jogger's mouth.' That mean anything to you?"

"I don't think so." I gave him my number so he could text me the notes and told him I'd look into it.

"Thanks," he said. His voice had gotten small. "Davis thinks we're better off with him on the run. Says it'd be worse if he was in jail."

"What do you think?"

He stared up at me for a moment, then said, "I want him to come home."

I sat down on the couch next to him. "I'm sure he'll show up."

I felt him leaning over until his shoulder was against mine. I wasn't wild about touching strangers, especially given that he didn't seem to have showered in some time, but I said, "It's all right to be scared, Noah." And then he turned his face away from me and started sobbing. "You're okay," I told him, lying. "You're okay. He'll come home."

"I can't think straight," he said, his little voice half strangled by the crying. "Ever since he left, I can't think straight." I knew how that felt—all my life, I'd been unable to think straight, unable to even finish having a thought because my thoughts came not in lines but in knotted loops curling in upon themselves, in sinking quicksand, in light-swallowing wormholes. "You're okay," I lied to him again. "You probably just need some rest." I didn't know what else to say. He was so small, and so alone.

"Will you let me know? If you find anything out about Dad, I mean."

"Yeah, of course."

After a while, he straightened up and wiped his face against his sleeve. I told him he should get some sleep. It was nearly midnight.

He put the bowl of Lucky Charms on the coffee table, stood up, and walked upstairs without saying good-bye.

I didn't know where to go, and having the bag of money in my hand was freaking me out a little, so in the end I just left the house. I looked up at the sky as I ambled toward Harold, and thought about the stars in Cassiopeia, centuries of light-time from me and from one another.

I swung the bag in my hand as I walked. It weighed almost nothing.

TEN

I TEXTED DAISY the next morning while I was still in bed.

Big news call when you can.

She called immediately.

"Hey," I said.

"I know he is a gigantic baby," she responded, "but I actually think upon close examination he is hot. And in general, quite charming, and very sexually open and comfortable, although we didn't *do it* or anything."

"I'm thrilled for you, so last night—"

"And he really seemed to like me? Usually I feel like boys are a bit afraid of me, but he wasn't. He holds you and you feel *held*, you know what I'm saying? Also he's already called me this morning, which I found cute instead of worrisomely overeager. But please do not think I am becoming the best friend who falls in love and ditches her bitches. Wait, oh God, I just said I'm in love. We've been hooking up for under twenty-four hours and I'm dropping L-bombs. What is happening to me? Why is this boy I've known since eighth grade suddenly so amazing?"

"Because you read too much romantic fan fiction?"

"There is literally no such thing," she answered. "How's Davis?"

"That's what I want to talk about. Can we meet somewhere? It's better if I can show you." I wanted to see her face when she saw the money.

"I already have a breakfast date, unfortunately."

"I thought you weren't ditching your bitches," I said.

"And I'm not. My breakfast date is with Mr. Charles Cheese. Alas. Can it wait till Monday?"

"Not really," I said.

"Okay, I get off work at six. Applebee's. Might have to multitask, though, because I'm trying to finish a story—don't take it personally okay he's calling I have to go thanks love you bye."

As I put down my phone, I noticed Mom standing in my doorway. "Everything okay?" she asked.

"Holy Helicopter Parenting, Mom."

"How was your date with that boy?"

"Which boy? There are so many. I have a spreadsheet just to keep track of them."

To kill time that morning, I went through Noah's file of entries from his dad's notes app. It was a long, seemingly random list—everything from book titles to quotes.

> Over time, markets will always seek to become more free.
>
> Experiential value.
>
> Floor five Stairway one
>
> Disgrace—Coetzee

It went on like that for pages, just little memos to himself that were inscrutable to anyone else. But the last four notes in the documents interested me:

> Maldives Kosovo Cambodia
>
> Never Tell Our Business to Strangers
>
> Unless you leave a leg behind
>
> The jogger's mouth

It was impossible to know when those notes had been written, and whether they'd all been written at once, but they certainly seemed connected: A quick search told me that Kosovo, Cambodia, and the Maldives were all nations that had no extradition treaty with the United States, meaning that Pickett might be allowed to stay in them without having to face criminal charges at home. *Never Tell Our Business to Strangers* was a memoir by a woman whose father lived on the run from the law. The top search result for "Unless you leave a leg behind" was a news article called "How White-Collar Fugitives Survive on the Lam"; the quote in question referred to how difficult it is to fake your own death.

"The jogger's mouth" made no sense to me, and searching turned up nothing except for a bunch of people jogging with their mouths open. But of course we all put ridiculous things in our notes apps that only make sense to us. That's what notes are *for*. Maybe he'd just seen a jogger with an interesting mouth. I felt bad for Noah, but eventually I set the list aside.

Harold and I made it to Applebee's half an hour early that afternoon. For some reason, I was scared to actually get out of the car, but if you pulled down the center segment of Harold's backseat, you could reach directly into the trunk. So I wiggled my way back there and fumbled around until I'd found the tote bag with the money, my dad's phone, and its car charger.

I stuffed the bag under the passenger seat, plugged in my dad's phone, and waited for it to charge enough to turn on.

Years ago, Mom had backed up all Dad's pictures and emails onto a computer and multiple hard drives, but I liked swiping through them on his phone—partly because that's how I'd always looked at them, but mostly because there was something magical about it being *his* phone, which still worked eight years after his body stopped working.

The screen lit up and then loaded the home screen, a picture of my mom and me at Juan Solomon Park, seven-year-old me on a playground swing, leaning so far back that my upside-down face was turned to the camera. Mom always said I remembered the pictures, not what was actually happening when they were taken, but still, I felt like I could remember—him pushing me on the swing, his hand as big as my back, the certainty that swinging away from him also meant swinging back to him.

I tapped over to his photos. He'd taken most of the pictures himself, so you rarely see him—instead, you see what he saw, what looked interesting to him, which was mostly me, Mom, and the sky broken up by tree branches.

I swiped right, watching us all get younger. Mom riding a tiny tricycle with tiny me on her shoulders, me eating breakfast with cinnamon sugar plastered all over my face. The only pictures he appeared in were selfies, but phones back then didn't have front-facing cameras, so he had to guess at the framing. The pictures were inevitably crooked, part of us out of the frame, but you could always see me at least, curling into Mom—I was a mama's girl.

She looked so young in those pictures—her skin taut, her face thin. He'd often take five or six pictures at once in the hopes of getting one right, and if you swiped through them like a flipbook, Mom's smile got bigger and smaller, my squirming six-year-old self moved this way or that, but Dad's face never changed.

When he fell, his headphones were still playing music. I do remember that. He was listening to some old soul song, and it was coming out of his earbuds loud, his body on its side. He was just lying there, the lawn mower stopped, not far from the one tree in our front yard. Mom told me to call 911, and I did. I told the operator my dad had fallen. She asked if he was breathing, and I asked Mom, and she said no, and the whole time this totally incongruous soul song was crooning tinnily through his earbuds.

Mom kept doing CPR on him until the ambulance came. He was dead the whole time, but we didn't know. We didn't know for sure until a doctor opened the door to the windowless hospital "family room" where we were waiting, and said, "Did your husband have a heart condition?" Past tense.

My favorite pictures of my dad are the few where he's out of focus—because that's how people are, really, and so I settled on one of those, a picture he'd taken of himself with a friend at a Pacers game, the basketball court behind them, their features blurred.

And then I told him. I told him that I lucked into some money and that I'd try to do right by it and that I missed him.

I'd put the phone and charger away by the time Daisy showed up. She was walking toward Applebee's when I called to her through Harold's open window. She came over and got into the passenger seat.

"Can you give me a ride home after this? My dad is taking Elena to some math thing."

"Yeah, of course. Listen, there's a bag under your seat," I said. "Don't freak out."

She reached down, pulled out the bag, and opened it. "*Oh, fuck*," she whispered. "Oh my God, Holmesy, what is this? Is this real?" Tears sprouted from her eyes. I'd never seen Daisy cry.

"Davis said it was worth it to him, that he'd rather give us the reward than have us snooping around."

"It's real?"

"Seems to be. I guess his lawyer is going to call me tomorrow."

"Holmesy, this is, this is—is this one hundred thousand dollars?"

"Yeah, fifty each. Do you think we can keep it?"

"Hell yes, we can keep it."

I told her about Davis calling it a rounding error, but I still worried that it might be dirty money or that I might be exploiting Davis or . . . but she shushed me. "Holmesy. I'm so fucking done with the idea that there's nobility in turning down money."

"But it's—like, we only got this money because we know someone."

"Yeah, and Davis Pickett only got his money because *he* knew someone, specifically his father. This is not illegal or unethical. It's *awesome*."

She was staring out the windshield. It had started to drizzle a little—one of those cloudy days in Indiana when the sky feels very close to the ground.

Out on Ditch Road, a stoplight turned yellow, then red. "I'm gonna go to college," she said. "And not at night."

"I mean, it's not enough to pay for all of college."

She smiled. "Yeah, I know it's not enough to pay for all of college, Professor Buzzkill. But it is fifty thousand dollars, which will make college a hell of a lot easier." She turned to me and grabbed me by the shoulders and shook me. "HOLMESY. BE HAPPY. WE ARE RICH." She pulled a single hundred-dollar bill from one of the stacks and pocketed it. "Let's have the finest meal Applebee's has to offer."

At our usual table, Daisy and I shocked Holly by ordering two sodas. When she returned with our drinks, she asked Daisy, "You want the Blazin' Texan burger?"

"Holly, what is your best steak?"

Holly, unamused as usual, answered, "None of them are that good."

"Well, then I'll have my usual Blazin' Texan burger, but

I'd like to upgrade my side to onion rings. And yes, I know it's extra."

Holly nodded, then turned her eyes to me. "Veggie burger," I said. "No cheese or mayonnaise or—"

"I know your order," Holly said. "Coupon?"

"Not today, Holly," Daisy answered. "Not today."

We spent most of dinner imagining how, precisely, Daisy would retire from Chuck E. Cheese's. "I want to go in tomorrow, totally normal day, and when I draw the short straw and have to get in the Chuckie costume, I just walk off with it. Walk right through the doors, into my brand-new car, take Chuckie home, get him taxidermied, and mount him on the wall like a hunting trophy."

"It's so weird, putting the heads of stuff you've killed on the wall," I said. "Davis's guesthouse was full of that stuff."

"Tell me about it," Daisy said. "Mychal and I were hooking up in the actual shadow of a stuffed moose head. BTW, thanks for walking in on us last night, perv."

"Sorry, I wanted to tell you that you're rich." She laughed and shook her head again in disbelief. "I ran into Noah, by the way, the little brother? He asked if I knew anything about his dad and showed me this list of his notes. Here," I said, and showed her the list on my phone. "His last note was 'the jogger's mouth.' That mean anything to you?" Daisy shook her head slowly. "I just feel bad for him," I said. "He was crying and everything."

"That kid is not your problem," Daisy said. "We're not in the helping-billionaire-orphans business; we're in the getting-rich business, and business is booming."

"Well, fifty thousand dollars isn't *rich*," I said. "I mean, it's less than half of what IU would cost," which was the state school a couple hours south of us in Bloomington.

Daisy went quiet for a long time, her eyes blanked by concentration.

"All right," she said at last. "Just did some mental math. Fifty thousand dollars is, like, five thousand nine hundred hours at my job. Which is, like, seven hundred eight-hour shifts, if you can even get a full shift, which usually you can't, so that's two years of working seven days a week, eight hours a day. Maybe that's not rich to you, Holmesy, but that's rich to me."

"Fair enough," I said.

"And it was all sitting in a box of Cheerios."

"Well, like half of it was in a box of shredded wheat."

"You know what makes you a solid BFF, Holmesy? That you even told me about the money. Like, I *hope* I am the sort of person who would go halvsies with you on a six-figure-lottery situation, but to be perfectly honest, I don't trust myself." She took a bite of her burger and mostly swallowed before saying, "This lawyer guy isn't going to try to take back the money, is he?"

"I don't think so," I said.

"We should go to a bank," she said. "Get it deposited now."

"Davis said we should wait to talk to the lawyer."

"You trust him?"

"Yeah. I really do."

"Aww, Holmesy, we've both fallen in love. Me with an artist, you with a billionaire. We're finally leading the debutante lives we've always deserved."

In the end, our meal cost less than thirty dollars, but we left Holly a twenty-dollar tip for putting up with us.

ELEVEN

I WAS WATCHING VIDEOS ON MY PHONE the next morning when the call came in. "Hello?" I said.

"Aza Holmes?"

"This is she."

"This is Simon Morris. I believe you're acquainted with Davis Pickett."

"Hold on." I slipped on some shoes, snuck past Mom, who was watching TV in the living room while grading tests, and went outside. I walked down to the edge of our yard and sat down facing the house.

"Okay, hi," I said.

"I understand that you've received a gift from Davis."

"Yeah," I said. "I split it with my friend; is that okay?"

"How you handle your financial affairs is unimportant to me. Ms. Holmes, you may find that if a teenager walks into a bank with a vast array of hundred-dollar bills, the bank will generally be suspicious, so I've spoken to one of our bankers at Second Indianapolis, and they'll accept your deposit. I've set an appointment for you at three fifteen P.M. on Monday at the branch at Eighty-Sixth Street and College Avenue. I believe your school day ends at two fifty-five, so you should have adequate time to get there."

"How do you know—"

"I'm thorough."

"Can I ask you a question?"

"You just have," he noted dryly.

"So you're taking care of Pickett's affairs while he is gone?"

"That's correct."

"And if Pickett shows up somewhere . . ."

"Then the pleasures and sorrows of his life will belong to him again. Until then, some of them fall to me. May I request that you come to your point?"

"I'm sorta worried about Noah."

"Worried?"

"He just seems really sad, and there's kind of no one there to look after him. I mean, isn't there any other family?"

"None with whom the Picketts have a good relationship. Davis has been declared an emancipated minor by the state and is his brother's legal guardian."

"I don't mean a legal guardian. I mean someone who actually, you know, looks after him. Like, Davis isn't a *parent*. I mean, they're not just gonna be alone forever, are they? What if their dad is dead or something?"

"Ms. Holmes, legal death is different from biological death. I trust that Russell is both legally and biologically living, but I *know* he is legally alive because Indiana law considers an individual alive until either biological evidence of their death emerges or seven years pass from the last evidence of life. So, the legal question—"

"I don't mean *legally*," I said. "I just mean, who's going to take care of him?"

"But I can only answer that question legally. And the legal answer is that I administer the financial affairs, the house manager administers the home affairs, and Davis is the guardian. Your concern is admirable, Ms. Holmes, but I assure you that everything is cared for, legally. Three fifteen tomorrow. Your banker's name is Josephine Jackson. Do you have any other questions of pertinence to your situation?"

"I don't think so."

"Well, you have my number. Be well, Ms. Holmes."

I felt fine the next day at school, until Daisy and I were on our way to the bank. I was driving, and Daisy was talking about how her most recent fic had sort of gone viral in the Star

Wars fan-fiction world and how she had tons of kudos on it and how she'd had to stay up all night to finish this paper on *The Scarlet Letter* and how she could maybe finally get some sleep now that she was "retiring" from Chuck E. Cheese's, and I felt fine. I felt like a perfectly normal person, who was not cohabitating with a demon that forced me to think thoughts I hated thinking, and I was just feeling, like, *I've been better this week. Maybe the medicine is working*, when from nowhere the thought appeared: *The medicine has made you complacent, and you forgot to change the Band-Aid this morning*.

I was pretty sure I had actually changed the Band-Aid right after waking up, just before I brushed my teeth, but the thought was insistent. *I don't think you changed it. I think this is last night's Band-Aid*. Well, it's not last night's Band-Aid because I definitely changed it at lunch. *Did you, though?* I think so. *You THINK so?* I'm pretty sure. *And the wound is open*. Which was true. It hadn't yet scabbed over. *And you left the same Band-Aid on for—God—probably thirty-seven hours by now, just letting it fester inside that warm, moist old Band-Aid*. I glanced down at the Band-Aid. It looked new. *You didn't*. I think I did. *Are you sure?* No, but that's actually progress if I'm not checking it every five minutes. *Yeah, progress toward an infection*. I'll do it at the bank. *It's probably already too late*. That's ridiculous. *Once the infection is in your bloodstream*—Stop that makes no sense it's not even red or swollen. *You know it doesn't have to be*—Please just stop I will change it at the bank—*YOU KNOW I'M RIGHT*.

"Did I go to the bathroom before lunch?" I asked Daisy quietly.

"Dunno," she said. "Um, you sat down after us, so I guess?"

"But I didn't say anything about it?"

"No, you didn't say, 'Greetings, lunch tablemates. I have just returned from the bathroom.'"

Felt the tension between the urge to pull over and change the Band-Aid and the certainty of Daisy thinking me crazy. Told myself I was fine, this was a malfunction in my brain, that thoughts were just thoughts, but when I glanced at the Band-Aid again I saw the pad was stained. I could see the stain. Blood. Or pus. Something.

I pulled into an optometrist's parking lot, took off the Band-Aid, and looked at the wound. It was red at the edges. The Band-Aid had dried blood on it. Like it hadn't been changed in some time.

"Holmesy, I'm sure you went to the bathroom. You *always* go to the bathroom."

"Doesn't matter now; it's infected," I said.

"No, it's not."

"You see this red?" I pointed at the inflamed skin on either side of the wound. "That's infection. That's a big problem." I rarely let anyone see my finger without the Band-Aid, but I wanted Daisy to understand. This was not like the other times. This was not irrational worry, because dried blood was unusual, even for when the callus was cracked open. It meant the Band-Aid had been on for way too long. This was not normal. Then again, didn't it always feel different? No, this felt different from the other differents. There was visible evidence of infection.

"It looks like your finger has looked every single time you've ever worried about it."

I squeezed some hand sanitizer onto the cut, felt a deep, stinging burn, unwrapped a new Band-Aid, and wrapped it around my finger. I sat there for a while, embarrassed, wishing I were alone, but also terrified. Couldn't get the redness and the swelling out of my mind, my skin responding to the invasion of parasitic bacteria. Hated myself. Hated this.

"Hey," Daisy said. She put a hand on my knee. "Don't let Aza be cruel to Holmesy, okay?"

This was different. The sting of the hand sanitizer was gone now, which meant the bacteria were back to breeding, spreading through my finger into the bloodstream. Why did I ever crack open the callus anyway? Why couldn't I just leave it alone? Why did I have to give myself a constant, gaping open wound on, of all places, my finger? The hands are the dirtiest parts of the body. Why couldn't I pinch my earlobe or my belly or my ankle? I'd probably killed myself with sepsis because of some stupid childhood ritual that didn't even prove what I wanted it to prove, because what I wanted to know was unknowable, because there was no way to be sure about *anything*.

It'll feel better if you reapply the hand sanitizer. Just a couple more times. It was 3:12. We had to get to the bank. I took off the Band-Aid, applied hand sanitizer, reapplied a Band-Aid. It was 3:13. Daisy said, "Do you want me to drive?" I shook my head. Started Harold up. Put him in reverse. Then back in park.

Took off the Band-Aid, applied more hand sanitizer. It stung less this time. Maybe that means they're mostly dead. Or maybe it means they're in too deep already, that they've gotten through the skin into the blood. Just look at it one more time. Does it look like the swelling is getting better? It's only been eight minutes too soon to tell. Stop. It was 3:15. "Holmesy," she said. "We need to go. I can drive."

I shook my head again, put the car into reverse, and this time succeeded in getting moving. "I wish I understood it," she told me as I drove. "Like, does it help to be reassuring or is it better to worry with you? Is there *anything* that makes it better?"

"It's infected," I whispered. "And I did it to myself. Like I always do. Opened the callus up and now it's infected." I was that fish, infected with a parasite, swimming close to the surface, trying to get myself eaten.

When we finally got to the bank, I stood in the back while Daisy introduced herself to a teller, and then we were escorted to a glassed-off private office in the back, where a thin woman in a black suit placed our cash into a machine that shuffled through the bills, counting them. We filled out a bunch of forms and then had brand-new bank accounts, complete with debit cards that would arrive in seven to ten days. The woman gave us five temporary checks to use until our real ones arrived, encouraged us not to make any major purchases for at least six months "while you learn to live with this windfall," and then started talking about the places we could put the money—college savings accounts or mutual funds or bonds or stocks—and I was trying to pay attention to her, but the problem was I wasn't really in the bank. I was inside my head, the torrent of thoughts screaming that I had sealed my fate by not changing the Band-Aid for over a day, that it was too late, and now I could feel the heat and soreness in my fingertip, and you know it's real once you can physically feel it, because the senses can't lie. Or can they? I thought, *It's happening*, the *it* too terrifying and vast to name with anything but a pronoun.

Driving to Daisy's apartment complex, I kept forgetting why I was stopped at a stoplight, and then I'd let off Harold's brake only to look up and notice, oh, right. The light is red.

You hear a lot about the benefits of insanity or whatever—like, Dr. Karen Singh had once told me this Edgar Allan Poe quote: "The question is not yet settled, whether madness is or is not the loftiest intelligence." I guess she was trying to make me feel better, but I find mental disorders to be vastly overrated. Madness, in my admittedly limited experience, is accompanied by no superpowers; being mentally unwell doesn't make you loftily intelligent any more than having the flu does. So I know I should've been a brilliant detective or whatever, but in actuality I was one of the least observant people I'd ever met. I was aware of absolutely nothing outside myself on the drive to Daisy's apartment building and then to my house.

I went to the bathroom when I got home and examined the cut. The swelling seemed down. Maybe. Maybe the light in the bathroom just wasn't strong enough for me to see clearly. I cleaned it with soap and water, patted it dry, applied hand sanitizer, and then rebandaged my finger. I also took my regular medication, and then a few minutes later an oblong white pill I'd been told to use when panicky.

I let the pill melt on my tongue into a vague sweetness and waited for it to kick in. I felt certain something was going to kill me, and of course I was right: Something is going to kill you, someday, and you can't know if this is the day.

After a while, my head got heavy, and I sat down on the couch in front of the TV. I didn't really have the energy to turn it on, so I just stared at the blank screen.

The oblong pill made me feel exceptionally groggy, but only from the bridge of my nose up. My body felt like its standard self, broken and insufficient in the usual ways, but my brain felt sloppy and exhausted, like the noodle legs of a runner post-marathon. Mom came home and plopped down next to me. "Long day," she said. "I don't mind students, Aza. It's the parents that make my job hard."

"Sorry," I said.

"How was your day?"

"Okay," I said. "I don't have a fever, do I?"

She pressed the back of her hand to my forehead. "I don't think so. Do you feel sick?"

"Just tired, I think." Mom turned on the TV, and I told her I was going to lie down and do some homework.

I read my history textbook for a while, but my consciousness felt like a camera with a dirty lens, so I decided to text Davis.

Me: *Hi.*

Him: *Hi.*

Me: *How are you?*

Him: *Pretty good, you?*

Me: *Pretty good.*

Him: *Let's continue this awkward silence in person.*

Me: *When?*

Him: *There is a meteor shower Thursday night. Should be a good one if it's not cloudy.*

Me: *Sounds great. See you then. I have to go my mom is here.*

She had, in fact, peeked her head in through the door. "What's up?" I asked.

"Want to make dinner together?"

"I need to read."

She came in, sat down on the edge of my bed, and said, "You feeling scared?"

"Kinda."

"Of what?"

"It's not like that. The sentence doesn't have, like, an object. I'm just scared."

"I don't know what to say, Aza. I see the pain on your face and I want to take it from you."

I hated hurting her. I hated making her feel helpless. I hated it. She was running her fingers through my hair. "You're all right," she said. "You're all right. I'm here. I'm not going anywhere." I felt myself stiffen a little as she kept playing with my hair. "Maybe you just need a good night's sleep," she said at last—the same lie I'd fed to Noah.

TWELVE

THE MORNING OF THE METEOR SHOWER, I arrived at school with Harold and discovered a bright orange Volkswagen Beetle parked in my usual spot. As I pulled in next to the car, I saw that Daisy was in the driver's seat. I rolled down my window and said, "Didn't Josephine the banker tell us not to make any purchases for six months?"

"I know, I know," she said. "But I talked the car sales dude down to eighty-four hundred dollars from ten thousand, so in a way I actually *saved* money. You know what the color's called?" She snapped. "Snap orange! Because it's *snappy*."

"Don't waste the money, okay?"

"Don't worry, Holmesy. This car is only going to appreciate in value. Liam is a future collector's item. I've named him Liam, by the way." I smiled—it was an inside joke that literally no one else would get.

As we walked across the parking lot, Daisy handed me a thick book, *Fiske Guide to Colleges*. "I also picked this up, but it turns out I don't need it because I'm definitely going to IU. I always knew that college was expensive, but some of these places cost almost a hundred grand *per year*. What do they do there? Are the classes on yachts? Do you get to live in a castle and get served by house-elves? Even Rich Me can't afford fancy college."

Certainly not if you're buying cars, I wanted to say, but instead I asked her about the Pickett disappearance. "You ever figure out what 'the jogger's mouth' was?"

"Holmesy," she said. "We got the reward. It's over."

"Right, I know," I said, and before I could say anything else, she spotted Mychal across the parking lot and ran off to hug him.

All morning, I lost myself in Daisy's college book. Every now and again, a bell would sound, and I'd move to a different room, sitting at a different desk, and then I'd go back to reading the college guide, holding it on my lap under the desk. I'd never really thought about going to college anywhere but Indiana University or Purdue—my mom had gone to Indiana and my dad to Purdue—and they were both cheap compared with going to school out of state.

But reading through the hundreds of colleges in this book, which were rated on everything from academics to cafeteria quality, I couldn't help but imagine myself at some small college somewhere on a hilltop in the middle of nowhere with two-hundred-year-old buildings. I read about one school where you could use the same library study carrel that Alice Walker had. Admittedly, fifty thousand would hardly make a dent in the tuition, but maybe I could get a scholarship. My grades were good, and I was a competent standardized test taker.

I let myself imagine it—taking classes like Politicized Geography and Nineteenth-Century British Women in Literature in small classrooms, everyone seated in a circle. I imagined the crunch of gravel paths under my feet as I walked from class to the library, where I'd study with friends, and then before dinner at a cafeteria that served everything from cereal to sushi, we'd stop at the college coffee shop and talk about philosophy or power systems or whatever you talk about in college.

It was so fun to imagine the possibilities—West Coast or East Coast? City or country? I felt like I might end up anywhere, and imagining all the futures I might have, all the Azas I might become, was a glorious and welcome vacation from living with the me I currently was.

I broke away from the college guide only for lunch. Across the table from me, Mychal was working on a new art project—meticulously tracing the waveforms of some song onto a sheet of thin, translucent paper—while Daisy regaled our lunch table with the story of her car purchase, without ever quite revealing how she came across the necessary funds. After I'd eaten a few bites of my sandwich, I took out my phone and texted Davis. *What time tonight?*

Him: *Looks like it's going to be overcast tonight so no meteor shower.*

Me: *My primary interest is not the meteor shower.*

Him: *Oh. Then after school?*

Me: *I've got a homework date with Daisy. Seven?*

Him: *Seven works.*

After school, Daisy and I locked ourselves in my room to study for a couple hours. "It's only been three days since I retired from Chuck E. Cheese, but it's already shocking how much easier school is," she said as she unzipped her backpack. She pulled out a brand-new laptop and set it up on my desk.

"Jesus, Daisy, don't spend it all at once," I said quietly, so Mom wouldn't hear. Daisy shot me a look. "What?"

"You already *had* a car and a computer," she said.

"I'm just saying you don't want to spend all of it."

She rolled her eyes a little, and I said *what* again, but she disappeared into her online world. I could see her screen from the bed—she was scrolling through comments on her stories as

I read one of Alexander Hamilton's *Federalist* essays for history. I kept reading the words but not understanding them, then circling back, reading the same paragraph over and over again.

Daisy was quiet for a few minutes, but at last said, "I try really hard not to judge you, Holmesy, and it's slightly infuriating when you judge me."

"I'm not judging—"

"I know you think you're poor or whatever, but you know nothing about being actually poor."

"Okay, I'll shut up about it," I said.

"You're so stuck in your head," she continued. "It's like you genuinely can't think about anyone else." I felt like I was getting smaller. "I'm sorry, Holmesy, I shouldn't say that. It's just frustrating sometimes." When I didn't respond, she kept talking. "I don't mean that you're a bad friend or anything. But you're slightly tortured, and the way you're tortured is sometimes also painful for, like, everyone around you."

"Message received," I said.

"I don't mean to sound like a bitch."

"You don't," I said.

"Do you know what I mean, though?" she asked.

"Yeah," I said.

We studied together quietly for another hour before she said she needed to leave for dinner with her parents. When she got up to leave, we both said, "I'm sorry," at the same time, then laughed. By the time Davis texted me at 6:52, I had mostly forgotten about it.

Him: *I'm in your driveway should I come in?*

Me: *No no no no nope no I will be out shortly.*

Mom was emptying the dishwasher. "Headed out to dinner," I told her, and then grabbed my coat and got out the door before she could inquire further.

"Hi," he said as I climbed into his car.

"Hi back," I said.

"Have you eaten?" he asked.

"I'm not really hungry, but we can get food somewhere if you are," I said.

"I'm good," he said, backing up. "I actually kind of hate eating. I've always had a nervous stomach."

"Me too," I said, and then my phone started ringing. "It's my mom. Don't say anything." I tapped to answer. "Hey."

"Tell the driver of that black SUV to turn around this instant and come back to our house."

"Mom."

"This isn't going further without me meeting him."

"You have met him. When we were eleven."

"I am your mother, and he is your—whatever he is—and I want to talk to him."

"Fine," I said, and hung up. "We, uh, need to go into the house if that's okay, and meet my mom."

"Cool."

Something in his voice reminded me that his mom was

dead, and I thought about how everyone always seemed slightly uncomfortable when discussing their fathers in front of me. They always seemed worried I'd be reminded of my fatherlessness, as if I could somehow forget.

I never realized how small my house was until I saw Davis seeing it—the linoleum in the kitchen rolling up in the corners, the little settling cracks in the walls, all our furniture older than I was, the mismatched bookshelves.

Davis looked huge and misplaced in our house. I couldn't remember the last time I'd seen a guy inside this room. He wasn't quite six feet tall, but somehow his presence made the ceilings seem low. I felt embarrassed of our dusty old books and the walls decorated with family photos instead of art. I knew I shouldn't be ashamed—but I was anyway.

"It's nice to see you, Ms. Holmes," Davis said, offering a handshake. My mom hugged him. We all sat down at our kitchen table, which almost never had more than two people at it—Mom and me. It seemed overfull.

"How are you, Davis?" she asked.

"Things are good. As you may have heard, I am kind of an orphan, but I am well. How are you?"

"Who looks after you these days?" she asked.

"Well, everybody and nobody, I guess," he said. "I mean, we have a house manager, and there's a lawyer guy who does the money stuff."

"You're a junior at Aspen Hall, yes?" I closed my eyes and tried to telepathically beg my mother not to attack him.

"Yes."

"Aza is not some girl from the other side of the river."

"Mom," I said.

"And I know you can have anything the moment you want it, and that can make a person think the world belongs to them, that people belong to them. But I hope you understand you are not entitled to—"

"*Mom*," I said again.

I shot Davis an apologetic look, but he didn't see, because he was looking at my mom. He started to say something, but then had to stop, because his eyes were welling up with tears.

"Davis, are you all right?" my mom asked. He tried to speak again but it devolved into a choked sob.

"Davis, I'm sorry, I didn't realize . . ."

Blushing, he said, "I'm sorry."

Mom started to reach a hand across the table, but then stopped herself. "I just want you to be good to my daughter," she said. "There's only one of her."

"We have to get going," I announced.

Mom and Davis continued their staring contest, but Mom finally said, "Back by eleven," and I grabbed Davis by the forearm and pulled him out the front door, shooting Mom a look as I went.

"Are you okay?" I asked as soon as we were safely inside his Escalade.

"Yeah," he said quietly.

"She's just really overprotective."

"I get it," he said.

"You don't need to be embarrassed."

"I'm not embarrassed."

"Then what are you?"

"It's complicated."

"I've got time," I told him.

"She's wrong that I can have anything I want whenever I want it."

"What do you want that you don't have?" I asked.

"A mother, for starters." He put the car into reverse and backed out of the driveway.

I wasn't sure what to say, so eventually I just said, "Sorry."

"You know that part of Yeats's 'The Second Coming' where it's, like, 'The best lack all conviction, while the worst are full of passionate intensity'?"

"Yeah, we read it in AP."

"I think it's actually worse to lack all conviction. Because then you just go along, you know? You're just a bubble on the tide of empire."

"That's a good line."

"Stole it from Robert Penn Warren," he said. "My good lines are always stolen. I lack all conviction." We drove across the river. Looking down, I could see Pirates Island.

"Your mom gives a shit, you know? Most adults are just hollowed out. You watch them try to fill themselves up with booze or money or God or fame or whatever they worship, and it all rots them from the inside until nothing is left but the money or booze or God they thought would save them. That's what my dad is like—he really disappeared a long time ago, which is maybe why it didn't bother me much. I wish he were here, but I've wished that for a long time. Adults think they're wielding power, but really power is wielding them."

"The parasite believes itself to be the host," I said.

"Yeah," he said. "Yeah."

As we walked up to the Pickett house, I could see two place settings at one corner of Davis's huge dining room table. A candle flickered between the settings, and the first floor of the house was lit a soft gold. My stomach was all turned around, and I had no desire to eat, but I followed him in. "I guess Rosa made us dinner," he said to me. "So we should at least have a few bites to be polite."

"Hi, Rosa," he said. "Thanks for staying late."

She pulled him into a big bear hug. "I made spaghetti. Vegetarian."

"You didn't need to do this," he said.

"My children are grown-ups, so you and Noah are the only little boys I have left. And when you tell me you have a date with your new girlfriend—"

"Not girlfriend," Davis said. "Old friend."

"Old friends make the best girlfriends. You eat. I'll see you tomorrow." She pulled him down into another hug and kissed him on the cheek. "Take something up to Noah so he doesn't starve," Rosa added, "and do your dishes. It's not too hard to wipe dishes clean and put them in a dishwasher, Davis."

"Got it," he said.

"Your life is so weird," I said as we sat down to eat at the table set for two, with a Dr Pepper in front of my spot and a Mountain Dew in front of his.

"I guess," he said. He raised his can of soda. "To weird," he said.

"To weird." We clinked cans and sipped.

"She acts like a parent," I said.

"Yeah, well, she's known me since I was a baby. And she cares about us. But she also gets paid to care about us, you know? And if she didn't . . . I mean, she'd have to find a different job."

"Yeah," I said. It seemed to me that one of the defining features of parents is that they don't get paid to love you.

He asked me about my school day, and I told him I'd had a fight with Daisy. I asked about his day at school, and he said, "It was okay. There's this rumor at school that I killed not only my dad, but also my mom . . . so. I don't know. I shouldn't let it get to me."

"That would get to anyone."

"I can take it, but I worry about Noah."

"How is Noah?"

"He climbed into bed with me last night and just cried. I felt so bad I loaned him my Iron Man."

"I'm sorry," I said.

"He's, just . . . I guess at some point, you realize that whoever takes care of you is just a person, and that they have no superpowers and can't actually protect you from getting hurt. Which is one thing. But Noah is starting to understand that maybe the person he thought was a superhero turns out sort of to be the villain. And that really sucks. He keeps thinking Dad is going to come home and prove his innocence, and I don't know how to tell him that, you know, Dad isn't innocent."

"Does the phrase 'the jogger's mouth' mean anything to you?"

"No, but the cops asked me that, too. Said it was in Dad's phone."

"Yeah."

"I mean, my father is many things—but a jogger is not one of them. He thinks exercise is irrelevant, because Tua is going to unlock the key to eternal life."

"Seriously?"

"Yeah, he believes Malik is going to be able to identify some factor in tuatara blood that makes them age slowly, and then he's going to 'cure death,'" Davis said, using air quotes.

"That's why his will leaves everything to Tua—he thinks he's going to be remembered as the man who ended death." I asked him if Tua would really get all of his dad's money, and he laughed a little and said, "Everything. The business, the house, the property. I mean, Noah and I have plenty of money for college and everything—but we're not gonna be rich."

"If you have plenty of money for college and everything, you're rich."

"True. And Dad doesn't owe us anything. I just wish he'd, you know, do the dad stuff. Take my brother to school in the morning, make sure he does his homework, not disappear in the middle of the night to escape prosecution, et cetera."

"I'm sorry."

"You say that a lot."

"I feel it a lot."

He looked up at me. "Have you ever been in love, Aza?"

"No. You?"

"No." He glanced down at my plate, then said, "Okay, if neither of us is going to eat, we should probably go outside. Maybe we'll catch a break in the clouds."

We put our coats back on and walked outside. It was a windy night, and I tucked my head into my chest as we walked, but when I glanced over at Davis, he was looking up.

In the distance, I could see that two of the poolside

recliners had been pulled out onto the golf course, near one of the flags marking a hole. The flag was whipping in the wind, and I could hear the white noise of traffic in the distance, but it was otherwise quiet, the cicadas and crickets silenced by the cold. We lay down on the loungers, next to each other but not touching, and looked up at the sky for a while. "Well, this is disappointing," he said.

"But it's still happening, right? Like, there is still a meteor shower. We just can't see it."

"Correct," he said.

"So, what would it look like?" I asked.

"Huh?"

"If it weren't cloudy, what would I be seeing?"

"Well." He took his phone out and opened it up to some stargazing app. "So, over here in the northern sky is the constellation Draco," he said, "which to me looks more like a kite than a dragon, but anyway, there would be meteors visible around here. There's not much moon tonight, so you could probably see five or ten meteors an hour. Basically, we're moving through dust left behind by this comet called Giacobini-Zinner, and it would be super beautiful and romantic if only we did not live in gloomy Indiana."

"It *is* super beautiful and romantic," I said. "We just can't see it."

I thought about him asking me if I'd ever been in love. It's a weird phrase in English, *in* love, like it's a sea you drown in or a town you live in. You don't get to be *in* anything else—in friendship or in anger or in hope. All you can be in is love. And I wanted to tell him that even though I'd never been in love, I knew what it was like to be *in* a feeling, to be not just surrounded by it but also permeated by it, the way my grandmother talked about God being everywhere. When my thoughts spiraled, I was *in* the spiral, and of it. And I wanted to tell him that the idea of being in a feeling gave language to something I couldn't describe before, created a form for it, but I couldn't figure out how to say any of that out loud.

"I can't tell if this is a regular silence or an awkward silence," Davis said.

"What gets me about that poem 'The Second Coming' . . . you know how it talks about the widening spiral?"

"The widening gyre," he corrected me. "'Turning and turning in the widening gyre.'"

"Right, whatever, the widening gyre. But the really scary thing is not turning and turning in the widening gyre; it's turning and turning in the *tightening* gyre. It's getting sucked into a whirlpool that shrinks and shrinks and shrinks your world until you're just spinning without moving, stuck inside a prison cell that is exactly the size of you, until eventually you realize that you're not actually *in* a prison cell. You *are* the prison cell."

"You should write a response," he said. "To Yeats."

"I'm not a poet," I said.

"You talk like one," he said. "Write down half the stuff you say and it would be a better poem than I've ever written."

"You write poetry?"

"Not really. Nothing good."

"Like what?" I asked. It was so much easier to talk to him in the dark, looking at the same sky instead of at each other. It felt like we didn't have bodies, like we were just voices talking.

"If I ever write something I'm proud of, I'll let you read it."

"I like bad poetry," I said.

"Please don't make me share my dumb poems with you. Reading someone's poetry is like seeing them naked."

"So I'm *basically* saying I want to see you naked," I said.

"They're just stupid little things."

"I want to hear one."

"Okay, like, last year I wrote one called 'Last Ducks of Autumn.'"

"And it goes . . ."

"The leaves are gone / you should be, too / I'd be gone if I were you / but then again, here I am / walking alone / in the frigid dawn."

"I quite like that," I said.

"I like short poems with weird rhyme schemes, because that's what life is like."

"That's what life is like?" I was trying to get his meaning.

"Yeah. It rhymes, but not in the way you expect."

I looked over at him. I suddenly wanted Davis badly

enough that I no longer cared why I wanted him, whether what wanted him was capitalized or lowercase. I reached over, touched his cold cheek with my cold hand, and began to kiss him.

When we came up for air, I felt his hands on my waist, and he said, "I, uh, wow."

I smirked at him. I liked feeling his body against mine, one of his hands tracing my spine. "Got any other poems?"

"I've been trying to write just couplets lately. Like, nature stuff. Like, 'the daffodil knows more of spring / than roses know of anything.'"

"Yup, that works, too," I said, and kissed him again. I felt my chest tighten, his cold lips and warm mouth, his hands pulling me closer to him through the layers of our coats.

I liked making out with so many layers on. Our breathing steamed up his glasses as we kissed, and he tried to take them off, but I pressed them up the bridge of his nose, and we were laughing together, and then he started kissing my neck, and a thought occurred to me: His tongue had been in my mouth.

I told myself to be in this moment, to let myself feel his warmth on my skin, but now his tongue was on my neck, wet and alive and microbial, and his hand was sneaking under my jacket, his cold fingers against my bare skin. It's fine you're fine just kiss him *you need to check something* it's fine just be fucking normal *check to see if his microbes stay in you* billions of people kiss and don't die *just make sure his microbes aren't going to permanently colonize you* come on please stop this *he could have campylobacter he could be a nonsymptomatic* E. coli *carrier get that and you'll need antibiotics and then you'll get* C. diff *and boom dead in four days* please fucking stop just kiss him *JUST CHECK TO MAKE SURE.*

I pulled away.

"You okay?" he asked.

I nodded. "I just, just need a little air." I sat up, turned away from him, pulled out my phone, and searched, "do bacteria of people you kiss stay inside your body," and quickly scrolled through a couple pseudoscience results before getting to the one actual study done on the subject. Around eighty million microbes are exchanged on average per kiss, and "after six-month follow-up, human gut microbiomes appear to be modestly but consistently altered."

His bacteria would be in me forever, eighty million of them, breeding and growing and joining my bacteria and producing God knows what.

I felt his hand on my shoulder. I spun around and squirmed away from him. My breath running away from me. Dots in my vision. You're fine he's not even the first boy you've kissed *eighty million organisms in me forever* calm down *permanently altering the microbiome* this is not rational *you need to do something* please *there is a fix here* please *get to a bathroom.* "What's wrong?"

"Uh, nothing," I said. "I, um, just need to use the restroom."

I pulled my phone back out to reread the study but resisted the urge, clicked it shut and slid it back into my pocket. But no, I had to check to see if it had said modestly altered or moderately altered. I pulled out my phone again, and brought up the study. Modestly. Okay. Modestly is better than moderately. *But consistently*. Shit.

I felt nauseated and disgusting, but also pathetic; I knew how I looked to him. I knew that my crazy was no longer a quirk, a simple matter of a cracked finger pad. Now, it was an irritation, like it was to Daisy, like it was to anyone who got close to me.

I was cold, but started to sweat anyway. I zipped my jacket up to my chin as I walked toward the house. I didn't want to run, but every second counted. Needed to get to a bathroom. Davis opened the back door for me and pointed me down a hallway toward a guest bathroom. I closed the door and locked it, shutting myself inside, and leaned against the countertop. I unzipped my jacket and stared at myself in the mirror. I took off the Band-Aid, opened up the cut with my thumbnail, then washed my hands and put on a new Band-Aid. I looked in the drawers beneath the sink for some mouthwash, but they didn't have any, so in the end, I just swished cold water around in my mouth and spit it out.

There, are we good? I asked myself, and I responded, *One more time to make sure*, and so I swished and gargled more water, spit it out. I patted my sweaty face dry with some toilet paper and walked back into the golden light of Davis's mansion.

He motioned for me to sit down, and put his arm around me. I didn't want his microbiota near me, but I let him keep his arm there, because I didn't want to seem like a freak. "Are you okay?"

"Yeah. Just, like, a little panicky."

"Was it something that I did? Should I do—"

"No, it's not about you."

"You can tell me."

"It's really not. I . . . just, kissing freaked me out a little, I guess."

"Okay, so no kissing yet. That's no problem."

"It will be," I said. "I have these . . . thought spirals, and I can't get out of them."

"Turning and turning in the tightening gyre," he said.

"I'm . . . this, like . . . this doesn't get better. You should know that."

"I'm not in a rush."

I leaned forward, looking at the hardwood floor. "I'm not gonna un-have this is what I mean. I've had it since I can remember and it's not getting better and I can't have a normal life if I can't kiss someone without freaking out."

"It's okay, Aza. Really."

"You might think that now, but you won't think that forever."

"But it's not forever," he said. "It's now. Can I get you anything? Glass of water or something?"

"Can we . . . can we just watch a movie or something?"

"Yes," he said. "Absolutely." He offered me his hand, but I got up on my own. As we walked toward the basement steps, Davis said, "Here at the Pickett residence, we have both kinds of movies—Star Wars and Star Trek. What would you prefer?"

"I'm not really a fan of space movies," I said.

"Great, then we'll watch *Star Trek IV: The Voyage Home*, forty percent of which is set right here on earth." I looked up at him and smiled, but I could not cinch the lasso on my thoughts, which were galloping all around my brain.

We walked down to the basement, where I tapped the F. Scott Fitzgerald novel to make the bookcase open. I sat down in one of the overstuffed leather recliners, grateful for the armrests between the seats. Davis appeared after a while with a Dr Pepper, placed it in the cup holder by my armrest, and sat down next to me. "How do you manage to be best friends with Daisy without liking space operas?"

"I'll watch them with her; I just don't *love* them," I said. *He's trying to treat you like you're normal and you're trying to respond like you're normal but everyone involved knows you are definitely not normal. Normal people can kiss if they want to kiss. Normal people don't sweat like you. Normal people choose their thoughts like they choose what to watch on TV. Everyone in this conversation knows you're a freak.*

"Have you read her fic?"

"I read a couple stories when she first started in middle school. They're not really my thing." I could feel the sweat glands opening on my upper lip.

"She's a pretty good writer. You should read them. You're actually kind of *in* some of them."

"Yeah, okay," I said quietly, and then at last he pulled out his phone and used an app to start the movie. I pretended to watch while settling all the way into the spiral. I kept thinking about that Pettibon painting, with its multicolored whirlpool, pulling your eye into the center of it. I tried to breathe in the Dr. Singh–sanctioned way without making it too obvious, but within a few minutes I was sweating in earnest, and he *definitely* noticed, because he'd seen this movie a hundred times, so really he was only watching it to watch *me* watch it, and I could feel his glances over at me, and even though I had my jacket zipped, he obviously had noticed the mad, wet mustache on my sopping upper lip.

I could feel the tension in the air, and I knew he was trying to figure out how to make me happy again. His brain was spinning right alongside mine. I couldn't make myself happy, but I could make people around me miserable.

When the movie ended, I told him I was tired, because that seemed the adjective most likely to get me where I needed to be—alone and in my bed. Davis drove me home, walked me to the door, and kissed me chastely on my sweaty lips. As I stood on my doormat, I waved at him. He backed out of the driveway, and then I went into the garage, opened Harold's trunk, and grabbed my dad's phone, because I felt like looking at his pictures.

I snuck past Mom, who was asleep on the couch in front of the TV. I found an old wall charger in my desk, plugged in Dad's phone, and sat there for a long time swiping through his photos, scrolling through all the pictures of the sky split open by tree branches.

"You know we've got those on the computer," Mom said gently from behind me. I hadn't heard her get up.

"Yeah," I said. I unplugged the phone and shut it off.

"Were you talking to him?"

"Kinda," I said.

"What were you telling him?"

I smiled. "Secrets."

"Ah, I tell him secrets, too. He's good at keeping them."

"The best," I said.

"Aza, I'm very sorry if I hurt Davis's feelings. And I've written him an apology note as well. I took it too far. But I also need you to understand—" I waved her away.

"It's fine. Listen, I gotta change." I grabbed clothes and then went to the bathroom, where I undressed, toweled off the sweat, and then let my body cool down in the air, my feet cold against the floor. I untied my hair, then stared at myself in the mirror. I hated my body. It disgusted me—its hair, its pinpricks of sweat, its scrawniness. Skin pulled over a skeleton, an animated corpse. I wanted out—out of my body, out of my thoughts, *out*—but I was stuck inside of this thing, just like all the bacteria colonizing me.

Knock on the door. "I'm *changing*," I said. I removed the Band-Aid, checked it for blood or pus, tossed it in the trash, and then applied hand sanitizer to my finger, the burn of it seeping into the cut.

I pulled on sweatpants and an old T-shirt of my mom's, and emerged from the bathroom, where Mom was waiting for me.

"You feeling anxious?" she said askingly.

"I'm fine," I answered, and turned toward my room.

I turned out the lights and got into bed. I wasn't tired, exactly, but I wasn't feeling too keen on consciousness, either. When Mom came in, a few minutes later, I pretended to be asleep so I wouldn't have to talk to her. She stood above me, singing this old song she'd sung whenever I couldn't sleep, as far back as I could remember.

It's a song soldiers in England used to sing to the tune of the New Year's song, "Auld Lang Syne." It goes, "We're here because we're here because we're here because we're here." Her pitch rose through the first half like a deep breath in, and then she sang it back down. "We're here because we're here because we're here because we're here."

Even though I was supposed to be basically grown up and my mother annoyed the hell out of me, I couldn't stop thinking until her lullaby finally put me to sleep.

THIRTEEN

DESPITE MY HAVING psychologically decompensated in his presence, Davis texted me the next morning before I even got out of bed.

Him: *Want to watch a movie tonight? Doesn't even have to be set in space.*

Me: *I can't. Another time maybe. Sorry I freaked out and for the sweating and everything.*

Him: *You don't even sweat an un-normal amount.*

Me: *I definitely do but I don't want to talk about it.*

Him: *You really don't like your body.*

Me: *True.*

Him: *I like it. It's a good body.*

I enjoyed being with him more in this nonphysical space, but I also felt the need to board up the windows of my self.

Me: *I feel kinda precarious in general, and I can't really date you. Or date anyone. I'm sorry but I can't. I like you, but I can't date you.*

Him: *We agree on that. Too much work. All people in relationships ever do is talk about their relationship status. It's like a Ferris wheel.*

Me: *Huh?*

Him: *When you're on a Ferris wheel all anyone ever talks about is being on the Ferris wheel and the view from the Ferris wheel and whether the Ferris wheel is scary and how many more times it will go around. Dating is like that. Nobody who's doing it ever talks about anything else. I have no interest in dating.*

Me: *Well, what do you have an interest in?*

Him: *You.*

Me: *I don't know how to respond to that.*

Him: *You don't need to. Have a good day, Aza.*

Me: *You too, Davis.*

I had an appointment with Dr. Karen Singh the next day after school. I sat on the love seat across from her and looked up at that picture of a man holding a net. I stared at the picture while we talked because the relentlessness of Dr. Singh's eye contact was a little much for me.

"How have you been?"

"Not great."

"What's going on?" she asked. In my peripheral vision, I could see her legs crossed, black short-heeled shoes, her foot tapping in the air.

"There's this boy," I said.

"And?"

"I don't know. He's cute and smart and I like him, but I'm not getting any better, and I just feel like if this can't make me happy, then what can?"

"I don't know. What can?"

I groaned. "That's such a psychiatrist move."

"Point taken. A change in personal circumstances, even a positive one, can trigger anxiety. So it wouldn't be uncommon to feel anxious as you develop a new relationship. Where are you with the intrusive thoughts?"

"Well, yesterday I was making out with him and had to stop everything because I couldn't stop thinking about how gross it was, so not great."

"About how gross what was?"

"Just how his tongue has its own particular microbiome and once he sticks his tongue in my mouth his bacteria become part of my microbiome for literally the rest of my life. Like, his tongue will sort of *always* be in my mouth until I'm dead, and then his tongue microbes will eat my corpse."

"And that made you want to stop kissing him."

"Well, yeah," I said.

"That's not uncommon. So part of you wanted to be kissing him and another part of you felt the intense worry that comes with being intimate with someone."

"Right, but I wasn't worried about intimacy. I was worried about microbial exchange."

"Well, your worry expressed itself as being about microbial exchange."

I just groaned at the therapy bullshit. She asked me if I'd taken my Ativan. I told her I hadn't brought it to Davis's house. And then she asked me if I was taking the Lexapro every day, and I was, like, not *every* day. The conversation devolved into her telling me that medication only works if you take it, and that I had to treat my health problem with consistency and care, and me trying to explain that there is something intensely weird and upsetting about the notion that you can only become yourself by ingesting a medication that changes your self.

When the conversation paused for a moment, I asked, "Why'd you put up that picture? Of that guy with the netting?"

"What aren't you saying? What are you scared to say, Aza?"

I thought about the real question, the one that remained constantly in the background of my consciousness like a ringing in the ears. I was embarrassed of it, but also I felt like saying it might be dangerous somehow. Like how you don't ever say Voldemort's name. "I think I might be a fiction," I said.

"How's that?"

"Like, you say it's stressful to have a change in circumstances, right?"

She nodded.

"But what I want to know is, is there a you independent of circumstances? Is there a way-down-deep me who is an actual, real person, the same person if she has money or not, the same person if she has a boyfriend or not, the same if she goes to this school or that school? Or am I only a set of circumstances?"

"I don't follow how that would make you fictional."

"I mean, I don't control my thoughts, so *they're* not really mine. I don't decide if I'm sweating or get cancer or *C. diff* or whatever, so my *body* isn't really mine. I don't decide any of that—outside forces do. I'm a story they're telling. I am circumstances."

She nodded. "Can you apprehend these outside forces?"

"No, I'm not *hallucinating*," I said. "It's . . . like, I'm just not sure that I am, strictly speaking, real."

Dr. Singh placed her feet on the floor and leaned forward, her hands on her knees. "That's very interesting," she said. "Very interesting." I felt briefly proud to be, for a moment anyway, not *not* uncommon. "It must be very scary, to feel that your self might not be yours. Almost a kind of . . . imprisonment?"

I nodded.

"There's a moment," she said, "near the end of *Ulysses* when the character Molly Bloom appears to speak directly to the author. She says, 'O Jamesy let me up out of this.' You're imprisoned within a self that doesn't feel wholly yours, like Molly Bloom. But also, to you that self often feels deeply contaminated."

I nodded.

"But you give your thoughts too much power, Aza. Thoughts are only thoughts. They are not you. You do belong to yourself, even when your thoughts don't."

"But your thoughts *are* you. I think therefore I am, right?"

"No, not really. A fuller formation of Descartes's philosophy would be *Dubito, ergo cogito, ergo sum*. 'I doubt, therefore I think, therefore I am.' Descartes wanted to know if you could really know that anything was real, but he believed his ability to doubt reality proved that, while *it* might not be real, he was. You are as real as anyone, and your doubts make you more real, not less."

The moment I got back home, I could feel Mom's nerves jangling about my visit with Dr. Singh, even though she was trying to be calm and normal. "How was it?" she asked, not looking back at me while grading tests on the couch.

"Good, I guess," I said.

"I want to apologize again for the way I spoke to Davis yesterday," she said. "You have every right to be upset with me."

"I'm not," I said.

"But I want you to be cautious, Aza. I can tell your anxiety is increasing—from your face to your fingertip."

I balled up my hand and said, "It's not him."

"What is it then?"

"There's no *reason*," I said, and turned on the TV, but she took the remote and muted it.

"You seem locked inside of your mind, and I can't know what's going on in there, and it scares me." I pressed my thumbnail against my fingertip through the Band-Aid, thinking it would scare her a lot more if she *could* see what was going on in there.

"I'm fine. Really."

"But you're not."

"Mom, tell me what to say. Seriously. Just . . . tell me what words I can say to make you calm down about it."

"I don't want to calm down. I want you to stop being in pain."

"Well, that's not how it works, okay? I have to go read for history."

I stood up, but before I could get to my room, she said, "Speaking of which, Mr. Myers told me today that your essay on the Columbian Exchange was the best he'd seen in all his years of teaching."

"He's been teaching like two years," I said.

"Four, but still," she said. "You're going places, Aza Holmes. Big places."

"Did you ever hear of Amherst?" I asked.

"Where?"

"Amherst. It's this college in Massachusetts. It's really good. It's ranked really high. I think I might want to go there—if I get in."

Mom started to say something but swallowed it, and then sighed. "We'll just have to see where the scholarships come from."

"Or Sarah Lawrence," I said. "That one seems good, too."

"Well, remember, Aza, a lot of those schools charge you just to apply, so we have to be selective. The whole process is rigged, from start to finish. They make you pay to find out you can't afford to go. We need to be realistic, and realistically, you're going to be close to home, okay? And not only because of money. I don't think you really want to be halfway across the country from everything you know."

"Yeah," I said.

"Okay, I get it. You don't want to talk to your mother. I love you anyway." She blew me a kiss and at last I escaped to my room.

I *did* have to read for history, but after I finished, I wasn't tired and I kept thinking about texting Davis.

I knew what I wanted to write, or at least what I was thinking about writing. I couldn't stop thinking about the text—writing it out, hitting send knowing I couldn't take it back, the sweaty heart-race of waiting for a reply.

I turned off my light, rolled over onto my side, and shut my eyes, but I couldn't shake the thought; so I reached over for my phone, clicked it awake, and wrote him. *When you said before that you like my body, what did you mean?*

I watched the screen for a few seconds, waiting for the . . . of his reply to appear, but it didn't, so I put the phone back onto the bedside table. My brain was quiet now that I'd done the thing it wanted me to do, and I was nearly asleep when I heard the phone vibrate.

Him: *I mean I like it.*

Me: *What about it?*

Him: *I like the way your shoulders slope down into your collarbone.*

Him: *And I like your legs. I like the curve of your calf.*

Him: *I like your hands. I like your long fingers and the insides of your wrists, the color of the skin there, the veins underneath it.*

Me: *I like your arms.*

Him: *They're skinny.*

Me: *They feel strong actually. Is this okay?*

Him: *Very.*

Me: *So, the curve of my calf? I never noticed it.*

Him: *It's nice.*

Me: *Is that it?*

Him: *I like your ass. I really really like your ass. Is this okay?*

Me: *Yes.*

Him: *I want to start a fan blog about your ass.*

Me: *Okay that's a little weird.*

Him: *I want to write fan fiction in which your amazing butt falls in love with your beautiful eyes.*

Me: *lol. You are really ruining the moment. You were saying...before...?*

Him: *That I like your body. I like your stomach and your legs and your hair and I like. Your. Body.*

Me: *Really?*

Him: *Really.*

Me: *What is wrong with me that texting is fun and kissing is scary?*

Him: *Nothing is wrong with you. Want to come over after school Monday? Watch a movie or something?*

I paused for a while before finally writing, *Sure.*

FOURTEEN

IN THE PARKING LOT before school on Monday, I told Daisy about the texting and the kissing and the eighty million microbes.

"When you put it that way, kissing is actually quite disgusting," she said. "On the other hand, maybe his microbes are *better* than yours, right? Maybe you're getting *healthier*."

"Maybe."

"Maybe you're gonna get superpowers from his microbes. She was a normal girl until she kissed a billionaire and became . . . MICROBIANCA, Queen of the Microbes." I just looked at her. "I'm sorry, is that not helpful?"

"It'll probably get less weird, right?" I said. "Like, each time we kiss and nothing bad happens, it'll get less scary. I mean, it's not like he's actually going to give me campylobacter." And then after a second, I added, "Probably."

Daisy started to say something, but then she saw Mychal walking toward her from across the parking lot. "You'll be fine, Holmesy. See you at lunch. Love you!" she said, and then took off toward Mychal. She threw her arms around him, and kissed him dramatically on the lips, one leg raised at the knee like she was in a movie or something.

I drove over to Davis's house straight from school. The wrought-iron gates at the entrance of the driveway were closed, and I had to get out to press the intercom button.

"Pickett estate," said a voice I recognized as Lyle's.

"Hi, it's Aza Holmes, Davis's friend," I said.

He didn't answer, but the gate began to creak open. I got back in Harold and drove up the driveway. Lyle was sitting in his golf cart when I arrived next to the house. "Hi," I said.

"Davis and Noah are at the pool," he said. "Can I give you a ride?"

"I can walk," I said.

"Take the ride," he responded flatly, gesturing to the space on the cart's bench beside him. I sat down, and he set off very slowly toward the pool. "How's Davis doing?" he asked me.

"Good, I think."

"Fragile—that's what he is. They both are."

"Yeah," I said.

"You gotta remember that. You ever lost somebody?"

"I have," I said.

"Then you know," he said as we approached the pool. Davis and Noah were sitting next to each other on the same pool lounger, both hunched forward, staring at the patio beneath them. I was thinking about Lyle saying *then you know*. I didn't, not really. Every loss is unprecedented. You can't ever know someone else's hurt, not really—just like touching someone else's body isn't the same as having someone else's body.

When Davis heard the golf cart pull up, he turned his head to me, nodded, and stood up.

"Hi," I said.

"Hey. I, uh, need a few minutes here. Sorry, uh, something came up with Noah. Lyle, why don't you show Aza around? Show her the lab, maybe? I'll meet you there in a bit, okay?"

I nodded and then got back into the golf cart. Lyle took out his cell phone. "Malik, you got a few minutes to give Davis's friend a tour? . . . We'll be there shortly." Lyle drove me past the golf course, asking me about my school and my grades and what my parents did for a living. I told him my mom was a teacher.

"Dad's not in the picture?"

"He's dead."

"Oh. I'm sorry."

We followed a packed-dirt path through a stand of trees

to a rectangular glass building with a flat roof. A sign outside read LABORATORY.

Lyle walked me to the door and opened it, but then said good-bye. The door closed behind me, and I saw Malik the Zoologist leaning over a microscope. He seemed not to have heard me walk in. The room was enormous, with a long black table in the center, like the ones from chemistry class. There were cabinets beneath it, and all kinds of equipment on top of the table, including some stuff I recognized—glass test tubes, bottles of liquids—and a lot of stuff I didn't. I walked over toward the table and looked at a circular machine with test tubes inside of it.

"Sorry about that," Malik said at last, "but these cells don't live very long outside the body, and Tua only weighs a pound and a half, so I try not to take more blood from her than necessary. That's a centrifuge." He walked over and held up a test tube that contained what looked like blood, then placed it carefully in a rack of tubes.

"So you're interested in biology?"

"I guess," I said.

He looked at the little pool of blood in the bottom of the test tube and said, "Did you know that tuatara can carry parasites—Tua carries salmonella, for instance—but they never get sick from them?"

"I don't know much about tuatara."

"Few people do, which is a real shame, because they're by

far the most interesting reptile species. Truly a glimpse into the distant past." I kept looking at the tuatara blood.

"It's hard for us to even imagine how successful they've been—tuatara have been around a thousand times longer than humans. Just think about that. To survive as long as the tuatara, humans would have to be in the first one-tenth of one percent of our history."

"Seems unlikely," I said.

"Very. Mr. Pickett loves that about Tua—how *successful* she is. He loves that at forty, she's probably still in the first quarter of her life."

"So he leaves his whole estate to her?"

"I can think of worse uses for a fortune," Malik said.

I wasn't sure that I could.

"But what fascinates me most, and is the focus of my research, is their molecular evolution rate. I apologize if this is boring." In fact, I liked listening to him. He was so excited, his eyes wide, like he genuinely loved his work. You don't meet a lot of grown-ups like that.

"No, it's interesting," I said.

"Have you taken bio?"

"Taking it now," I said.

"Okay, so you know what DNA is." I nodded. "And you know that DNA mutates? That's what has driven the diversity of life."

"Yeah," I said.

"So, look." He walked over to a microscope connected to a computer and brought an image of a vaguely circular blob up on the screen. "This is a tuatara cell. As far as we can tell, tuatara haven't changed much in the last two hundred million years, okay? They look the same as their fossils. And tuatara do *everything* slowly. They mature slowly—they don't stop growing until they're thirty. They reproduce slowly—they lay eggs only once every four years. They have a very slow metabolism. But despite doing everything slowly and having not changed much in two hundred million years, tuatara have a faster rate of molecular mutation than any other known animal."

"Like, they're evolving faster?"

"At a *molecular* level, yes. They change more rapidly than humans or lions or fruit flies. Which raises all kinds of questions: Did all animals once mutate at this rate? What happened to slow down molecular mutation? How does the animal itself change so little when its DNA is mutating so rapidly?"

"And do you know the answers?"

He laughed. "Oh no no no. Far from it. What I love about science is that as you learn, you don't really get answers. You just get better questions."

I heard a door open behind me. Davis. "Movie?" he asked.

I told Malik thanks for the tour, and he said, "Anytime. Perhaps next time you'll be ready to pet her."

I smiled. "I doubt it."

Davis and I didn't hug or kiss or anything; we just walked next to each other on the dirt path for a while until he said, "Noah got in trouble in school today."

"What happened?"

"I guess he got caught with some pot."

"Jesus, I'm sorry. Did he get arrested?"

"Oh, no, they don't involve the police with stuff like that." I wanted to tell him the police sure as hell got involved with stuff like that at White River High School, but I stayed quiet. "He's getting suspended, though."

It was just cold enough that I could see the air steam out of my mouth. "Maybe that'll be good for him."

"Well, he's been suspended twice before, and it hasn't helped him so far. I mean, who brings pot to school when they're thirteen? It's like he *wants* to get in trouble."

"I'm sorry," I said.

"He needs a dad," Davis said. "Even a shitty dad. And I can't—like, I have no fucking idea what to do with him. Lyle tried to talk to him today, but Noah's just so monosyllabic—*cool, yeah, 'sup, right*. I can tell he misses Dad, but I can't *do* anything about it, you know? Lyle isn't his father. I'm not his father. Anyway, I just really needed to vent, and you're the only person I can talk to at the moment."

The *only* rolled over me. I could feel my palms starting to sweat. "Let's watch that movie," I said at last.

Down in the theater, he said to me, "I was trying to think of space movies you might like. This one is ridiculous, but also kind of awesome. If you don't like it, you can pick the next ten movies we watch. Deal?"

"Sure," I said. The movie was called *Jupiter Ascending*, and it *was* both ridiculous and kind of awesome. A few minutes in, I reached over to hold his hand, and it felt okay. Nice, even. I liked his hands and the way his fingers intertwined with mine, his thumb turning little circles in the soft skin between my thumb and forefinger.

As the movie reached one of its many climaxes, I giggled at something ridiculous and he said, "Are you enjoying this?"

And I said, "Yeah, it's silly but great."

I felt like he was still looking at me, so I glanced over at him. "I can't tell if I'm misreading this situation," he said, and the way he was smiling made me want to kiss him so much. Holding hands felt good when it often hadn't before, so maybe this would be different now, too.

I leaned over the sizable armrest between us and kissed him quickly on the lips, and I liked the warmth of his mouth. I wanted more of it, and I raised my hand to his cheek and started really kissing him now, and I could feel his mouth opening, and I just wanted to be with him like a normal person would. I wanted to feel the brain-fuzzing intimacy I'd felt when texting with him, and I liked kissing him. He was a good kisser.

But then the thoughts came, and I could feel his spit alive in my mouth. I pulled away as subtly as I could manage.

"You okay?"

"Yeah," I said. "Yeah, totally. Just want to . . ." I was trying to think of what a normal person would say, like maybe if I could just say and do whatever normal people say and do, then he would believe me to be one, or maybe that I could even become one.

"Take it slow?" he suggested.

"Yeah," I said. "Yeah, exactly."

"Cool." He nodded toward the movie. "I've been waiting for this scene. You'll love it. It's bonkers."

There's an Edna St. Vincent Millay poem that's been rumbling around inside me ever since I first read it, and part of it goes, "Blown from the dark hill hither to my door / Three flakes, then four / Arrive, then many more." You can count the first three flakes, and the fourth. Then language fails, and you have to settle in and try to survive the blizzard.

So it was with the tightening spiral of my thoughts: I thought about his bacteria being inside of me. I thought about the probability that some percentage of said bacteria were malicious. I thought about the *E. coli* and campylobacter and *Clostridium difficile* that were very likely an ongoing part of Davis's microbiota.

A fourth thought arrived. Then many more.

"I have to go to the bathroom," I said. "I'll be right back."

I emerged from the basement to find the dying light of the day shining through the windows, making the white walls look a little pink. Noah, playing a video game on the couch, said, "Aza?"

I spun around and entered a bathroom. I washed my face, stared at myself in the mirror, watching myself breathe. I watched myself for a long time, trying to figure a way to shut it off, trying to find my inner monologue's mute button, *trying*.

And then I pulled the hand sanitizer out of my jacket and squeezed a glob of it into my mouth. I gagged a little as I swished the burning slime of it around my mouth, then swallowed.

"You watching *Jupiter Ascending*?" Noah asked as I left the bathroom.

"Yeah."

"Dope." I turned to leave, but then he said, "Aza?" I walked over to him and sat next to him on the couch.

"Nobody wants to find him."

"Your dad, you mean?"

"It's like I can't think about anything else. I . . . it's . . . Do you think, like, he would really disappear and not even text us? Do you think maybe he's trying and we just haven't figured out how to listen?"

I felt so bad for the kid. "Yeah, maybe," I said. "Or maybe he's just waiting until it's safe."

"Right," Noah said. "Yeah, that makes sense. Thanks." I was starting to stand up when he said, "But couldn't he have sent an email? They can't trace that stuff if you just use public Wi-Fi. Couldn't he have texted us from a phone he picked up somewhere?"

"Maybe he's scared," I said. I was trying to help, but maybe there was no helping.

"Will you keep looking, though?"

"Yeah," I said. "Yeah, sure, Noah."

He reached over to pick up his video game controller, my sign to go back downstairs.

Davis had paused the movie in the midst of a starfighter battle, and the bright light from a suspended explosion was reflected in his glasses as he turned to me. I sat down next to him, and he asked, "You all right?"

"I'm really sorry," I said.

"Is there something I should do differen—"

"No, it has nothing to do with you. It's just, like, I just . . . I can't talk about it right now." My head was spinning, and I was trying to keep my mouth turned away from him so he wouldn't smell the hand sanitizer on my breath.

"That's fine," he said. "I like us. I like that we've got our own way of doing things."

"You don't mean that."

"I do." I was staring at the frozen movie screen, waiting for him to un-pause it. "I overheard you talking to Noah."

I could still feel his spit in my mouth, and the respite the hand sanitizer had provided was dwindling away. If I could still feel his spit, it was probably still in there. *You might need to drink more of it*. This is ridiculous. Billions of people kiss, and nothing bad happens to them. *You know you'll feel better if you drink more.*

"He needs to see somebody," I said. "A psychologist or something."

"He needs a father."

Why did you even try to kiss him? You should've known. You could've had a normal night, but you chose this. Right now needs to be about Noah, not me. *His bacteria are swimming in you. They're on your tongue right now. Even pure alcohol can't kill them all.*

"Do you just want to watch the movie?"

I nodded, and we sat next to each other, close but not touching, for the next hour, as the spiral tightened.

FIFTEEN

AFTER I GOT HOME THAT NIGHT, I went to bed but not to sleep. I kept starting texts to him and then not sending them, until finally I put the phone down and took my laptop out. I was wondering what had happened to Davis's online life—where he'd gone once he shut down his social media profiles.

The google hits related to Davis were overwhelmingly about his father—"Pickett Engineering CEO Reveals in Interview He Won't Leave a Dime to His Teenage Children," etc. Davis hadn't updated his Instagram, Facebook, Twitter, or blog since the disappearance, and searches for his two usernames, dallgoodman and davisnotdave02, turned up only links to other people.

So I started looking for similar usernames: dallgoodman02,

davisnotdave, davisnotdavid, then guessing at Facebook and blog URLs. And then after more than an hour, just after midnight, it finally occurred to me to search for the phrase, "the leaves are gone you should be, too."

A single link came up, to a blog with the username isnotid02. The site had been created two months earlier, and like Davis's previous journal, most of the entries began with a quote from someone else and then concluded with a short, cryptic essay. But this site also had a tab called *poems*. I clicked over to the journal and scrolled down until I reached the first entry:

> "In three words I can sum up everything I've learned about life: It goes on." —ROBERT FROST
>
> Fourteen days since the mess began. My life isn't worse, exactly—just smaller. Look up long enough and you start to feel your infinitesimality. The difference between alive and not—that's something. But from where the stars are watching, there is almost no difference between varieties of alive, between me and the newly mown grass I'm lying on right now. We are both astonishments, the closest thing in the known universe to a miracle.

> "And then a Plank in Reason, broke / And I dropped down, and down—" —EMILY DICKINSON

There are about a hundred billion stars in the Milky Way—one for every person who ever lived, more or less. I was thinking about that beneath the sky tonight, unseasonably warm, as good a showing of stars as one gets around here. Something about looking up always makes me feel like I'm falling.

Earlier, I heard my brother crying in his room, and I stood next to the door for a long time, and I know he knew I was there because he tried to stop sobbing when the floorboards creaked under my footstep, and I just stood out there for the longest time, staring at his door, unable to open it.

"Even the silence / has a story to tell you."

—JACQUELINE WOODSON

The worst part of being truly alone is you think about all the times you wished that everyone would just leave you be. Then they do, and you are left being, and you turn out to be terrible company.

"The world is a globe—the farther you sail, the closer to home you are." —TERRY PRATCHETT

Sometimes I open Google Maps and zoom in on random places where he might be. S came by last night to walk us through what happens now—what happens if he's found, what happens if he's not—and at one point he said, "You understand that I'm referring now not to the physical person but to the legal entity." The legal entity is what hovers over us, haunting our home. The physical person is in that map somewhere.

"I am in love with the world." —MAURICE SENDAK

We always say that we are beneath the stars. We aren't, of course—there is no up or down, and anyway the stars surround us. But we say we are beneath them, which is nice. So often English glorifies the human—we are whos, other animals are thats—but English puts us beneath the stars, at least.

Eventually, a *she* showed up.

"What's past is prologue." —WILLIAM SHAKESPEARE

Seeing your past—or a person from your past—can for me at least be physically painful. I'm overwhelmed by a melancholic ache—and I want the past back, no matter the cost. It doesn't matter that it won't come back, that it never even actually existed as I remember it—I want it back. I want things to be like they were, or like I remember them having been: Whole. But she

> doesn't remind me of the past, for some reason. She feels present tense.

The next entry was posted late the night he'd given me the money, and more or less confirmed that the she was me.

> "Awake, dear heart, awake. Thou hast slept well. Awake." —WILLIAM SHAKESPEARE
>
> I wonder if I fucked it up. But if I hadn't done it, I'd have wondered something else. Life is a series of choices between wonders.
>
> "The isle is full of noises." —WILLIAM SHAKESPEARE
>
> The thought, would she like me if I weren't me, is an impossible thought. It folds in upon itself. But what I mean is would she like me if the same body and soul were transported into a different life, a lesser life? But then, of course, I wouldn't be me. I would be someone else. The past is a snare that has already caught you. A nightmare, Dedalus said, from which I am trying to awake.

And then the most recent entry:

> "This thing of darkness I / Acknowledge mine." —WILLIAM SHAKESPEARE

She noted, more than once, that the meteor shower
was happening, beyond the overcast sky, even if we
could not see it. Who cares if she can kiss? She can see
through the clouds.

It was only after reading every journal entry that I noticed the ones about me began with quotes from *The Tempest*. I felt like I was invading his privacy, but it was a public blog, and spending time with his writing felt like spending time with him, only not as scary. So I clicked over to the *poems* section.

The first one went:

My mother's footsteps
Were so quiet
I barely heard her leave.

Another:

You must never let truth get in the way of beauty,
Or so e. e. cummings believed.
"This is the wonder that's keeping the stars apart,"
He wrote of love and longing.
That often got him laid I'm sure,
Which was the poem's sole intent.
But gravity differs from affection:
Only one is constant.

And then the first poem, written on the same day as the first journal entry, two weeks after his father's disappearance.

> He carried me around my whole life—
> Picked me up, took me here and there, said
> Come with me. I'll take you. We'll have fun.
> We never did.
> You don't know a father's weight
> Until it's lifted.

As I reread the poem, my phone buzzed. Davis. *Hi.*

Me: *Hi.*

Him: *Are you on my blog right now?*

Me:…*Maybe. Is that okay?*

Him: *I'm just glad it's you. My analytics said someone from Indianapolis has been on the site for 30 minutes. I got nervous.*

Me: *Why?*

Him: *I don't want my terrible poems published in the news.*

Me: *Nobody would do that. Also stop saying your poems are terrible.*

Him: *How did you find it?*

Me: *Searched "the leaves are gone you should be too." Nothing anyone else would know to search.*

Him: *Sorry if I sound paranoid I just like posting there and don't want to have to delete it.*

Him: *It was nice to see you tonight.*

Me: *Yeah.*

I saw the . . . that meant he was typing, but no words came, so after a while, I wrote him.

Me: *Do you want to facetime?*

Him: *Sure.*

My fingers were trembling a little when I tapped the button to start a video call. His face appeared, gray in the ghostlight of his phone, and I held a finger up to my mouth and whispered, "*Shh*," and we watched each other in silence, our barely discernible faces and bodies exposed through our screens' dim light, more intimate than I could ever be in real life.

As I looked at his face looking at mine, I realized the light that made him visible to me came mostly from a cycle: Our screens were lighting each of us with light from the other's bedroom. I could only see him because he could see me. In the fear and excitement of being in front of each other in that grainy silver light, it felt like I wasn't really in my bed and he wasn't really in his. Instead, we were together in the non-sensorial place, almost like we were inside the other's consciousness, a closeness that real life with its real bodies could never match.

After we hung up, he texted me. *I like us. For real.*

And somehow, I believed him.

SIXTEEN

AND FOR A WHILE, we found ways to be us—hanging out IRL occasionally, but texting and facetiming almost every night. We'd found a way to be on a Ferris wheel without talking about being on a Ferris wheel. Some days I fell deeper into spirals than others, but changing the Band-Aid sort of worked, and the breathing exercises and the pills and everything else sort of worked.

And my life continued—I read books and did homework, took tests and watched TV with my mom, saw Daisy when she wasn't busy with Mychal, read and reread that college guide and imagined the array of futures it promised.

And then one night, bored and missing the days when Daisy and I spent half our lives together at Applebee's, I read her Star Wars stories.

Daisy's most recent story, "A Rey of Hot," had been

published the week before. I was astonished to see it had been read thousands of times. Daisy was kind of famous.

The story, narrated by Rey, takes place on Tatooine, where lovebirds Rey and Chewbacca have stopped off to pick up some cargo from an eight-foot-tall dude named Kalkino. Chewie and Rey are accompanied by a blue-haired girl named Ayala, whom Rey describes as "my best friend and greatest burden."

They meet up with Kalkino at a pod race, where Kalkino offers the team two million credits to take four boxes of cargo to Utapau.

"I've got a weird feeling about this," Ayala said.

I rolled my eyes. Ayala couldn't get anything right. And the more she worried, the worse she made everything. She had the moral integrity of a girl who'd never been hungry, always shitting on the way Chewie and I made a living without noticing that our work provided her with food and shelter. Chewie owed Ayala a life debt because her father had died saving Chewie years ago, and Chewie was a Wookiee of principle even when it wasn't convenient. Ayala's morals were all convenience because easy living was the only kind of living she'd ever known.

Ayala mumbled, "This isn't right." She reached into her mane of blue hair and plucked out a strand, then twirled it around her finger. A nervous habit, but then all her habits were nervous.

I kept reading, my gut clenching as I did. Ayala was horrible. She interrupted Chewie and Rey while they were making out on board the *Millennium Falcon* with an annoying question about the hyperdrive "that a reasonably competent five-year-old could've figured out." She screwed up the shipment by opening one of the cargo cases, revealing power cells that shot off so much energy they almost blew up the ship. At one point, Daisy wrote, "Ayala wasn't a bad person, just a useless one."

The story ended with the triumphant delivery of the power cells. But because one had lost some of its energy when Ayala opened the box, the recipients knew our intrepid heroes had seen the cargo, and a bounty was placed on their heads—or should I say *our* heads—all of which meant the stakes would be even higher in next week's story.

There were dozens of comments. The most recent one was, "I LOVE TO HATE AYALA. THANK YOU FOR BRINGING HER BACK." Daisy had replied to that comment with, "Thx! Thx for reading!"

I read through the stories in reverse chronological order and discovered all the previous ways Ayala had ruined things for Chewie and Rey. The only time I'd ever done anything worthwhile was when, overcome by anxiety, I threw up on a Hutt named Yantuh, creating a momentary distraction that allowed Chewie to grab a blaster and save us from certain death.

I stayed up too late reading, and then later still thinking about what I'd say to Daisy the next morning, my thoughts careening between furious and scared, circling around my bedroom like a vulture. I woke up the next morning feeling wretched—not just tired, but terrified. I now saw myself as Daisy saw me—clueless, helpless, useless. Less.

As I drove to school, my head pounding from sleeplessness, I kept thinking about how I'd been scared of monsters as a kid. When I was little, I knew monsters weren't, like, *real*. But I also knew I could be hurt by things that weren't real. I knew that made-up things mattered, and could kill you. I felt like that again after reading Daisy's stories, like something invisible was coming for me.

I expected the sight of Daisy to piss me off, but when I actually saw her, sitting on the steps outside school, bundled up against the cold, a gloved hand waving at me, I felt like—well, like I deserved it, really. Like Ayala was the thing Daisy had to do to live with me.

She stood up as I approached. "You okay, Holmesy?" Daisy asked. I nodded. I couldn't really say anything. My throat felt tight, like I might start to cry.

"What's wrong?" she asked.

"Just tired," I said.

"Holmesy, don't take this the wrong way, but you look like you just got off work from your job playing a ghoul at a haunted house, and now you're in a parking lot trying to score some meth."

"I'll be sure not to take that the wrong way."

She put her arm around me. "I mean, you're still gorgeous, of course. You can't ungorgeous yourself, Holmesy, no matter how hard you try. I'm just saying you need some *sleep*. Do some self-care, you know?" I nodded and shrugged off her embrace. "We haven't hung out in forever just the two of us," she said. "Maybe I can come over later?"

I wanted to tell her no, but I was thinking about how Ayala always said no to everything, and I didn't want to be like my fictional self. "Sure."

"Mychal and I are having a homework night, but I should have about a hundred and forty-two minutes after school if we go straight to your house, which just happens to be the running time of *Attack of the Clones*."

"A homework night?" I asked.

Mychal appeared from behind me and said, "We're reading *A Midsummer Night's Dream* to each other for English."

". . . seriously?"

"What?" Daisy said. "It's not my fault we're adorable. But first, Yoda lightsaber battling at your house after school. Cool?"

"Cool."

"It's a date," she said.

Six hours later, we lay on the floor next to each other, bodies propped up with couch cushions, and watched Anakin Skywalker and Padmé fall for each other in extremely slow motion. Daisy considered *Attack of the Clones* to be the most underrated Star Wars film. I thought it was kinda crap, but it was fun to watch Daisy watch it. Her mouth literally moved with each line of dialogue.

I was looking at my phone mostly, scrolling through articles about Pickett's disappearance, looking for anything that might connect to joggers or a jogger's mouth. I'd meant it when I told Noah I'd keep looking—but the clues we had just didn't seem much like clues.

"I want to like Jar Jar, because hating Jar Jar is so cliché, but he was *the worst*," Daisy said. "I actually killed him years ago in my fic. It felt amazing." My stomach turned, but I concentrated on my phone. "What are you looking at?" she asked.

"Just reading about the Pickett investigation, seeing if there's anything new. Noah's really screwed up about it, and I . . . I don't know. I just want to help him somehow."

"Holmesy, we got the reward. It's over. Your problem is you don't know when you've won."

"Yeah," I said.

"I mean, Davis gave us the reward so that we would drop it. So, drop it."

"Yeah, okay," I said. I knew she was right, but she didn't have to be such an asshole about it.

I thought the conversation was over, but a few seconds later she paused the movie and continued talking. "It's just, like, this isn't going to be some story where the poor, penniless girl gets rich and then realizes that truth matters more than money and establishes her heroism by going back to being the poor, penniless girl, okay? Everyone's life is better with Pickett disappeared. Just let it be."

"No one's taking away your money," I said quietly.

"I love you, Holmesy, but be smart."

"*Got it*," I said.

"Promise?"

"Yeah, I promise."

"And we break hearts, but we don't break promises," she said.

"You say that's your 'motto,' but you spend ninety-nine percent of your time with Mychal now."

"Except right now I'm hanging out with you and Jar Jar Binks," she said.

We went back to watching the movie. As it ended, she squeezed my arm and said, "I love you," then raced off to Mychal's place.

SEVENTEEN

LATER THAT NIGHT, I got a text from Davis.

Him: *You around?*

Me: *I am. You want to facetime?*

Him: *Could I possibly see you irl?*

Me: *I guess, but I'm less fun irl.*

Him: *I like you irl. Is now good?*

Me: *Now's good.*

Him: *Dress warm. It's cold out, and the sky is clear.*

Harold and I drove over to the Pickett compound. He's not much for cold weather, and it seemed to me I could hear something in his engine tightening up, but he held it together for me, that blessed car.

The walk from the driveway to Davis's house was frigid, even in my winter coat and mittens. You never think much about weather when it's good, but once it gets cold enough to see your breath, you can't ignore it. The weather decides when you think about it, not the other way around.

As I approached, the front door opened for me. Davis was sitting on the couch next to Noah, playing their usual starfighter video game. "Hi," I said.

"Hey," Davis said.

"'Sup," Noah added.

"Listen, bud," Davis said as he stood up. "I'm gonna go for a walk with Aza before she debundles. Back in a bit, cool?" He reached over and mussed Noah's hair.

"Cool," Noah said.

"I read Daisy's stories," I told him as we walked. The grass of the golf course was still cut perfectly short, even though the only golfer in the family had now been missing for months.

"They're pretty good, right?"

"I guess. I was distracted by how terrible Ayala is."

"She's not all bad. Just anxious."

"She causes one hundred percent of the problems in the stories."

He nudged his shoulder against me sweetly. "I kind of liked her, but I guess I'm biased."

We walked around the whole property until we eventually stopped at the pool. Davis tapped a button on his phone and the pool cover rolled away. We sat down on lounge chairs next to each other, and I watched the water from the pool steam into the cold air as Davis lay back to look up at the sky. "I don't understand why he's so stuck inside himself, when there is this endlessness to fall into."

"Who is?"

"Noah." I noticed he'd reached into his coat pocket. He pulled something out and twirled it in his palm. At first, I thought it might be a pen, but then as he moved it rhythmically through his fingers, like a magician playing with cards, I realized it was the Iron Man. "Don't judge me," he said. "It's been a bad week."

"I just don't think Iron Man is much of a superh—"

"You're breaking my heart, Aza. So, you see Saturn up there?" Using his Iron Man as a pointer, he told me how you can tell the difference between a planet and a star, and where different constellations were. And he told me that our galaxy was a big spiral, and that a lot of galaxies were. "Every star we can see right now is in that spiral. It's huge."

"Does it have a center?"

"Yeah," he said. "Yeah, the whole galaxy is rotating around this supermassive black hole. But very slowly. I mean, it takes our solar system like two hundred twenty-five million Earth years to orbit the galaxy."

I asked him if the spirals of the galaxy were infinite, and he said no, and then he asked about my spirals.

I told him about this mathematician Kurt Gödel, who had this really bad fear of being poisoned, so much so that he couldn't bring himself to eat food unless it was prepared by his wife. And then one day his wife got sick and had to go into the hospital, so Gödel stopped eating. I told Davis how even though Gödel must've known that starvation was a greater risk than poisoning, he just couldn't eat, and so he starved to death. At seventy-one. He cohabitated with the demon for seventy-one years, and then it got him in the end.

When I'd finished the story, he asked, "Do you worry that will happen to you?"

And I said, "It's so weird, to know you're crazy and not be able to do anything about it, you know? It's not like you believe yourself to be normal. You know there is a problem. But you can't figure a way through to fixing it. Because you can't be sure, you know? If you're Gödel, you just can't be sure your food isn't poisoned."

"Do you worry that will happen to you?" he asked again.

"I worry about a lot of things."

We kept on talking, for so long that the stars moved above us, until eventually he asked, "Wanna swim?"

"Bit cold," I said.

"Pool's heated," he answered. He stood up and pulled off his shirt, then kicked out of his jeans while I watched. I liked watching him take off his jeans. He was skinny, but I liked his body—the small but sinewy muscles in his back, his goose-bumped legs. Shivering, he jumped into the water. "Magnificent," he said.

"I don't have a bathing suit."

"Well, if you have a bra and underwear that's *basically* a bikini." I laughed and took off my coat, then stood up.

"Do you mind turning around?" I asked him. He turned toward the dimly lit terrarium, where the billionaire-in-waiting was hiding somewhere in her artificial forest.

I wriggled out of my jeans and pulled off my shirt. I felt naked even though technically I wasn't, but I dropped my hands to my sides and said, "Okay, you can look." I slid into the warmth of the pool next to him; he put his hands on my waist under the water, but didn't try to kiss me.

The terrarium was behind him, and now that my eyes were fully adjusted to the dark I could see the tuatara on a branch, staring at us through one of her redblack eyes. "Tua's watching us," I said.

"She's such a perv," Davis answered, and then turned to look at the animal. Her green skin had some kind of yellow moss growing on it, and I could see her teeth as she breathed with her mouth slightly open. Her miniature crocodile tail flickered suddenly, and Davis startled, curling into me, then laughed. "I hate that thing," he said.

It was freezing when we got out. We didn't have any towels, so we carried our clothes in our arms and ran back to the house. Noah was still on the couch playing the same game. I hustled past him and jogged up the marble stairs.

Once we were dressed, we went to Davis's bedroom. He put the Iron Man on his bedside table, then knelt down to show me how his telescope worked. He plugged some coordinates into a remote control, and the telescope moved itself. When it stopped, Davis stooped to look through the lens, then cleared the way for me.

"That's Tau Ceti," he said. The way the telescope was zoomed in, I couldn't see anything but darkness and one jittering disk of white light. "Twelve light-years away, similar to our sun but a little smaller. Two of its planets actually might be habitable—probably not, but maybe. It's my favorite star." I didn't know what I was supposed to be seeing—it was just a circle like any other. But then he explained.

"I like to look at it and think about how the sun's light looks to someone in Tau Ceti's solar system. Right now, they're seeing our light from twelve years ago—in the light they're seeing, my mom has three years to live. This house has just been built, and Mom and Dad are always fighting about the layout of the kitchen. In the light they see, you and I are just kids. We've got the best and the worst of it in front of us."

"We still have the best and the worst of it in front of us," I said.

"I hope not," he said. "I sure as hell hope the worst is behind me."

I pulled away from Tau Ceti's twelve-year-old light and looked up at Davis. I took his hand, and part of me wanted to tell him I loved him, but I wasn't sure if I really did. Our hearts were broken in the same places. That's something like love, but maybe not quite the thing itself.

It sucked having a dead person in your family, and I knew what he meant, about seeking solace in the old light. Three years from now, I knew, he'd find a different favorite star, one with older light to gaze upon. And when time caught up with that one, he'd love a farther star, and a farther one, because you can't let the light catch up with the present. Otherwise you'd forget.

That's why I liked looking at my dad's pictures. It was the same thing, really. Photographs are just light and time.

"I should go," I said quietly.

"Can I see you this weekend?"

"Yeah," I said.

"Could we hang out at your house next time, maybe?"

"Sure," I said. "If you don't mind being harassed by my mother."

He assured me he didn't, and then we hugged good-bye,

and as I left him alone in his room, he knelt back down to the telescope.

When I got home that night, I told Mom that Davis wanted to come over this weekend. "Is he your boyfriend?" she asked.

"I guess so," I said.

"He respects you as an equal?"

"Yeah."

"He listens to you as much as you listen to him?"

"Well, I'm not great at talking. But yes. He listens to me. He's really, really sweet, and also at some point you just have to trust me, you know?"

She sighed. "All I want in this world is to keep you. Keep you from hurt, keep you from stress, all that." I hugged her. "You know I love you."

I smiled. "Yeah, Mom. I know you love me. You definitely don't have to worry about that."

After going to bed that night, I checked in on Davis's blog.

> "Doubt thou that the stars are fire, / Doubt that the sun doth move." —WILLIAM SHAKESPEARE
>
> It dothn't move, of course—well, it does, but not around us. Even Shakespeare assumed fundamental

truths about the fundament that turned out to be wrong. Who knows what lies I believe, or you do. Who knows what we shouldn't doubt.

Tonight, under the sky, she asked me, "Why do all the ones about me have quotes from *The Tempest*? Is it because we are shipwrecked?"

Yes. Yes, it is because we are shipwrecked.

I hit refresh after reading it, just in case, and there was a new entry, posted minutes before.

"There's an expression in classical music. It goes, 'We went out to the meadow.' It's for those evenings that can only be described in that way: There were no walls, there were no music stands, there weren't even any instruments. There was no ceiling, there was no floor, we all went out to the meadow. It describes a feeling."

—TOM WAITS

I know she's reading this right now. (Hi.) I felt like we went out to the meadow tonight, only we weren't playing music. In the best conversations, you don't even remember what you talked about, only how it felt. It was like we weren't even there, lying together by the pool. It felt like we were in some place your body can't visit, some place with no ceiling and no walls and no floor and no instruments.

And that really should have ended my evening. But instead of going to sleep, I decided to torture myself by reading more Ayala stories.

I didn't understand how Davis could like her. She was horrible—totally self-centered and perpetually annoying. At one party scene, Rey observed, "Of course, when Ayala's around, it's never *really* a party, because at parties, people have fun."

Eventually, I clicked away from the site, but I couldn't bring myself to put away the computer and go to sleep. Instead, I ended up on Wikipedia, reading about fan fiction and Star Wars, and then I found myself reading the same old articles about the human microbiota and studies of how people's microbial makeup had shaped and, in some cases, killed them.

At one point, I came across this sentence: "Mammal brains receive a constant stream of interoceptive input from the GI tract, which combines with other interoceptive information from within the body and contextual information from the environment before sending an integrated response to target cells within the GI tract through what is commonly called the 'gut-brain informational axis' but might be better described as the 'gut-brain informational *cycle*.'"

I realize that's not the sort of sentence that fills most people with horror, but it stopped me cold. It was saying that my bacteria were affecting my thinking—maybe not directly, but through the information they told my gut to send to my brain. *Maybe you're not even thinking this thought. Maybe your thinking's infected.* Shouldn't've been reading these articles. Should've gone to sleep. *Too late now.*

I checked the light under the door to make sure Mom had gone to sleep and then snuck over to the bathroom. I changed the Band-Aid, looking carefully at the old one. There was blood. Not a lot, but blood. Faintly pink. It isn't infected. It bleeds because it hasn't scabbed over. *But it could be*. It isn't. *Are you sure? Did you even clean it this morning?* Probably. I always clean it. *Are you sure?* Oh, for fuck's sake.

I washed my hands, put on a new Band-Aid, but now I was being pulled all the way down. I opened the medicine cabinet quietly. Took out the aloe-scented hand sanitizer. I took a gulp, then another. Felt dizzy. You can't do this. This shit's pure alcohol. It'll make you sick. *Better do it again.* Poured some more of it on my tongue. That's enough. You'll be clean after this. *Just get one last swallow down.* I did. Heard my gut rumbling. Stomach hurt.

Sometimes you clear out the healthy bacteria and that's when C. diff *comes in. You gotta watch out for that.* Great, you tell me to drink it, then tell me not to.

Back in my room, sweating over the covers, body clammy, corpse-like. Can't get my head straight. Drinking hand sanitizer is not going to make you healthier, you crazy fuck. *But they can talk to your brain. THEY can tell your brain what to think, and you can't. So, who's running the show?* Stop it, please.

I tried not to think the thought, but like a dog on a leash I could only get so far from it before I felt the strangling pull against my throat. My stomach rumbled.

Nothing worked. Even giving in to the thought had only provided a moment's release. I returned to a question Dr. Singh had first asked me years ago, the first time it got this bad: *Do you feel like you're a threat to yourself?* But which is the threat and which is the self? I wasn't *not* a threat, but couldn't say to whom or what, the pronouns and objects of the sentence muddied by the abstraction of it all, the words sucked into the non-lingual way down. *You're a we. You're a you. You're a she, an it, a they.* My kingdom for an I.

Felt myself slipping, but even that's a metaphor. Descending, but that is, too. Can't describe the feeling itself except to say that I'm not me. Forged in the smithy of someone else's soul. Please just let me out. Whoever is authoring me, let me up out of this. Anything to be out of this.

But I couldn't get out.

Three flakes, then four arrive.

Then many more.

EIGHTEEN

MOM WOKE ME UP AT 6:50. "Sleep through your alarm?" she asked.

I squinted. It was still dark in my room. "I'm fine," I said.

"You sure?"

"Yeah," I said, and pulled myself out of bed.

I was at school just thirty-two minutes later. I didn't look my best, but I'd long ago given up trying to impress the student body of White River High School.

Daisy was sitting alone on the front steps. "You look sleepy," she said as I walked up. It was cloudy, the kind of day where the sun is a supposition.

"Long night. How are you?"

"Great, except I haven't seen nearly enough of my best friend lately. You want to hang out later? Applebee's?"

"Sure," I said.

"Also, my mom had to borrow my car, so can we just go together?"

I made it through lunch, through the standard post-lunch encounter with Mom worrying over my "tired eyes," through history and statistics. In each room the soul-sucking fluorescent light coated everything in a film of sickness, and the day droned on until the final bell released me at last. I made it to Harold, sat down in the driver's seat, and waited for Daisy.

I hadn't been sleeping much. Hadn't been thinking straight. That sanitizer is basically pure alcohol; you can't keep drinking that. Should probably call Dr. Singh, but then you'll have to talk to her answering service and tell a stranger that you're crazy. Can't bear the thought of Dr. Singh calling back, voice tinged with sympathy, asking whether I'm taking the medication every day. Doesn't work anyway. Nothing does. Three different medications and five years of cognitive behavioral therapy later, and here we are.

I startled awake at the sound of Daisy opening the passenger door. "You okay?" she asked.

"Yeah," I said. I turned the car on. Felt my spine straightening. I reversed out of the parking spot and then waited in line to leave campus. "You barely even changed my name," I said. My voice felt squeaky, but I was finding it.

"Huh?"

"Ayala, Aza. Beginning of the alphabet to the end and back. Gave her compulsions. Gave her my personality. Anyone reading it would know how you really feel about me. Mychal. Davis. Everyone at school, probably."

"Aza," Daisy said. My real name sounded wrong in her voice. "You're not—"

"Oh, fuck off."

"I've been writing them since I was eleven, and you've *never read a single one*."

"You never asked."

"First, I *did* ask. A bunch of times. And then I got tired of you saying you'd read them and never doing it. And second, I shouldn't *have* to ask. You could take three seconds away from your nonstop fucking contemplation of yourself to think about other people's interests. Look, I came up with Ayala in like seventh grade. And it was a dick move, but she's her own character now. She's not you, okay?" We were still inching our way through the student parking lot. "I mean, I love you, and it's not your fault, but your anxiety does kind of invite disasters."

At last I pulled off campus and headed north up Meridian toward the highway. She kept talking, of course. She always did. "I'm sorry, okay? I should've let Ayala die years ago. But yeah, you're right, it is kind of a way of coping with—I mean, Holmesy, you're *exhausting*."

"Yeah, all our friendship has gotten you in the last couple months is fifty thousand dollars and a boyfriend. You're right, I'm a terrible person. What'd you call me in that story? Useless. I'm useless."

"Aza, she's *not you*. But you are . . . extremely self-centered. Like, I know you have the mental problems and whatever, but they do make you . . . you know."

"I don't know, actually. They make me what?"

"Mychal said once that you're like mustard. Great in small quantities, but then a lot of you is . . . a lot."

I didn't say anything.

"I'm sorry. I shouldn't've said that."

We were stopped at a red light, and when it turned green I was somewhat ungentle with Harold's accelerator. I could feel the heat in my cheeks, but couldn't tell if I was about to start crying or screaming. Daisy kept going. "But you know what I mean. Like, what are my parents' names?"

I didn't answer. I didn't know the answer. I just took a long breath, trying to push my heartbeat down into my chest. I didn't need Daisy to point out what a shitshow I was. I knew.

"What are their jobs? When was the last time you were at my apartment—five years ago? We're supposed to be best friends, Holmesy, and you don't even know if I have any fucking pets. You have no idea what it's like for me, and you're so, like, pathologically uncurious that you don't even know what you don't know."

"You have a cat," I whispered.

"You just have no fucking clue. It's all so fucking easy for you. I mean, you think you and your mom are poor or whatever, but you got braces. You got a car and a laptop and all that shit, and you think it's *natural*. You think it's just normal to have a house with your own room and a mom who helps you with your homework. You don't think you're privileged, but you have everything. You don't know what it's like for me, and you don't *ask*. I share a room with my annoying eight-year-old sister whose name you don't know and then you judge me for buying a car instead of saving it all for college, but *you don't know*. You want me to be some selfless, proper heroine who's too good for money, but that's bullshit, Holmesy. Being poor doesn't purify you or whatever the fuck. It just sucks. You don't know my life. You haven't taken the time to find out, and you don't get to judge me."

"Her name is Elena," I said quietly.

"You think it's hard for you and I'm sure it is from inside your head, but . . . you can't get it, because your privileges are just oxygen to you. I thought the money, I thought it would make us the same. I've always been trying to keep up with you, trying to type as fast on my phone as you can on your laptop, and I thought it would make us closer, but it just made me feel . . . like you're spoiled, kinda. Like, you've had this all along, and you can't even know how much easier it makes everything, because you don't ever think about anybody else's life."

I felt like I might throw up. We merged onto the highway. My head was careening—I hated myself, hated her, thought she was right and wrong, thought I deserved it and didn't.

"You think it's easy for me?"

"I don't mean—"

I turned to her. "STOP TALKING. Jesus Christ, you haven't shut up in ten years. I'm sorry it's not fun hanging out with me because I'm stuck in my head so much, but imagine being *actually* stuck inside my head with no way out, with no way to ever take a break from it, because that's my life. To use Mychal's clever little analogy, imagine eating NOTHING BUT mustard, being stuck with mustard ALL THE TIME and if you hate me so much then stop asking me to—"

"HOLMESY!" she shouted, but too late. I looked up only in time to see that I'd kept accelerating while the traffic had slowed. I couldn't even get my foot to the brake before we slammed into the SUV in front of us. A moment later, something slammed into us from behind. Tires screeching. Honking. Another crash, this one smaller. Then silence.

I was trying to catch my breath, but I couldn't, because every breath hurt.

I swore, but it just came out as *ahhhhggg*. I reached for the door only to realize my seat belt was still on. I looked over at Daisy, who was looking back at me. "Are you okay!" she shouted. I realized I was groaning with each exhalation. My ears were ringing. "Yeah," I said. "You?" The pain made me feel dizzy. Darkness encroached at the edge of my vision. "I think so," she said. The world narrowed into a tunnel as I struggled for breath. "Stay in the car, Holmesy. You're hurt. Do you have your phone? We gotta call 911."

The phone. I unbuckled my seat belt and pushed my door open. I tried to stand, but the pain brought me back into Harold's seat. Fuck. *Harold*. A woman wearing a business suit knelt down to my eye level. She told me not to move, but I had to. I lifted myself up, and the pain blinded me for a minute, but then the black dots scattered so I could see the damage.

Harold's trunk was as crumpled as his hood—he looked like a seismograph reading, except for the passenger compartment, which was perfectly intact. He never failed me, not even when I failed him.

I leaned on Harold's side as I staggered back to the trunk. I tried to lift the trunk gate, but it was crushed. I started pounding on the trunk with my hands, screaming with every breath, "Fuck oh God, oh God, oh God. He's totaled. He's totaled."

"You're kidding me," Daisy said as she walked to the back of Harold. "You're upset about the goddamned car? It's a *car*, Holmesy. We almost *died*, and you're worried about your *car*?"

I pounded on the trunk again, until Harold's license plate slid off, but I couldn't get it open.

"Are you *crying* about the *car*?"

I could see the latch; I just couldn't get it pried open, and whenever I tried to lift, the pain in my ribs made my vision cloud up, but I finally wrested the trunk open enough to reach my arm inside. I fumbled around until I found my dad's phone. The screen was shattered.

I held the power button to turn it on, but beneath the branches of broken glass, the screen only glowed a cloudy gray. I pulled myself back to the driver's-side door and slumped into Harold's seat, my forehead on the steering wheel.

I knew the pictures were backed up, that nothing had really been lost. But it was his phone, you know? He'd held it, talked into it. Taken my picture with it.

I ran my thumb across the shattered glass and cried until I felt a hand on my shoulder. "My name's Franklin. You've been in a car accident. I'm a firefighter. Try not to move. An ambulance is on its way. What's your name?"

"Aza. I'm not hurt."

"Just hang tight for me, Aza. Do you know what day it is?"

"It's my dad's phone," I said. "This is his phone, and . . ."

"Is this his car? Are you worried he'll be upset? Aza, I've been doing this for a long time, and I can promise, your dad's not mad at you. He's relieved you're okay."

I felt like I was getting ripped apart from the inside, the

supernova of my selves simultaneously exploding and collapsing. It hurt to cry, but I hadn't cried in so long, and I didn't really want to stop. "Where are you having pain?" he asked.

I pointed toward the right side of my rib cage. A woman approached, and they began a conversation about whether I'd need a backboard. I tried to say that I felt dizzy and then felt myself falling, even though there was really nowhere to fall.

I woke up staring at the ceiling of an ambulance, strapped to a backboard, a man holding an oxygen mask over my face, the sirens distant, my ears still ringing. Then falling again, down and down, and then on a hospital bed in a hallway, Mom over me, makeup dripping from her red eyes. "My baby, oh Lord. Baby, are you all right?"

"I'm fine," I said. "I think I just cracked a rib or something. Dad's phone is broken."

"It's okay. We have everything backed up. They called me and told me you were hurt but they didn't tell me if you were . . ." she said, and then started crying. She sort of collapsed into Daisy, which is when I noticed Daisy was there, a red welt on her collarbone.

I turned away from them and looked up at the bright fluorescent light above my bed, feeling the hot tears on my face, and finally my mom said, "I can't lose you, too."

A woman came in and took me away to get a CT scan,

and I was sort of relieved to be away from both my mom and Daisy for a while, not to feel the swirl of fear and guilt over being such a failure as a daughter and a friend.

"Car accident?" the woman asked as she pushed me past the word *kindness* painted in calligraphy on the wall.

"Yeah," I said.

"Those seat belts will hurt ya while saving your life," she said.

"Yeah. Am I gonna need antibiotics?"

"I'm not your doctor. She'll be in after we get the test."

They put something in my IV that made me feel like I was pissing my pants, then ran me through the cylinder of the CT machine, and eventually returned me to the shivering nerves of my mother. I couldn't shake the crack in her voice when she said she couldn't lose me, too. I felt her nerves as she paced around the room, texting with my aunt and uncle in Texas, pressing long breaths through pursed lips, dabbing at her eye makeup with a tissue.

Daisy didn't say much, for once. "It's okay if you want to go home," I said to her at one point.

"Do you want me to go home?" she asked.

"Up to you," I said. "Seriously."

"I'll stay," she answered, and sat quietly, her eyes glancing from me to my mom and back again.

NINETEEN

"GOOD NEWS AND BAD NEWS," announced a woman in navy-blue scrubs upon entering the room. "Bad news, you have a lacerated liver. Good news, it's a mild laceration. We'll watch you closely for a couple days, so we can make sure your bleeding doesn't increase, and you'll be sore for several weeks, but I'm ordering you pain medication now so you'll be comfortable. Questions."

"She's going to be okay?" my mom asked.

"Yes. If the bleeding worsens, surgery will be necessary, but based on the radiologist's report, I think that's very unlikely. As liver lacerations go, this is about as good as they get. Your daughter is really quite lucky, in the scheme of things."

"She's going to be okay," my mom said again.

"As I said, we'll keep a close eye on her for a couple days, and then she'll have about a week of bed rest. Within six or so weeks, she should be her old self."

My mother dissolved into tears of gratitude as I turned over that phrase, *her old self*. "Do I need antibiotics?" I asked.

"You shouldn't. If we had to do surgery, you would, but as of now, no." A shiver of relief rolled through me. No antibiotics. No increased risk of *C. diff.* Just needed to get the hell out of here, then.

The doctor asked me about my medications, and I told her. She made some notes in the chart and then said, "Someone will be by shortly to take you upstairs, and we'll get you something for the pain before that."

"Wait," I said. "What do you mean upstairs?"

"As I said, you'll need to spend a couple nights here so that you can—"

"Wait, no no no no. I can't stay in the hospital."

"Baby," my mom said. "You have to."

"No, I really can't. I really, this is, like, the one place I absolutely cannot stay tonight. Please. Just let us go home."

"That would be inadvisable."

Oh no. Listen, it's okay. Most people admitted to the hospital go home healthier than they left it. Almost everyone, really. *C. diff* infections are only common in postsurgical patients. You won't even be on antibiotics. *Oh no no no no no no no.*

Of all the places to end up in the tightening gyre, here we were, on the fourth floor of a hospital in Carmel, Indiana.

Daisy left once I'd gotten upstairs but Mom stayed, lying on her side in the reclining chair next to my hospital bed, facing me.

I could feel her breath on me that night as she slept, her lips parted, smudged eyes closed, the microbes from her lungs floating across my cheek. I couldn't roll over onto my side because even with the medication the pain was paralyzing, and when I turned my head, her breath just blew my hair across my face, so I lived with it.

She stirred, her eyes locked to mine. "You okay?"

"Yeah," I said.

"Does it hurt?" I nodded. "You know Sekou Sundiata, in a poem, he said the most important part of the body 'ain't the heart or the lungs or the brain. The biggest, most important part of the body is the part that hurts.'" Mom put her hand on my wrist and fell back asleep.

Even though I was pretty high on morphine or whatever, I couldn't sleep. I could hear beeping in the rooms next to mine, and it wasn't particularly dark, and well-meaning strangers kept showing up to pull blood out of my body and/or check my blood pressure, and most of all, I knew: I knew that *C. diff* was invading my body, that it was floating in the air. On my phone, I paged through patients' stories of how they went into the hospital for a gallbladder surgery or a kidney stone, and they'd come out destroyed.

The thing about *C. diff* is that it's inside of everyone. We all have it, lurking there; it's just that sometimes it grows out of control and takes over and begins attacking your insides. Sometimes it just happens. Sometimes it happens because you ingest someone else's *C. diff*, which is slightly different from your own, and it starts mixing with yours, and *boom*.

I felt these little jolts through my arms and legs as my brain whirred through thoughts, trying to figure out how to make this okay. My IV line beeping. Couldn't even say when I last changed the Band-Aid on my finger. The *C. diff* both inside me and around me. It could survive months outside a body, waiting for a new host. The combined weight of all large animals in the world—human, cow, penguin, shark—is around 1.1 billion tons. The combined weight of the earth's bacteria is 400 billion tons. They overwhelm us.

For some reason, I started hearing that song "Can't Stop Thinking About You" in my head. The more I thought about that song, the weirder it got. Like, the chorus—*can't stop can't stop can't stop thinking about you*—imagines that it is somehow sweet or romantic to be unable to turn your thoughts away from someone, but there's nothing romantic or pretty about a boy thinking about you the way you think about *C. diff*. Can't stop thinking. Trying to find something solid to hold on to in this rolling sea of thought. The spiral painting. Daisy hates you and she should. Davis's microbe-soaked tongue on your neck. Your mom's warm breaths. Hospital gown clinging to your back soaked with sweat. And in the way-down deep, some me screaming, *get me out of here get me out of here get me out please I'll do anything*, but the thoughts just keep spinning, the tightening gyre, the jogger's mouth, the stupidity of Ayala, Aza, and Holmesy and all my irreconcilable selves, my self-absorption, the filth in my gut, *think about anything other than yourself you disgusting narcissist.*

I took my phone and texted Daisy: *I'm so sorry I haven't been a good friend. I can't stop thinking about it.*

She wrote back immediately: *It's fine. How are you?*

Me: *I do care about your life and I'm sorry I haven't shown it.*

Daisy: *Holmesy calm down everything is fine I'm sorry we fought we'll make up it will be fine.*

Me: *I'm just really sorry. I can't think straight.*

Daisy: *Stop apologizing. Are you on sweet pain meds?*

I didn't reply, but I couldn't stop thinking about Daisy, about Ayala, and most of all about the bugs inside and outside of me, and I knew I was being selfish by even making a big deal out of it, making other people's real *C. diff* infections about my hypothetical one. Reprehensible. Pinched my finger with my thumbnail to attest to this moment's reality, but can't escape myself. Can't kiss anyone, can't drive a car, can't function in the actual sensate populated world. How could I even fantasize about going to some school far away where you pay a fortune to live in dorms full of strangers, with communal bathrooms and cafeterias and no private spaces to be crazy in? I'd be stuck here for college, if I could ever get my thinking straightened enough to attend. I'd live in my house with Mom, and then afterward, too. I could never become a functioning grown-up like this; it was inconceivable that I'd ever have a career. In job interviews they'd ask me, *What's your greatest weakness?* and I'd explain that I'll probably spend a good portion of the workday terrorized by thoughts I'm forced to think, possessed by a nameless and formless demon, so if that's going to be an issue, you might not want to hire me.

Thoughts are just a different kind of bacteria, colonizing you. I thought about the gut-brain information axis. *Maybe you're already gone. The prisoners run the jail now.* Not a person so much as a swarm. Not a bee, but the hive.

I couldn't stand my mother's breath on my face. My palms were sweating. I felt my self slipping away. *You know how to deal with this.* "Can you turn over?" I whispered, but she responded only with breath. *You just need to stand up.*

I picked up my phone to text Daisy, but now the letters blurred out on the screen, and the full panic gripped me. See the hand sanitizer mounted on the wall near the door. *It's the only way* that's stupid if it worked alcoholics would be the healthiest people in the world *you're just going to sanitize your hands and your mouth* please fucking think about something else *stand up* I HATE BEING STUCK INSIDE YOU *you are me* I am not *you are we* I am not *you want to feel better you know how to feel better* it'll just make me barf *you'll be clean you can be sure* I can never be sure *stand up* not even a person just a deeply flawed line of reasoning *you want to stand up* the doctor said stay in bed and the last thing needed is a surgery *you will get up and wheel your IV cart* let me up out of this *wheel your IV cart to the front of the room* please *and you will pump the hand sanitizer foam into your hands, clean them carefully, and then you will pump more foam into your hands and you will put that foam in your mouth, swish it around your filthy teeth and gums.* But that stuff has alcohol in it that my damaged liver will have to process *DO YOU WANT TO DIE OF* C. DIFF no but this is not rational *THEN GET UP AND WHEEL YOUR IV CART TO THE CONTAINER OF HAND SANITIZER MOUNTED ON THE GODDAMNED WALL YOU IDIOT.* Please let me go. I'll do anything. I'll stand down. You can have this body. I don't want it anymore. *You will stand up.* I will not. I am my way not my will. *You will stand up.* Please. *You will go to the hand sanitizer.* Cogito, ergo non sum. Sweating *you already have it* nothing hurts like this *you've already got it* stop please God stop *you'll never be free of this* you'll never be free of this *you'll never get your self back* you'll never get your self back *do you want to die of this* do you want to die of this *because you will* you will *you will* you will *you will* you will.

I pulled myself to standing. For a moment, I thought I might faint as the pain blazed through me. I grabbed hold of the IV pole and took a few shuffling steps. I heard my mom stirring. I didn't care. Pressed the dispenser, rubbed the foam all through my hands. Pressed it again, and shoved a scoop of it into my mouth.

"Aza, what are you doing?" my mom asked. I was so fucking embarrassed, but I did it again, because I had to. "Aza, stop it!"

I heard my mom getting up, and knew my window was closing, so I took a third shot of the foam and stuffed it into my mouth, gagging. A spasm of nausea lurched through me, and I vomited, the pain in my ribs blinding, as Mom grabbed me by the arm. There was yellow bile all over my pale blue hospital gown.

A voice came from inside a speaker somewhere behind me. "This is Nurse Wallace."

"My daughter is vomiting. I think she drank hand sanitizer."

I knew how disgusting I was. I knew. I knew now for sure. I wasn't possessed by a demon. I was the demon.

TWENTY

THE NEXT MORNING, you wake up in a hospital bed, staring up at ceiling tiles. Gingerly, carefully, you assess your own consciousness for a moment. You wonder, *Is it over?*

"The hospital food didn't look so good, so I made you some breakfast," your mother says. "Cheerios." You look down at your body, rendered mostly formless by a bleached white blanket.

You say, "Cheerios aren't something you make," and your mom laughs. At the end of your bed you see a huge bouquet of flowers resting on a table, ostentatiously huge, complete with a crystal vase. "From Davis," your mother says. Nearer to you, hovering above your formless body, a tray of food. You swallow. You look at the Cheerios, bobbing in milk. Your body hurts. A thought crosses your mind: *God only knows what you inhaled while you were asleep.*

It's not over.

You lie there, not even thinking really, except to try to consider how to describe the hurt, as if finding the language for it might bring it up out of you. If you can make something real, if you can see it and smell it and touch it, then you can kill it.

You think, it's like a brain fire. Like a rodent gnawing at you from the inside. A knife in your gut. A spiral. Whirlpool. Black hole.

The words used to describe it—despair, fear, anxiety, obsession—do so little to communicate it. Maybe we invented metaphor as a response to pain. Maybe we needed to give shape to the opaque, deep-down pain that evades both sense and senses.

For a moment, you think you're better. You've just had a successful train of thought, with an engine and a caboose and everything. Your thoughts. Authored by you. And then you feel a wave of nausea, a fist clenching from within your rib cage, cold sweat hot forehead *you've got it it's already inside of you crowding out everything else taking you over and it's going to kill you and eat its way out of you* and then in a small voice, half strangled by the ineffable horror, you barely squeeze out the words you need to say. "I'm in trouble, Mom. Big trouble."

TWENTY-ONE

THE ARC OF THE STORY GOES LIKE THIS: Having descended into proper madness, I begin to make the connections that crack open the long-dormant case of Russell Pickett's disappearance. My dogged obsessiveness leads me to ignore all manner of threats, and the risk to the fortune Daisy and I have stumbled into. I focus only on the mystery, and embrace the belief that solving it is the ultimate Good, that declarative sentences are inherently better than interrogative ones, and in finding the answer despite my madness, I simultaneously find a way to live with the madness. I become a great detective, not in spite of my brain circuitry, but because of it.

I'm not sure who I walk into the sunset with in the proper story, Davis or Daisy, but I walk into it. You see me backlit, an eclipse silhouetted by the eight-minute-old light of our home star, holding hands with somebody.

And along the way, I realize that I have agency over myself, that my thoughts are—as Dr. Singh liked to say—only thoughts. I realize that my life is a story that I'm telling, and I'm free and empowered and the captain of my consciousness and yeah, no. That's not how it went down.

I did not become dogged or declarative, nor did I walk off into the sunset—in fact, for a while there, I saw hardly any natural light at all.

What happened was relentlessly and excruciatingly dull: I lay in a hospital bed and *hurt*. My ribs hurt, my brain hurt, my thoughts hurt, and they did not let me go home for eight days.

At first, they figured me for an alcoholic—that I'd gone for the hand sanitizer because I was so desperate for a drink. The truth was so much weirder and less rational that nobody really seemed to buy it until they contacted Dr. Singh. When she arrived at the hospital, she pulled a chair up to the edge of my bed. "Two things happened," she said. "First, you're not taking your medication as prescribed."

I told her I'd taken it almost every day, which *felt* true, but wasn't. "I felt like it was making me worse," I eventually confessed.

"Aza, you're an intelligent young woman. Surely you don't think drinking hand sanitizer while hospitalized for a lacerated liver marks forward progress in your mental health journey." I just stared at her. "As I'm sure they explained to you, drinking hand sanitizer is *dangerous*—not only because of the alcohol, but because it contains chemicals that when ingested can *kill* you. So we're not moving forward with the idea that the medicine you stopped taking was making you worse." She said it all so forcefully that I just nodded.

"And the second thing that happened is that you experienced in the accident a serious trauma, and this would be challenging for anyone." I kept staring. "We need to get you on a different medication, one that works better for you, that you can tolerate, and that you'll take."

"None of them work."

"None of them have worked *yet*," she corrected.

Dr. Singh came by each morning, and then in the afternoon another doctor visited to assess my liver situation. Both were a relief if for no other reason than my omnipresent mother was forced to leave the room briefly.

On the last day, Dr. Singh sat down next to the side of my bed and placed a hand on my shoulder. She'd never touched me before. "I recognize that a hospital setting has probably not been great for your anxiety."

"Yeah," I said.

"Do you feel you are a threat to yourself?"

"No," I said. "I'm just really scared and having a lot of invasives."

"Did you consume hand sanitizer yesterday?"

"No."

"I'm not here to judge you, Aza. But I can only help if you're being honest."

"I am being honest. I haven't." For one thing, they'd taken the wall-mounted sanitizer station out of my room.

"Have you thought about it?"

"Yeah."

"You don't have to be afraid of that thought. Thought is not action."

"I can't stop thinking about getting *C. diff*. I just want to be sure that I'm not . . ."

"Drinking hand sanitizer won't help."

"But what *will* help?"

"Time. Treatment. Taking your meds."

"I feel like a noose is tightening around me and I want out, but struggling only cinches the knot. The spiral just keeps tightening, you know?"

She looked me dead in the eye. I thought she might cry or something, the way she was looking at me. "Aza, you're going to survive this."

Even after they let me go home, Dr. Singh still came to my house twice a week to check on my progress. I had switched to a different medication, which Mom made sure I took every morning, and I wasn't allowed to get up except to go to the bathroom lest I re-lacerate my liver.

I was out of school for two weeks. Fourteen days of my life reduced to one sentence, because I can't describe anything that happened during those days. It hurt, all the time, in a way language could not touch. It was boring. It was predictable. Like walking a maze you know has no solution. It's easy enough to say what it was like, but impossible to say what it was.

Daisy and Davis both tried to visit, but I wanted to be alone, in bed. I didn't read or watch TV; neither could adequately distract me. I just lay there, almost catatonic, as my mother hovered, perpetually near, breaking the silence every few minutes with a question-phrased-as-a-statement. Each day is a little better? You're feeling okay? You're improving? The inquisition of declarations.

I didn't even turn on my phone for a while, a decision endorsed by Dr. Singh. When I finally did power it up, I felt an insoluble fear. I both wanted to find a lot of text messages and didn't.

Turns out I had over thirty messages—not just from Daisy and Davis, although they had written, but also from Mychal and other friends, and even some teachers.

I returned to school on a Monday morning in early December. I wasn't sure if the new medication was working, but I also wasn't wondering whether to take it. I felt ready, like

I had returned to the world—not my old self, but myself nonetheless.

Mom drove me to school. Harold had been totaled, and anyway, I was too scared of driving.

"Excited or nervous?" Mom asked me. She drove with both hands on the steering wheel, ten and two o'clock.

"Nervous," I said.

"Your teachers, your friends, they all understand, Aza. They just want you well and will support you one hundred percent, and if they don't, I will crush them."

I smiled a little. "Everyone knows, is all. That I went crazy or whatever."

"Oh, sweetie," she said. "You didn't *go* crazy. You've always been crazy." Now I laughed, and she reached over to squeeze my wrist.

Daisy was waiting on the front steps. Mom stopped the car, and I got out, the weight of the backpack still tender against my ribs. It was a cold day, but the sun was bright even though it had just risen, and I kept blinking away the light. It had been a while since I'd spent much time outside.

Daisy looked different. Her face brighter somehow. It took me a second to realize she'd gotten a haircut, a just-under-the-chin bob that looked really good.

"Can I hug you without lacerating your liver?"

"I like the new hairstyle," I said as we hugged.

"You're sweet, but we both know it's a disaster."

"Listen," I said. "I'm really sorry."

"Me too, but we have forgiven each other and now we will live happily ever after."

"Seriously, though," I said. "I feel terrible about—"

"I do, too," she said. "You gotta read my new story, man. It's a fifteen-thousand-word apology set on postapocalyptic Jedha. What I want to say to you, Holmesy, is that yes, you are exhausting, and yes, being your friend is work. But you are also the most fascinating person I have ever known, and you are not like mustard. You are like pizza, which is the highest compliment I can pay a person."

"I'm just really sorry, Daisy, for not being—"

"Jesus Christ, Holmesy, you can sure hold a grudge against yourself. You are my favorite person. I want to be buried next to you. We'll have a shared tombstone. It'll read, 'Holmesy and Daisy: They did everything together, except the nasty.' Anyway, how are you?" I shrugged. "Want me to keep talking?" I nodded. "You know how sometimes people will say, like, oh, *she really loves the sound of her voice*? I do seriously love the sound of my voice. I've got a voice for radio." She turned and started walking up the stairs to get in line for the metal detectors. "So I know what you're wondering: Daisy, are you still dating Mychal? Where's your car? What happened to your hair? The answers are no, sold, and a cut became necessary after Elena intentionally put three pieces of chewed bubble gum in my hair while I was sleeping. It's been a long two weeks, Holmesy. Should I elaborate?"

I nodded.

"With pleasure," she answered as we cleared the metal detectors. "So with Mychal it really boiled down to my need to be young and wild and free—like, I had this near-death experience and then thought, *Do I really want to waste my youth in a capital-R Relationship*? And so I was, like, 'Let's see other people,' and he was, like, 'No,' and I was, like, 'Please,' and he was, like, 'I want to be in a monogamous relationship,' and I was, like, 'I just don't want the weight of this, like, Thing dominating my life,' and he was, like, 'I'm not a thing,' and then we broke up. I think technically he dumped me in the end, but it was one of those things where you'd need, like, a three-judge panel to determine who was technically at fault.

"Anyway, then with the car, it turns out that cars are expensive to own and also it turns out that they can hurt you, so I got a refund because I had it less than sixty days, and now I'm just going to Uber everywhere for the rest of my life, because then it's kind of like I have *every* car, and also as a rich person I deserve to be chauffeured. Should I keep going?"

We'd reached my locker now, and I was surprised to find that I remembered the combination. There were so many human bodies around me. I kind of couldn't believe it. I pulled my locker open. I hadn't done any homework. I was behind on everything. The hallway was so loud, so crowded. "Yeah," I said.

"No problem. I can do this *all day*. This is another reason we're destined to be together—you're so good at not talking.

So, with Elena, she put gum in my hair on purpose while I was sleeping, and the next morning I was, like, 'Why is there chewed gum in my hair?' and she was, like, 'Ha-ha!' I was, like, 'Elena, you have no understanding of humor. It isn't funny just to make someone's life worse. Like, if I broke your leg, would that be funny?' And she was, like, 'Ha-ha!' So I got this fancy haircut, and believe you me, I paid for it out of Elena's college fund. My parents made me set up a college fund for Elena, BTW.

"In other news, the whole Mychal thing has made our lunch table a little awkward, so we're going to have a two-person picnic outside. I know it's *slightly* cold, but trust me, sitting next to Mychal in the cafeteria is far colder. Are you so ready to go to biology right now and just absolutely murder it? Like, in forty-seven minutes, the dead and bloodless carcass of honors biology will be laid before your feet. God, a lot happened since you lost your mind. Is that rude to say?"

"Actually, the problem is that I *can't* lose my mind," I said. "It's inescapable."

"That is precisely how I feel about my virginity," Daisy said. "Another reason Mychal and I were doomed—he doesn't want to have sex unless he's *in love*, and yes, I know that virginity is a misogynistic and oppressive social construct, but I still want to lose it, and meanwhile I've got this boy hemming and hawing like we're in a Jane Austen novel. I wish boys didn't have all these feelings I have to manage like a fucking psychiatrist." Daisy walked me to the door of my classroom, opened it, and then walked me to my desk. I sat down. "You know I love you, right?" I nodded. "My whole life I thought I was the star of an overly earnest romance movie, and it turns out I was in a goddamned buddy comedy all along. I gotta go to calc. Good to see you, Holmesy."

Daisy had brought leftover pizza for our picnic, and we sat underneath our school's one big oak tree, halfway to the football field. It was frigid, and both of us were bundled into our winter coats, hoods up, my jeans stiff on the frozen ground.

I didn't have gloves, so I tucked my fists into the coat. It was no weather for a picnic.

"I've been thinking a lot about Pickett," Daisy said.

"Yeah?"

"Yeah, just—while you were gone, I kept thinking about how weird it is to leave your kids like that, without even saying good-bye. I almost feel bad for him, to be honest. Like, what has to be wrong with him that he doesn't at least buy a burner phone somewhere and text his kids and tell them he's okay?"

I felt worse for the thirteen-year-old who wakes up every morning thinking that maybe today is the day. And then he plays video games every night to distract from the dull ache of knowing your father doesn't trust or love you enough to be in contact, your father who privileged a tuatara over you in his estate plans. "I feel worse for Noah than for Pickett," I said.

"You've always empathized with that kid," she said. "Even when you can't with your best friend." I shot her a glance and she laughed it off, but I knew she wasn't kidding.

"So, what *do* your parents do?" I asked.

Daisy laughed again. "My dad works at the State Museum. He's a security guard there. He likes it, because he's really into Indiana history, but mostly he just makes sure nobody touches the mastodon bones or whatever. My mom works at a dry cleaners in Broad Ripple."

"Have you told them about the money yet?"

"Yeah. That's how Elena got that college fund. They made me put ten grand in it. My dad was, like, 'Elena would do the same for you if she came into some money.' Like hell she would."

"They weren't mad?"

"That I came home one day with fifty thousand dollars? No, Holmesy, they weren't mad."

Inside the arm of my coat, I could feel something seeping from my middle fingertip. I'd have to change the Band-Aid before history, have to go through the whole annoying ritual of it. But for now, I liked being next to Daisy. I liked watching my warm breath in the cold.

"How's Davis?" she asked.

"Haven't talked to him," I said. "I haven't talked to anyone."

"So it was pretty bad."

"Yeah," I said.

"I'm sorry."

"Yeah, it's not your fault."

"Did you . . . do you think about killing yourself?"

"I thought about not wanting to be that way anymore."

"Are you still . . ."

"I don't know." I let out a long, slow breath, and watched the steam of it disappear in the winter air. "I think maybe I'm like the White River. Non-navigable."

"But that's not the point of the story, Holmesy. The point of the story is they built the city anyway, you know? You work with what you have. They had this shit river, and they managed to build an okay city around it. Not a great city, maybe. But not bad. You're not the river. You're the city."

"So, I'm not bad?"

"Correct. You're a solid B-plus. If you can build a B-plus city with C-minus geography, that's pretty great."

I laughed. Beside me, Daisy lay down and motioned for me to lie next to her. We were looking up, our heads near the trunk of that lone oak tree, the sky smoke-gray above us past our fogged breath, the leafless branches intersecting overhead.

I don't know if I'd ever told Daisy about that—if she lay down at precisely that moment because she knew how much I loved seeing the sky cut up. I thought about how branches far from one another could still intersect in my line of vision, like how the stars of Cassiopeia were far from one another, but somehow near to me.

"I wish I understood it," she said.

"It's okay," I said. "Nobody gets anybody else, not really. We're all stuck inside ourselves."

"You just, like, hate yourself? You hate being yourself?"

"There's no self to hate. It's like, when I look into myself, there's no actual me—just a bunch of thoughts and behaviors and circumstances. And a lot of them just don't feel like they're mine. They're not things I want to think or do or whatever. And when I look for the, like, Real Me, I never find it. It's like those nesting dolls, you know? The ones that are hollow, and then when you open them up, there's a smaller doll inside, and you keep opening hollow dolls until eventually you get to the smallest one, and it's solid all the way through. But with me, I don't think there is one that's solid. They just keep getting smaller."

"That reminds me of a story my mom tells," Daisy said.

"What story?"

I could hear her teeth chattering when she talked but neither of us wanted to stop looking up at the latticed sky. "Okay, so there's this scientist, and he's giving a lecture to a huge audience about the history of the earth, and he explains that the earth was formed billions of years ago from a cloud of cosmic dust, and then for a while the earth was very hot, but then it cooled enough for oceans to form. And single-celled life emerged in the oceans, and then over billions of years, life got more abundant and complex, until two hundred fifty thousand or so years ago, humans evolved, and we started using more advanced tools, and then eventually built spaceships and everything.

"So he gives this whole presentation about the history of earth and life on it, and then at the end, he asks if there are any questions. An old woman in the back raises her hand, and says, 'That's all fine and good, Mr. Scientist, but the truth is, the earth is a flat plane resting on the back of a giant turtle.'

"The scientist decides to have a bit of fun with the woman and responds, 'Well, but if that's so, what is the giant turtle standing upon?'

"And the woman says, 'It is standing upon the shell of another giant turtle.'

"And now the scientist is frustrated, and he says, 'Well, then what is *that* turtle standing upon?'

"And the old woman says, 'Sir, you don't understand. It's turtles all the way down.'"

I laughed. "It's turtles all the way down."

"It's turtles all the way fucking down, Holmesy. You're trying to find the turtle at the bottom of the pile, but that's not how it works."

"Because it's turtles all the way down," I said again, feeling something akin to a spiritual revelation.

I stopped at Mom's classroom for the last few minutes of lunch. I closed the door behind me and sat down at a desk opposite her. I glanced up at the clock on the wall. 1:08. I had six minutes. I didn't want more.

"Hey," I said.

"First day back going well?" She blew her nose into a Kleenex. She had a cold, but she'd spent all her sick days on me being sick.

"Yeah," I said. "So listen, Davis gave me some money. A lot of money. About fifty thousand dollars. I haven't spent it or anything. I'm saving it for college." Her face tightened. "It was a gift," I said again.

"When?" she asked.

"Um, a couple months ago."

"That's not a gift. A necklace is a gift. Fifty thousand dollars is . . . not a gift. If I were you, I'd return that money to Davis," she said. "You don't want to feel indebted to him."

"But I'm not you," I said. "And I don't."

After a second, she said, "That's true. You're not." I waited for her to say something more, to tell me why I was wrong to keep the money.

At last, she said, "Your life is yours, Aza, but I think if you look at your mental health the last couple months . . ."

"The money didn't cause that. I've been sick for a long time."

"Not like this. I need you to be well, Aza. I can't lose—"

"God, Mom, please stop saying that. I know you're not trying to make me feel pressure, but it feels like I'm *hurting* you, like I'm committing assault or something, and it makes me feel ten thousand times worse. I'm doing my best, but I can't stay sane for you, okay?"

After a minute she said, "The day you came home after the accident, I carried you to the bathroom, and I carried you back to bed and tucked the covers up to your chin, and I realized that I'll probably never pick you up again. You're right. I keep saying I can't lose you, but I will. I am. And that's a hard thought. That's a hard, hard thought. But you're right. You're not me. You make your own choices. And if you're saving it for your education, making responsible decisions, well, then, I'm—" She never finished the sentence, because the bell beeped from on high.

"Okay," I said.

"Love you, Aza."

"I love you, too, Mom." I wanted to say more, to find a way to express the magnetic poles of my love for my mother: *thank you I'm sorry thank you I'm sorry*. But I couldn't bring myself to, and anyway, the bell had rung.

Before I could get to history, Mychal intercepted me. "Hey, how's it going?" he asked.

"I'm okay, you?"

"Daisy and I broke up."

"I heard."

"I'm kinda devastated."

"Sorry."

"And she isn't even upset about it, which just makes me feel pathetic. She thinks I should get over it, but everything reminds me of her, Holmesy, and seeing her ignore me, not show up to lunch, all that—can you, um, talk to her for me?"

Right then, I spotted Daisy halfway down the crowded hallway, her head down. "Daisy!" I shouted. She kept walking, so I yelled again, louder. She looked up and picked her way toward us through the crowd.

I pulled her and Mychal together. "Both of you can talk to me about each other, but you can't talk to each other about each other. And you're going to fix that, because it's annoying. Cool? Cool. I have to go to history."

Daisy texted me during class. *Thanks for that. We've decided to just be friends.*

Me: *Cool.*

Her: *But the kind of friends who kiss right after deciding to just be friends.*

Me: *I'm sure this will work out perfectly.*

Her: *Everything always does.*

Since I had my phone out, and we were watching a video in class anyway, I decided to text Davis. *Sorry not to reply for so long. Hi. I miss you.*

He wrote back immediately. *When can I see you?*

Me: *Tomorrow?*

Him: *Seven at Applebee's?*

Me: *Sounds good.*

TWENTY-TWO

I THOUGHT I'D BE FINE driving Mom's silver Toyota Camry to Applebee's that night, but I couldn't shake memories of the accident. It seemed surreal and miraculous to me that so many cars could drive past one another without colliding, and I felt certain that each set of headlights headed my way would inevitably veer into my path. Remembered the crunching sound of Harold's death, the silence that followed, the agony in my ribs. Thought about the biggest part being the part that hurts, about my dad's phone, gone forever. Tried to let myself have the thoughts, because to deny them was to just let them take over. It sort of worked—like everything else.

I made it to Applebee's fifteen minutes early. Davis was already there, and he hugged me in the entryway before we got seated. A thought appeared in my mind undeniable as the sun in a clear sky: *He's going to want to put his bacteria in your mouth.*

"Hi," I said.

"I missed you," he said.

After the nervous-making car trip, my brain was revving up. I told myself that having a thought was not dangerous, that thoughts aren't actions, that thoughts are just thoughts.

Dr. Karen Singh liked to say that an unwanted thought was like a car driving past you when you're standing on the side of the road, and I told myself I didn't have to get into that car, that my moment of choice was not whether to have the thought, but whether to be carried away by it.

And then I got in the car.

I sat down in the booth and instead of sitting across from me, he sat next to me, his hip against mine. "I talked to your mom a few times," he said. "I think she's coming around to me."

Who cares if he wants his bacteria in my mouth? Kissing is nice. Kissing feels good. I want to kiss him. *But you don't want to get campylobacter.* I won't. *You'll be sick for weeks. Might have to take antibiotics.* Stop. *Then you'll get* C. diff. *Or you'll get Epstein-Barr from the campylobacter.* Stop. *That could paralyze you, all because you kissed him when you didn't even actually want to because it's fucking gross, inserting your tongue into someone else's mouth.* "Are you there?" he asked.

"What, yeah," I said.

"I asked how you're feeling."

"Good," I said. "Honestly not good right now, but good in general."

"Why not good right now?"

"Can you sit across from me?"

"Um, yeah, of course." He got up and moved around to the opposite bench, which made me feel better. For a moment, anyway.

"I can't do this," I said.

"Can't do what?"

"This," I said. "I can't, Davis. I don't know if I'll ever be able to. Like, I know you're waiting for me to get better, and I really appreciate all your texts and everything. It's . . . it's incredibly sweet, but, like, this is probably what better looks like for me."

"I like this you."

"No, you don't. You want to make out and sit on the same side of the table and do other normal couple things. Because of course you do."

He didn't say anything for a minute. "Maybe you just don't find me attractive?"

"It's not that," I said.

"But maybe it is."

"It's not. It's not that I don't want to kiss you or that I don't like kissing or whatever. I . . . my brain says that kissing is one of a bunch of things that will, like, kill me. Like, actually kill me. But it's not even about *dying*, really—like, if I knew I was dying, and I kissed you good-bye, literally my last thought wouldn't be about the fact that I was dying; it would be about the eighty million microbes that we'd just exchanged. I know that when you just touched me, it didn't give me a disease, or it probably didn't. God, I can't even say that it *definitely* didn't because I'm so fucking scared of it. I can't even call it anything but it, you know? I just can't."

I could tell I was hurting him. I could see it in the way he kept blinking. I could see that he didn't understand it, that he couldn't. I didn't blame him. It made no sense. I was a story riddled with plot holes.

"That sounds really scary," he said. I just nodded. "Do you feel like you're getting better?" Everyone wanted me to feed them that story—darkness to light, weakness to strength, broken to whole. I wanted it, too.

"Maybe," I said. "Honestly, I feel really fragile. I feel like I've been taped back together."

"I know that feeling."

"How are you?" I asked.

He shrugged.

"How's Noah?" I asked.

"Not good."

"Um, unpack that for me," I said.

"He just misses Dad. It's like Noah's two people, almost: There's the miniature dudebro who drinks bad vodka and is the king of his little gang of eighth-grade pseudo-badasses. And then the kid who crawls into bed with me some nights and cries. It's almost like Noah thinks if he screws up enough, Dad will be forced to come out of hiding."

"He's heartbroken," I said.

"Yeah, well. Aren't we all. It's . . . I don't really want to talk about my life, if that's okay." It occurred to me that Davis probably liked what infuriated Daisy—that I didn't ask too many questions. Everyone else was so relentlessly curious about the life of the billionaire boy, but I'd always been too stuck inside myself to interrogate him.

Slowly, the conversation sputtered. We started talking to each other like people who used to be close—catching each other up on our lives rather than living them together. By the time he paid the bill, I knew that whatever we'd been, we weren't anymore.

Still, once I was home and under the covers, I texted him. *You around?*

You can't do it the other way, he replied. *And I can't do it this way.*

Me: *Why?*

Him: *It makes me feel like you only like me at a distance. I need to be liked close up.*

I kept typing and deleting, typing and deleting. I never ended up replying.

The next day at school, I was walking across the cafeteria to our lunch table when I was intercepted by Daisy. "Holmesy, we have to talk privately." She sat me down at a mostly empty lunch table, a few seats away from some freshmen.

"Did you break up with Mychal again?"

"No, of course not. The magic of being Just Friends is that you *can't* break up. I feel like I've unlocked the secret of the universe with this Just Friends thing. But no, we're going on an adventure."

"We are?"

"Do you feel like you've recovered your wits enough that you could, for instance, sneak underneath the city of Indianapolis to attend a guerrilla art show?"

"A what?"

"Okay, so remember how I had that idea for Mychal to make those photographic montages of exonerated prisoners?"

"Well, it was mostly his i—"

"Let's not get lost in the details, Holmesy. The point is he made it and submitted it to this supercool arts collective Known City, and they are putting it in this one-night-only gallery show they're doing Friday night called Underground Art, where they turn part of the Pogue's Run tunnel into an art gallery." Pogue's Run was the tunnel that emptied into the White River that Pickett's company had been hired to expand, the work they'd never finished. Seemed an odd place for an art show.

"I don't really want to spend Friday night at an illegal art gallery."

"It's not *illegal*. They have permission. It's just super underground. Like, literally underground." I scrunched up my face. "It's like the coolest thing ever to happen in Indianapolis, and my Just Friend has art *in the show*. Obviously don't feel obligated to be there, but . . . do be there."

"I don't want to be a third wheel."

"I am going to be nervous and surrounded by people cooler than me and I'd really like my best friend to be there."

I opened the Ziploc bag containing my peanut butter and honey sandwich and took a bite.

"You're thinking about it," she said, excitement in her voice.

"I'm thinking about it," I allowed.

And then, after I swallowed, I said, "All right, let's do it."

"Yes! Yes! We will pick you up at six fifteen on Friday; it's going to be amazing."

The way she smiled at me made it impossible not to smile back. In a quiet voice, not even sure she could hear me, I said, "I love you, Daisy. I know you say that to me all the time and I never say it, but I do. I love you."

"Ahh, fuck. Don't go all soft on me, Holmesy."

Mychal and Daisy showed up at my doorstep at six fifteen sharp. She was wearing a dress-and-tights combo dwarfed by her huge puffer coat, and Mychal was wearing a silver-gray suit that was slightly too big for him. I had on a long-sleeve T-shirt, jeans, and a coat. "I didn't know I was supposed to dress up for the sewer," I said sheepishly.

"The *art* sewer." Daisy smiled. I wondered whether maybe I should change, but she just grabbed me and said, "Holmesy, you look radiant. You look like . . . like yourself."

I sat in one of the backseats in Mychal's minivan, and as he drove south on Michigan Road, Daisy started playing one of our favorite songs, "You're the One." Mychal was laughing as Daisy and I screamed the lyrics to each other. She sang lead, and I belted out the background voice that just repeated, "You're everything everything everything," and I felt like I was. You're both the fire and the water that extinguishes it. You're the narrator, the protagonist, and the sidekick. You're the storyteller and the story told. You are somebody's something, but you are also your you.

As Daisy switched the song to a romantic ballad that she and Mychal were singing, I started thinking about turtles all the way down. I was thinking that maybe the old lady and the scientist were both right. Like, the world is billions of years old, and life is a product of nucleotide mutation and everything. But the world is also the stories we tell about it.

Mychal turned off Michigan at Tenth Street, and we drove for a while until we reached a pool supply store with a flickering backlit sign saying ROSENTHAL POOLS. The parking lot was already half full. Daisy stopped the music as Mychal pulled into a spot. We got out and found ourselves surrounded by a weird mix of twenty-something hipsters and middle-aged couples. Everyone but us seemed to know one another, and the three of us stood next to Mychal's car for a long time in silence, just watching the scene, until a middle-aged woman in an all-black outfit walked over and said, "Are you here for the event?"

"I'm, um, Mychal Turner," Mychal said. "I have a, um, a picture in the show."

"*Prisoner 101*?"

"Yeah. That's me."

"I'm Frances Oliver. I think *Prisoner 101* is one of the strongest pieces in the gallery. And I'm the curator, so I should know. Come, come, let's head on down together. I would be fascinated to learn more about your process."

Frances and Mychal began walking across the parking lot, but every few seconds Frances would pause and say, "Oh, I must introduce you to . . ." and we'd stop for a while to meet an artist or a collector or a "funding partner." Slowly, he was swallowed by all the people who loved *Prisoner 101* and wanted to talk with him about it, and after we stood behind him for a while, Daisy finally grabbed him by the hand and said, "We're gonna head down to the show. Enjoy this. I'm so proud of you."

"I can come with," he said, turning away from a gaggle of art students from Herron, the art college in town.

"No, have fun. You gotta meet all these people, so they'll buy your pictures." He smiled, kissed her, and returned to his crowd of fans.

When Daisy and I reached the edge of the parking lot, we saw through the trees a flashlight waving back and forth in the air, so we wound our way down a little hill toward the light until the brush opened up into a wide concrete basin. A tiny stream of water—I could easily step over it—bubbled along its bottom. We walked toward the bearded man waving the flashlight, who introduced himself as Kip and handed us hard hats with lanterns and a flashlight. "Follow the tunnel in for two hundred yards, then take your first left, and you'll be in the gallery."

The light from my helmet followed the creek downstream. In the distance, I could see the start of the tunnel, a light-sucking square cut into a hillside. There was an overturned shopping cart just outside the start of the culvert, trapped against a moss-covered boulder. As we walked toward the tunnel's entrance, I looked up at the black silhouettes of leafless maple trees splitting up the sky.

The creek ran along the left side of the Pogue's Run tunnel; we walked on a slightly elevated concrete sidewalk to the right of the creek. The smell enveloped us immediately—sewage and the sickly sweet smell of rot. I thought my nose would get used to it, but it never did.

A few steps in, we began to hear rodents scurrying along the creek bed. We could hear voices, too—echoey, unintelligible conversations that seemed to be coming from all sides of us. Our headlamps lit up the graffiti that lined the walls—spray-painted tags in bubble letters, but also stenciled images and messages. Daisy's light lingered on one image featuring a portly rat drinking a bottle of wine with the caption, THE RAT KING KNOWS YOUR SECRETS. Another message, scrawled in what looked like white house paint, read, IT'S NOT HOW YOU DIE. IT'S WHO YOU DIE.

"This is a little creepy," Daisy whispered.

"Why are you whispering?"

"Scared," she whispered. "Has it been two hundred yards yet?"

"Dunno," I said. "But I hear people up there." I turned around and shone my light back toward the tunnel's entrance, and a couple of middle-aged men behind us waved. "See, it's fine."

The creek wasn't really a body of water anymore so much as a slow-moving puddle; I watched a rat scamper across it without ever getting its nose wet. "That was a rat," Daisy said, her voice clenched.

"It lives here," I said. "We're the invaders." We kept walking. The only light in the world seemed to be the yellow beams of headlamps and flashlights—it was almost like everyone down there had become beams of light, bouncing along the tunnel in little groups.

Ahead of us, I saw headlamps turning to the left, into a square side tunnel, about eight feet high. We jumped over the trickling creek, past a sign that read, A PICKETT ENGINEERING PROJECT, and into the concrete side tunnel.

You could only see the artwork by the light of headlamps and flashlights, so the paintings and photographs lining the walls seemed to come in and out of focus. To see all of Mychal's picture, you had to stand against the opposite wall of the tunnel. It really was an amazing artwork—*Prisoner 101* looked as real as anyone, but he was made from pieces of the one hundred mugshots Mychal had found of men convicted of murder and then exonerated. Even up close, I couldn't tell that *Prisoner 101* wasn't real.

The rest of the art was cool, too—big abstract paintings of hard-edged geometric shapes, an assemblage of old wooden chairs precariously stacked to the ceiling, a huge photograph of a kid jumping on a trampoline alone in a vast harvested cornfield—but Mychal's was my favorite, and not just because I knew him.

After a while, we heard a clamor of voices approach, and the gallery became crowded. Someone had set up a stereo, and music began reverberating through the tunnel. Plastic cups were passed around, and then bottles of wine, and the place got louder and louder, and even though it was freezing down there, I started to feel sweaty, so I asked Daisy if she wanted to go for a walk.

"A walk?"

"Yeah, just, I don't know, down the tunnel or something."

"You want to go for a walk down the tunnel."

"Yeah. I mean, we don't have to."

She pointed into the darkness beyond the reach of our headlamps. "You're proposing that we just walk into that void."

"Not for like a *mile* or anything. Just to see what there is to see."

Daisy sighed. "Yeah, okay. Let's go for a walk."

It only took a minute for the air to feel crisper. The tunnel ahead of us was pitch-black, and it curved in a long, slow arc away from the party until we couldn't see the light from it anymore. We could still hear the music and the people talking over it, but it felt distant, like a party you drive past.

"I don't understand how you can be so inhumanly calm down here, fifteen feet below downtown Indianapolis, ankle deep in rat shit, but you have a panic attack when you think your finger is infected."

"I don't know," I said. "This just isn't scary."

"It objectively *is*," she said.

I reached up and clicked off my headlamp. "Turn off your light," I said.

"Hell, no."

"Turn it off. Nothing bad will happen." She clicked off her light, and the world went dark. I felt my eyes trying to adjust, but there was no light to adjust to. "Now you can't see the walls, right? Can't see the rats. Spin around a few times and you won't know which way is in and which way is out. This is scary. Now imagine if we couldn't talk, if we couldn't hear each other's breathing. Imagine if we had no sense of touch, so even if we were standing next to each other, we'd never know it.

"Imagine you're trying to find someone, or even you're trying to find yourself, but you have no senses, no way to know where the walls are, which way is forward or backward, what is water and what is air. You're senseless and shapeless—you feel like you can only describe what you are by identifying what you're not, and you're floating around in a body with no control. You don't get to decide who you like or where you live or when you eat or what you fear. You're just stuck in there, totally alone, in this darkness. That's scary. This," I said, and turned on the flashlight. "This is control. This is power. There may be rats and spiders and whatever the hell. But we shine the light on them, not the other way around. We know where the walls are, which way is in and which way is out. This," I said, turning off my light again, "is what I feel like when I'm scared. This"—I turned the flashlight back on—"is a walk in the fucking park."

We walked for a while in silence. "It's that bad?" she asked finally.

"Sometimes," I said.

"But then your flashlight starts working again," she said.

"So far."

As we kept walking, through the tunnel, the music behind us growing fainter, Daisy calmed down a bit. "I'm thinking of killing off Ayala," she said. "Would you take that personally?"

"Nah," I said. "I was just starting to like her, though."

"Did you read the most recent one?"

"The one where they go to Ryloth to deliver power converters? I loved the scene where Rey and Ayala are waiting for that dude in a bar, and they're just talking. I like your action scenes and everything, but the just talking is my favorite. Also, I liked that I got to hook up with a Twi'lek. Or, Ayala did, I guess. Your writing makes me feel like it's real, like I'm really there."

"Thanks," she said. "Now you're making me think maybe I shouldn't kill her."

"I don't mind if you kill her. Just make her die a hero."

"Oh, of course. She has to. I was thinking I'd make it some *Rogue One*–style sacrifice for the common good. If that sounds okay?"

"Works for me," I told her.

"God, is the smell getting worse?" she asked.

"It's not getting better," I acknowledged. It smelled more

like rotting garbage and unflushed toilets, and as we passed an offshoot to the tunnel, Daisy said she wanted to turn around, but in the distance ahead of us I could see a pinprick of gray light, and I wanted to see what was at the end.

As we walked, the sounds of the city grew slowly louder and the smell improved because we were close to open air. The gray light grew larger until we reached the edge of the tunnel. It was open and unfinished—the tiny trickle of water that was supposed to be diverted from the White River was instead dripping down into it, two stories below us.

I looked up. It was past ten o'clock, but I'd never seen the city look so blindingly bright. I could see everything: the green moss on the boulders in the river below; the golden frothy bubbles at the base of the waterfall; the trees in the distance bent over the water like the roof of a chapel; the power lines sagging across the river below us; a great silver grain mill absurdly still in the moonlight; neon Speedway and Chase Bank signs in the distance.

Indianapolis is so flat you can never really look down on it; it's not a town with million-dollar views. But now I had one, in the most unexpected place, the city stretching out below and beyond me, and it took a minute before I remembered that this was nighttime, that this silver-lit landscape is what passed, aboveground, for darkness.

Daisy surprised me by sitting down, her legs dangling over the concrete edge. I sat down on the other side of the trickle of water, and we looked at the same scene together for a long time.

We went out to the meadow that night, talking about college and kissing and religion and art, and I didn't feel like I was watching a movie of our conversation. I was having it. I could listen to her, and I knew she was listening to me.

"I wonder if they'll ever finish this thing," Daisy said at one point.

"I kind of hope not," I said. "I mean, I'm all for clean water, but I kind of want to be able to come here again in like ten or twenty years or something. Like, instead of going to my high school reunion, I want to be here." *With you*, I wanted to say.

"Yeah," she said. "Keep Pogue's Run filthy, because the view from the unfinished water treatment tunnel is spectacular. Thanks, Russell Pickett, for your corruption and incompetence."

"Pogue's *Run*," I mumbled. "Wait, where does Pogue's Run start? Where is its mouth?"

"The mouth of a river is where it ends, not where it begins. This is the mouth." I watched her realize it. "Pogue's *Run*. Holy shit, Holmesy. We're in the jogger's mouth."

I stood up. I felt for some reason like Pickett might be right behind us, like he might push us off the edge of his tunnel and into the river below. "*Now* I'm a little freaked out," I said.

"What are we gonna do?"

"Nothing," I said. "Nothing. We're gonna turn around, walk back to the party, hang out with fancy art people, and get home by curfew." I started walking back toward the distant music. "I'll tell Davis, so he knows. We let him decide whether to tell Noah. Other than that, we don't say a word."

"All right," she said, hustling to catch up to me. "I mean, is he down here *right now*?"

"I don't know," I said. "I don't think it's for us to know."

"Right," she said. "How could he have been down here this whole time, though?" I had a guess, but didn't say anything. "God, that smell . . ." she said, her voice trailing off as she said it.

You'd think solving mysteries would bring you closure, that closing the loop would comfort and quiet your mind. But it never does. The truth always disappoints. As we circulated around the gallery, looking for Mychal, I didn't feel like I'd found the solid nesting doll or anything. Nothing had been fixed, not really. It was like the zoologist said about science: You never really find answers, just new and deeper questions.

We finally found Mychal leaning against the wall opposite his photograph, talking to two older women. Daisy cut in and took his hand. "I hate to break up this party," she said, "but this famous artist has a curfew."

Mychal laughed, and the three of us made our way out of

the tunnel, into the silver-bright parking lot, and then into Mychal's minivan. The moment my door slid shut, he said, "That was the best night of my life thank you for being there oh my God that was just the best thing that's ever happened to me I feel like I might be an artist, like a proper one. That was so, so amazing. Did you guys have fun?"

"Tell us all about it," Daisy said, not exactly answering his question.

When I got home, Mom was sitting at the kitchen table, drinking a mug of tea. "What is that *smell*?" she asked.

"Sewage, body odor, mold—a mix of things."

"I'm worried, Aza. I'm worried you're losing your connection to reality."

"I'm not," I said. "I'm just tired."

"Tonight, you're gonna stay up and talk to me."

"About what?"

"About where you were, what you were doing, who you were doing it with. About your *life*."

So I told her. I told her that Daisy and Mychal and I had attended a one-night art show beneath downtown, and that Daisy and I had walked to the end of Pickett's unfinished tunnel, and I told her about going out to the meadow, and I told her about the jogger's mouth, about thinking Pickett was maybe down there, about the stench.

"You're going to tell Davis?" she asked.

"Yeah."

"But not the police?"

"No," I said. "If I tell the police, and he is dead down there, Davis and Noah's house won't even be theirs anymore. It'll be owned by a tuatara."

"A tua-what-a?"

"A tuatara. It looks like a lizard, but it isn't a lizard. Descended from the dinosaurs. They live for like a hundred and fifty years, and Pickett's will leaves everything to his pet tuatara. The house, the business, everything."

"The madness of wealth," my mother mumbled. "Sometimes you think you're spending money, but all along the money's spending you." She glanced down at her cup of tea, and then back up to me. "But only if you worship it. You serve whatever you worship."

"So we gotta be careful what we worship," I said. She smiled, then shooed me off to the shower. As I stood underneath the water, I wondered what I'd worship as I got older, and how that would end up bending the arc of my life this way or that. I was still at the beginning. I could still be anybody.

TWENTY-THREE

I WOKE UP THE NEXT MORNING, a Saturday, feeling truly rested, frozen rain plinking against my bedroom window. Indianapolis winters rarely feature the sort of beautiful snow that you can ski and sled in; our usual winter precipitation is a conglomeration called "wintry mix," involving ice pellets, frozen rain, and wind.

It wasn't even that cold—maybe thirty-five—but the wind was howling outside. I got up, dressed, ate some cereal, took a pill, and watched a bit of TV with Mom. I spent the morning procrastinating—I'd pull out my phone, start to text him, and then put it away. Then pull it out again, but no. Not yet. It never seemed like the right time. But of course, it never is the right time.

I remember after my dad died, for a while, it was both true and not true in my mind. For weeks, really, I could conjure him into being. I'd imagine him walking in, soaked in sweat, having finished mowing the lawn, and he'd try to hug me but I'd squirm out from his arms because even then sweat freaked me out.

Or I'd be in my room, lying on my stomach, reading a book, and I'd look over at the closed door and imagine him opening it, and then he would be in the room with me, and I'd be looking up at him as he knelt down to kiss the top of my head.

And then it became harder to summon him, to smell his smell, to feel him lifting me up. My father died suddenly, but also across the years. He was still dying, really—which meant I guess that he was still living, too.

People always talk like there's a bright line between imagination and memory, but there isn't, at least not for me. I remember what I've imagined and imagine what I remember.

I finally texted Davis just after noon: *We need to talk. Can you come over to my house today?*

He replied, *Nobody's here to look after Noah. Can you come over here?*

I need to talk to you alone, I wrote. I wanted Davis to have the choice whether or not to tell his brother.

I can be there at five thirty.

Thanks. See you then.

The day moved agonizingly slowly. I tried reading, texting Daisy, and watching TV, but nothing would make the time speed up. I wasn't sure whether life would be better frozen in this moment, or on the other side of the moment that was coming.

By four forty-five, I was reading in the living room while Mom paid bills. "Davis is coming over in a little bit," I told her.

"Okay. I've got a couple errands to run. You need anything at the grocery store?"

I shook my head.

"You feeling anxious?"

"Is there any way we can make a deal where I tell you when I have a mental health concern instead of you asking?"

"It's impossible for me not to worry, baby."

"I know, but it's also impossible not to feel the weight of that worry like a boulder on my chest."

"I'll try."

"Thanks, Mom. I love you."

"I love you, too. So much."

I scrolled through my endless TV options, none of them particularly compelling, until I heard Davis's knock—soft and unsteady—on the door.

"Hey," I said, and hugged him.

"Hey," he said. I motioned to the couch for him to sit down. "How've you been?"

"Listen," I said. "Davis, your dad. I know where the jogger's mouth is. It's the mouth of Pogue's Run, where the company had that unfinished project."

He winced, then nodded. "You're sure?"

"Pretty sure," I said. "I think he might be down there. Daisy and I were there last night, and . . ."

"Did you see him?"

I shook my head. "No. But the run's mouth, the jogger's mouth. It makes sense."

"It's just a note from his phone, though. You think he's just been down there this whole time? Hiding in a sewer?"

"Maybe," I said. "But . . . well, I don't know."

"But?"

"I don't want to worry you, but there was a bad smell. A really bad smell down there."

"That could've been anything," he said. But I could see the fear on his face.

"I know, yeah, totally, it could be anything."

"I never thought . . . I never let myself think—" And then his voice caught. The cry that finally came out of him felt like the sky ripping open. He sort of fell into me, and I held him on the couch. Felt his rib cage heave. It wasn't only Noah who missed his father. "Oh God, he's dead, isn't he?"

"You don't know that," I said. But he kind of did. There was a reason there had been no trail and no communication: He'd been gone all along.

He lay down and I lay down with him, the two of us barely fitting on the musty couch. He kept saying *what do I do, what do I do*, his head on my shoulder. I wondered whether it was a mistake to tell him. *What do I do?* He asked it again and again, pleading.

"You keep going," I told him. "You've got seven years. No matter what actually happened, he'll be legally alive for seven years, and you'll have the house and everything. That's a long time to build a new life, Davis. Seven years ago, you and I hadn't even met, you know?"

"We've got nobody now," he mumbled. I wished I could tell him that he had me, that he could count on me, but he couldn't.

"You have your brother," I said.

That made him split open again, and we cuddled together for a long time, until Mom came home with the groceries. Davis and I both jumped to a seating position, even though we hadn't been doing anything.

"Sorry to interrupt," Mom said.

"I was just headed out," Davis said.

"You don't have to," Mom and I said simultaneously.

"I kinda do," he said. He leaned over and hugged me with one arm. "Thank you," he whispered, although I wasn't sure I'd done him any favors.

Davis stopped at the doorway for a second, looked back at Mom and me in what must have seemed to him like domestic bliss. I thought he might say something, but he just waved, shyly and awkwardly, and disappeared out the front door.

It was a quiet night in the Holmes household. Could've been any night, really. I worked on a paper about the Civil War for history class. Outside, the day—which had never been particularly bright—dissolved into darkness. I told Mom I was going to sleep, changed into pajamas, brushed my teeth, changed the Band-Aid over the scab on my fingertip, crawled into bed, and texted Davis. *Hi.*

When he didn't reply, I wrote Daisy. *Talked to Davis.*

Her: *How'd it go?*

Me: *Not great.*

Her: *Want me to come over?*

Me: *Yeah.*

Her: *On my way.*

An hour later, Daisy and I were lying next to each other on my bed, computers on our stomachs. I was reading the new Ayala story. Every time I giggled at something, she'd say, "What's funny?" and I'd tell her. After I finished it, we just lay there, in bed together, staring up at the ceiling.

"Well," Daisy said after a while, "it all worked out in the end."

"How's that?"

"Our heroes got rich and nobody got hurt."

"*Everyone* got hurt," I pointed out.

"What I mean is that no one got *injured*."

"I lacerated my liver!"

"Oh, right. I forgot about that. At least no one died."

"Harold died! And possibly Pickett!"

"Holmesy, I am trying to have a happy ending here. Stop screwing it up for me."

"I'm so Ayala," I answered.

"*So* Ayala."

"The problem with happy endings," I said, "is that they're either not really happy, or not really endings, you know? In real life, some things get better and some things get worse. And then eventually you die."

Daisy laughed. "As always, Aza 'And Then Eventually You Die' Holmes is here to remind you of how the story really ends, with the extinction of our species."

I laughed. "Well, that is the only real ending, though."

"No, it's not, Holmesy. You pick your endings, and your beginnings. You get to pick the frame, you know? Maybe you don't choose what's in the picture, but you decide on the frame."

Davis never wrote me back, not even after I texted him a few days later. But he did update his blog.

> "And, like the baseless fabric of this vision, / The cloud-capp'd towers, the gorgeous palaces, / The solemn temples, the great globe itself, / Yea, all which it inherit, shall dissolve / And, like this insubstantial pageant faded, / Leave not a rack behind."
>
> —WILLIAM SHAKESPEARE
>
> I get that nothing lasts. But why do I have to miss everybody so much?

TWENTY-FOUR

A MONTH LATER, just after Christmas vacation ended, I got up early and poured a couple bowls of cereal for Mom and me. I was eating in front of the TV when she walked in, still wearing pajamas, flustered. "Late late late," she said. "Hit snooze too many times."

"I made you breakfast," I told her, and when she joined me on the couch, she said, "Cheerios aren't something you *make*." I laughed as she took a few bites, then ran off to get dressed. Always a flurry of movement, my mother.

When I turned back to the TV, a red breaking news band was scrolling across the bottom of the screen. I saw a reporter standing in front of the gates of the Pickett compound. I fumbled for the remote and unmuted the TV.

"Our sources indicate that while Pickett has not been

positively identified, authorities believe the body found in an offshoot of the Pogue's Run tunnel is indeed that of billionaire construction magnate Russell Davis Pickett, Sr. One source close to the investigation told Eyewitness News that Pickett likely died of exposure within quote 'a few days' of his disappearance, and while we have no official confirmation, several sources tell us that Pickett's body was discovered by police after an anonymous tip."

I texted Davis immediately. *Just saw the news. I'm so sorry, Davis. I know I've said that to you a lot, but I am. I'm just so sorry.*

He didn't reply right away, so I added, *I want you to know it wasn't Daisy or me who tipped off the cops. We never said anything to anyone.*

Now I saw the . . . of his typing. *I know. It was us. Noah and I decided together.*

Mom came in, putting earrings in while slipping on her shoes. She must've overheard the last bit of the story, because she said, "Aza, you should reach out to Davis. This is going to be a very hard day for him."

"I was just texting him," I said. "They were the ones who told the cops where to look."

"Can you imagine, that whole estate is going to a lizard?" They could've waited seven years, at least, before Pickett was declared dead—seven more years of that house, seven more years of getting anything they wanted—but they'd decided to let it go to a tuatara.

"I guess they couldn't leave their dad down there," I said. "Maybe I shouldn't have told him about the jogger's mouth." This was, after all, my fault. An icy dread passed over me. I'd forced them to choose between abandoning their father and abandoning their lives.

"Be kind to yourself," Mom said. "Obviously knowing the truth mattered more to him than the house, and it's not like he'll be thrown out onto the streets, Aza."

I tried to listen to her, but the undeniable feeling had sprung up in me. For a moment I tried to resist, but only a moment. I slipped off the Band-Aid and dug my nail into the callus of my finger, opening up a cut where the previous one had finally healed.

As I washed and rebandaged it in the bathroom, I stared at myself. I would always be like this, always have this within me. There was no beating it. I would never slay the dragon, because the dragon was also me. My self and the disease were knotted together for life.

I was thinking about Davis's journal, of that Frost quote, "In three words I can sum up everything I've learned about life—it goes on."

And you go on, too, when the current is with you and when it isn't. Or at least that's what I whispered wordlessly to myself. Before I left the bathroom, I texted him again. *Can we hang out sometime?*

I saw the . . . appear, but he never replied.

"We should get going," Mom said. I opened the bathroom door, pulled a jacket and a knit hat from the coatrack, and entered our frigid garage. I shimmied my fingertips under the garage door, lifted it up, and sat down in the passenger seat while Mom finished making her morning coffee. I kept looking at my phone, waiting for his reply. I was cold but sweating, the sweat soaking into my ski hat. I thought of Davis, hearing his own name on the news again. *You go on*, I told myself, and tried through the ether to say it to him, too.

Over the next few months, I kept going. I got better without ever quite getting well. Daisy and I started a Mental Health Alliance and a Fan-Fiction Workshop so that we could list some proper extracurriculars on next year's college applications, even though we were the only two members of both clubs. We hung out most nights, at her apartment or at Applebee's or at my house, sometimes with Mychal but usually not—usually it was just the two of us, watching movies or doing homework or just talking. It was so easy to go out into the meadow with her.

I missed Davis, of course. The first few days, I kept checking my phone, waiting for him to reply, but slowly I understood that we were going to be part of each other's past. I still missed him, though. I missed my dad, too. And Harold. I missed everybody. To be alive is to be missing.

And then one night in April, Daisy and I were over at my house, watching the one-night-only reunion of our favorite band, who were performing at some third-tier music awards show. They'd just brilliantly lip-synced their way through "It's Gotta Be You," when someone knocked. It was almost eleven o'clock, too late for visitors, and I felt a shiver of nerves as I opened the door.

It was Davis, wearing a plaid button-down and skinny jeans. He was holding a huge box.

"Um, hi," I said.

"This is for you," he told me, and handed me the box, which wasn't as heavy as I expected. I carried it inside and placed it on our dining room table, and when I turned back, he was already walking away.

"Wait," I said. "Come here." I reached my hand out for his. He took it, and we walked together into my backyard. The river was swollen, and you could hear it churning down there in the darkness somewhere. The air felt warm on the skin of my forearms as I lay down on the ground beneath the big ash tree in our backyard. He lay down next to me, and I showed him what the sky looked like from my house, all split up by the branches that were just beginning to sprout leaves.

He told me that he and Noah were moving, to Colorado, where Noah had gotten into some boarding school for troubled kids. Davis would finish high school out there, at a public school. They'd rented a house. "It's smaller than our current place," he said. "But on the other hand, no tuatara."

He asked me how I was doing, and I told him that I felt okay much of the time. Four weeks between visits to Dr. Singh now.

"So when are you leaving?" I asked him.

"Tomorrow," he said, and that killed the conversation for a while.

"Okay, so," I said at last, "what am I looking at?"

He laughed a little. "Well, you've got Jupiter up there, of course. Very bright tonight. And there's Arcturus." He squirmed a bit to turn around and pointed toward another part of the sky. "And there's the Big Dipper, and if you follow the line of those two stars, right there, that's Polaris, the North Star."

"Why'd you tell the cops to look down there?" I asked.

"It was eating Noah up, not knowing. I realized . . . I guess I realized I had to be a big brother, you know? That's my full-time occupation now. That's who I am. And he needed to know why his father wasn't in touch with him more than he needed all the money, so that's what we did."

I reached down and squeezed his hand. "You're a good brother."

He nodded. I could see in the gray light that he was crying a little. "Thanks," he said. "I kind of just want to stay here in this particular instant for a really long time."

"Yeah," I said.

We settled into a silence, and I felt the sky's bigness above me, the unimaginable vastness of it all—looking at Polaris and realizing the light I was seeing was 425 years old, and then looking at Jupiter, less than a light-hour from us. In the moonless darkness, we were just witnesses to light, and I felt a sliver of what must have driven Davis to astronomy. There was a kind of relief in having your own smallness laid bare before you, and I realized something Davis must have already known: Spirals grow infinitely small the farther you follow them inward, but they also grow infinitely large the farther you follow them out.

And I knew I would remember that feeling, underneath the split-up sky, back before the machinery of fate ground us into one thing or another, back when we could still be everything.

I thought, lying there, that I might love him for the rest of my life. We did love each other—maybe we never said it, and maybe love was never something we were in, but it was something I felt. I loved him, and I thought, maybe I will never see him again, and I'll be stuck missing him, and isn't that so terrible.

But it turns out not to be terrible, because I know the secret that the me lying beneath that sky could not imagine: I know that girl would go on, that she would grow up, have children and love them, that despite loving them she would get too sick to care for them, be hospitalized, get better, and then get sick again. I know a shrink would say, *Write it down, how you got here.*

So you would, and in writing it down you realize, love is not a tragedy or a failure, but a gift.

You remember your first love because they show you, prove to you, that you can love and be loved, that nothing in this world is deserved except for love, that love is both how you become a person, and why.

But underneath those skies, your hand—no, my hand—no, our hand—in his, you don't know yet. You don't know that the spiral painting is in that box on your dining room table, with a Post-it note stuck to the back of the frame: *Stole this from a lizard for you.—D.* You can't know yet how that painting will follow you from one apartment to another and then eventually to a house, or how decades later, you'll be so proud that Daisy continues to be your best friend, that growing into different lives only makes you more fiercely loyal to each other. You don't know that you'd go to college, find a job, make a life, see it unbuilt and rebuilt.

I, a singular proper noun, would go on, if always in a conditional tense.

But you don't know any of that yet. We squeeze his hand. He squeezes back. You stare up at the same sky together, and after a while he says, *I have to go*, and you say, *Good-bye*, and he says, *Good-bye, Aza*, and no one ever says good-bye unless they want to see you again.

ACKNOWLEDGMENTS

I'd first like to thank Sarah Urist Green, who read many, many, many versions of this story with immense thoughtfulness and generosity. Thanks also to Chris and Marina Waters; my brother, Hank, and sister-in-law, Katherine; my parents, Sydney and Mike Green; my in-laws, Connie and Marshall Urist; and Henry and Alice Green.

Julie Strauss-Gabel has been my editor for more than fifteen years now, and I will never be able to adequately express my gratitude for the faith and wisdom she showed during the six years we spent working together on this book. Thanks also to Anne Heausler for kind and contentious copyediting, and to the entire team at Dutton, especially Anna Booth, Melissa Faulner, Rosanne Lauer, Steve Meltzer, and Natalie Vielkind.

I am profoundly indebted to Elyse Marshall, friend and publicist and confidante and fellow traveler, and to many people at Penguin Random House who've helped to make my books and share them with readers. I want to especially thank Jen Loja, Felicia Frazier, Jocelyn Schmidt, Adam Royce, Stephanie Sabol, Emily Romero, Erin Berger, Helen Boomer, Leigh Butler, Kimberly Ryan, Deborah Kaplan, and Lindsey Andrews. Thanks as well to Don Weisberg, and to the brilliant Rosianna Halse Rojas, whose insight and guidance informed every page of this book.

Ariel Bissett, Meredith Danko, Hayley Hoover, Zulaiha Razak, and Tara Covais Varsov read drafts of this manuscript with great care and thoughtfulness. Joanna Cardenas provided invaluable insight and feedback. And for all kinds of help, thanks to Ilene Cooper, Bill Ott, Amy Krouse Rosenthal, Rainbow Rowell, Stan Muller, and Marlene Reeder.

Jodi Reamer and Kassie Evashevski, agents extraordinaire, are the best advocates an author could hope for—and also the most patient. Thanks to Phil Plait for astronomy help; E. K. Johnston for Star Wars expertise; Ed Yong for his book *I Contain Multitudes*; David Adam for his book *The Man Who Couldn't Stop*; Elaine Scarry for her book *The Body in Pain*; Stuart Hyatt for introducing me to Pogue's Run; and to James Bell, Michala Irons, Tim Riffle, Lea Shaver, and Shannon James for their legal expertise. With all that noted, geography, the law, power converters, the night sky, and everything else in this novel are imagined and treated fictitiously, and any mistakes are entirely my own.

Lastly, Dr. Joellen Hosler and Dr. Sunil Patel have made my life immeasurably better by providing the kind of high-quality mental health care that unfortunately remains out of reach for too many. My family and I are grateful. If you need mental health services in the United States, please call the SAMHSA treatment referral helpline: 1-877-SAMHSA7. It can be a long and difficult road, but mental illness is treatable. There is hope, even when your brain tells you there isn't.

A READERS GUIDE TO

TURTLES ALL THE WAY DOWN

JOHN GREEN

A CONVERSATION WITH JOHN GREEN

***Turtles All the Way Down* vividly conveys the experience of being inside Aza's head—even for those who do not personally deal with OCD and anxiety. What was it like bringing that experience to the page?**

It was hard! I always feel bad complaining about writing, because writing is much easier than most jobs, but being with Aza in her pain was definitely challenging for me.

I think we often approach psychic pain through metaphor or simile. We can say what the pain is *like*—it's like a knife stabbing the mind, like a blizzard, like a blankness descending upon us. But something is always lost in the process of metaphor making. You lose the immediacy of the pain, and the true terror of it. In writing this story, I wanted to find some kind of direct form of expression for Aza's torment, so that readers could glimpse not just what her pain is like, but what her pain *is*.

You've been very open about your own anxiety and obsessive-compulsive disorder and have been an advocate for those with mental illness. What were the challenges of crafting a protagonist with a disorder similar to yours?

I had to write with enough distance from myself to feel safe, and so Aza has different foci of her obsessive concerns and different behaviors she uses to manage them. It was uncomfortable, especially at first, to write about this thing that's been such a big part of my life. But in other ways, writing was helpful. It can be really isolating to live with mental illness, not least because it's so hard to explain to people around you what's going on, and I wrote the book partly because I wanted to give people in my life a sense of how obsessive thought spirals can consume one's consciousness.

Throughout the book, you emphasize the idea that there's no magical cure for mental illness. Why was it important to you to convey that message?

We really like stories that involve conquering obstacles and overcoming adversity. I love those stories too. But that hasn't been my experience with mental illness, and I didn't really want it to be Aza's. For me, it's not something I expect to defeat in my life. It's not like a battle I expect to win. It's something I expect to live with. I wanted Aza to find a path toward a rich and fulfilling life without experiencing some miracle cure.

How does this book fit into the current conversation about mental health?

That's for readers to decide, not me! I do think progress has been made in destigmatizing mental illness, but there's still a long way to go. I'm not an expert, and I'm definitely not a psychologist, but in my experience, stigmatization can compound the isolating effects of psychic pain. I remember how alone I felt in it in high school and it was a big part of what made my overwhelming fear so difficult to bear.

In the acknowledgments, you refer to Ed Yong's book *I Contain Multitudes*. How did that book influence *Turtles*—or your own thinking in general?

That book was so helpful to me. Aza's thinking around microbes is obviously irrational, but she's right that we are inundated with microscopic life, and that humans are by cell count about 50 percent microbial. Reading *I Contain Multitudes*, I kept thinking about how bacteria really do shape who we are—they affect our health, but they also communicate with our brain through the gut-brain information axis. They seem to tell us what kind of foods to crave, and our microbiomes may even be linked to anxiety and major depression. So, a lot of *Turtles All the Way Down* came out of reading that book and thinking about the relationship between "self" and these beings within us that aren't us.

The epigraph at the beginning of *Turtles All the Way Down* is from the philosopher Arthur Schopenhauer, "Man can do what he wills / but he cannot will what he wills." Why is that quote meaningful for you?

That's my experience of being a person. Like, I am not worried about free will; I am worried about my inability to define my will.

In the book, Aza is really freaked out by the feeling that her thoughts seem to come from outside of her. If you can't choose your thoughts, then who exactly are you? Who's running the ship here? Am I really the captain of my consciousness, or are outside forces shaping my self so completely that "I" don't really exist as a sovereign thing? For Aza, that's not an abstract question of mere philosophy; it really is critical to her survival that she find a way to imagine herself as a coherent, integrated self despite the fact that many of her thoughts do not feel like they are hers.

Aza shares a last name with Sherlock Holmes. *Turtles All the Way Down* begins with a mystery—the disappearance of a famous billionaire. Were you inspired by the famous detective?

I loved Sherlock Holmes growing up (and still do). But as a person who struggles with obsessiveness, I find it odd that Sherlock's obsessiveness is often linked to his powers of observation. That may be true to some people's experiences, but in my case, obsessiveness makes me a terrible detective, because when I'm unwell I struggle to apprehend anything about the world outside my self. (For that matter, I also find it difficult to accurately or rationally assess what's happening inside of my self as well.) So I wanted to write a mystery where the detective's brain disorder is distinctly unhelpful—not just preventing her from solving the mystery, but also hijacking the plot itself.

What inspired you to use the "turtles all the way down" story as a metaphor for Aza's experience?

I love that story first because so often when I am caught in an obsessive thought spiral, I am looking for the bottom turtle, for some *certainty* that will allow me to cinch shut my worries. But there is no bottom turtle, because it's turtles all the way down!

When Aza and Daisy discuss the story in the book, they're focused on something else, though—the ways that the old woman is right. The world is the stories we tell about it. Those stories shape the actual world, and they shape our actual lives. And so we must be careful which stories we tell ourselves, and which stories we share.

Aza and Daisy have a great friendship. You deeply explore the love of self and the love between friends and family in the novel. Why is this important?

I wanted to write about all the different kinds of love that can sustain and support you. I think one learns to imagine one's self as a singular noun in part through loving and being loved. I wanted to explore how that happens—through romantic love, but also through other loves. Romantic love is really important for a lot of people, but it's not the only kind of love that matters. When I was in high school, it was the love of my friends that got me through.

How did you approach writing about Aza's mom? Has being a parent affected your writing?

I think as parents, we desperately want to take pain away from our kids, and we want to—I want to save my kids from all the hurt that the world has in it. And you can't. And that's so difficult. It's so hard to reconcile yourself to that. If Aza has to learn to live with her pain, Aza's mom has to learn that she can't take it away.

In general, I have become much more interested in parents as characters since I became a parent. Like, I used to shuffle all the adults out of my books as quickly as possible. And now I'm like, "Hold on. Let's listen to your mother for a minute. She might have a point here."

QUESTIONS FOR DISCUSSION

1. John Green's depiction of Aza's mental health is different from what is often seen in literature and other media. How does *Turtles All the Way Down* change the way you think about mental health?

2. The *San Francisco Chronicle* said, "Green finds language to describe the indescribable." What is the significance of having language to understand Aza's experience? How does finding a vocabulary for the indescribable help people to connect?

3. Aza's mental illness means it's hard for her to see outside herself, which doesn't always make her a good friend. How does that impact Daisy?

4. Was it a betrayal for Daisy to have created Ayala in her fan fiction as an outlet for her frustrations with Aza? Would Aza have been able to understand Daisy's resentments if confronted with them directly?

5. Aza says, "Of course, you pretend to be the author. You have to . . . You think you're the painter, but you're the canvas." As readers, we know Aza is narrating her own story. Once we start to tell our own stories, are we fictionalizing ourselves?

6. Davis and Aza have both lost a parent. How have they each processed grief? How does that common experience impact their relationship?

7. Harold, the car that once belonged to her father, and her father's phone hold a lot of emotional significance for Aza. Why does interacting with those objects make Aza feel close to him?

8. Several characters in the novel process their emotions through fiction and poetry. If you were to use a quote from this novel to begin an essay about your life, which would it be and why? What other literary quotes are particularly resonant for you?

9. Daisy tells Aza, "Your privileges are just oxygen to you." Money and privilege are central to the novel. How does economic status color each character's experiences and decisions? Their understanding of themselves and others?

10. The last few paragraphs of *Turtles All the Way Down* zoom out to reframe Aza's time perspective of her own story. How does this shift change the way you think about Aza? How does it change the way you think about mental illness?

11. Daisy says, "You pick your endings, and your beginnings. You get to pick the frame, you know? Maybe you don't choose what's in the picture, but you decide on the frame." What does that mean to you?

12. The title, *Turtles All the Way Down*, refers to a theory of the universe. Aza and Daisy interpret this idea in different ways. How do you interpret Daisy's story?

MARINA WATERS

JOHN GREEN is the author of *Looking for Alaska*; *An Abundance of Katherines*; *Paper Towns*; *Will Grayson, Will Grayson* (with David Levithan); and *The Fault in Our Stars*. His books have received many accolades, including a Printz Medal, a Printz Honor, and an Edgar Award. John has twice been a finalist for the *LA Times* Book Prize and was selected by *TIME* magazine as one of the 100 Most Influential People in the World. With his brother, Hank, John has co-created many online video projects, including Vlogbrothers and the educational channel Crash Course. He lives with his family in Indianapolis, Indiana.

You can visit John online at **johngreenbooks.com**

Looking for Alaska

WINNER OF THE MICHAEL L. PRINTZ AWARD
A LOS ANGELES TIMES BOOK PRIZE FINALIST • A *NEW YORK TIMES* BESTSELLER • A *USA TODAY* BESTSELLER • A PBS GREAT AMERICAN READ SELECTION OF AMERICA'S 100 MOST-LOVED NOVELS • NPR'S TOP TEN BEST-EVER TEEN NOVELS • *TIME* MAGAZINE'S 100 BEST YOUNG ADULT NOVELS OF ALL TIME

Miles Halter is fascinated by famous last words—and tired of his safe life at home. He leaves for boarding school to seek what the dying poet François Rabelais called "The Great Perhaps." Much awaits Miles at Culver Creek, including Alaska Young, who will pull Miles into her labyrinth and catapult him into the Great Perhaps.

Looking for Alaska brilliantly chronicles the indelible impact one life can have on another. A modern classic, this stunning debut marked #1 bestselling author John Green's arrival as a groundbreaking new voice in contemporary fiction.

"A gem of modern literature."
—*GUARDIAN*

★ "What sings and soars in this gorgeously told tale is Green's mastery of language and the sweet, rough edges of Pudge's voice."
—*KIRKUS*

PB: 978-0-14-240251-1 • HC: 978-0-525-47506-4

An Abundance of Katherines

A MICHAEL L. PRINTZ HONOR BOOK • A LOS ANGELES TIMES BOOK PRIZE FINALIST • A *NEW YORK TIMES* BESTSELLER

When it comes to relationships, Colin Singleton's type is girls named Katherine. And when it comes to girls named Katherine, Colin is always getting dumped. Nineteen times, to be exact. On a road trip miles from home, this anagram-happy, washed-up child prodigy has ten thousand dollars in his pocket, a bloodthirsty feral hog on his trail, and an overweight, Judge Judy–loving best friend riding shotgun—but no Katherines. Colin is on a mission to prove The Theorem of Underlying Katherine Predictability, which he hopes will predict the future of any relationship, avenge Dumpees everywhere, and finally win him the girl. Love, friendship, and a dead Austro-Hungarian archduke add up to surprising and heart-changing conclusions in this ingeniously layered comic novel about reinventing oneself.

★ "Fully fun, challengingly complex and entirely entertaining."
—*KIRKUS*

★ "Laugh-out-loud funny . . . a coming-of-age American road trip that is at once a satire of and tribute to its many celebrated predecessors."
—*HORN BOOK*

PB: 978-0-14-241070-7 • HC: 978-0-525-47688-7

Paper Towns

WINNER OF THE EDGAR AWARD FOR BEST YOUNG ADULT MYSTERY
#1 *NEW YORK TIMES* BESTSELLER • A *USA TODAY* BESTSELLER

When Margo Roth Spiegelman beckons Quentin Jacobsen in the middle of the night—dressed like a ninja and plotting an ingenious campaign of revenge—he follows her. Margo's always planned extravagantly, and, until now, she's always planned solo. After a lifetime of loving Margo from afar, things are finally looking up for Q. . . until day breaks and she has vanished. Always an enigma, Margo has now become a mystery. But there are clues. And they're for Q.

★ "Green's prose is astounding—from hilarious, hyperintellectual trash talk and shtick, to complex philosophizing, to devastating observation and truths. . . . Profoundly moving."
—SLJ

★ "Stellar, with deliciously intelligent dialogue and plenty of mind-twisting insights . . . a powerfully great read."
—VOYA

PB: 978-0-14-241493-4 • HC: 978-0-525-47818-8

The Fault in Our Stars

***TIME* MAGAZINE'S #1 FICTION BOOK OF THE YEAR**
A *TODAY SHOW* BOOK CLUB PICK • #1 *NEW YORK TIMES* BESTSELLER
#1 *WALL STREET JOURNAL* BESTSELLER • #1 *USA TODAY* BESTSELLER
#1 INTERNATIONAL BESTSELLER

Despite the tumor-shrinking medical miracle that has bought her a few years, Hazel has never been anything but terminal, her final chapter inscribed upon diagnosis. But when a gorgeous plot twist named Augustus Waters suddenly appears at Cancer Kid Support Group, Hazel's story is about to be completely rewritten.

Insightful, bold, irreverent, and raw, *The Fault in Our Stars* brilliantly explores the funny, thrilling, and tragic business of being alive and in love.

"Damn near genius . . . *The Fault in Our Stars* is a love story, one of the most genuine and moving ones in recent American fiction, but it's also an existential tragedy of tremendous intelligence and courage and sadness."
—LEV GROSSMAN, *TIME* MAGAZINE

"The greatest romance story of this decade."
—ENTERTAINMENT WEEKLY

"This is a book that breaks your heart—not by wearing it down, but by making it bigger until it bursts."
—ATLANTIC

★ "In its every aspect, this novel is a triumph."
—BOOKLIST

PB: 978-0-14-242417-9 • HC: 978-0-525-47881-2

CRITICAL ACCLAIM FOR

TURTLES ALL THE WAY DOWN

A *New York Times* Notable Book • A *New York Times* Critics' Top Book of the Year • An NPR Best Book of the Year • A *TIME* Best Book of the Year • A *Wall Street Journal* Best Book of the Year • A *Boston Globe* Best Book of the Year • An *Entertainment Weekly* Best Book of the Year • A *Seventeen* Best Book of the Year • A *Southern Living* Best Book of the Year • A *Publishers Weekly* Best Book of the Year • A *Booklist* Editors' Choice Selection • A *BookPage* Best Book of the Year • An *SLJ* Best Book of the Year • An A.V. Club Best Book of the Year • A Bustle Best Book of the Year • A BuzzFeed Best Book of the Year • A PopSugar Best Book of the Year • A Vulture Best Book of the Year

#1 *New York Times* Bestseller

#1 *Wall Street Journal* Bestseller

#1 Indie Bestseller

#1 International Bestseller

Featured on *60 Minutes, Fresh Air, Studio 360, Good Morning America, The TODAY Show*

"So surprising and moving and true that I became completely unstrung, incapable of reading it to my husband without breaking down. One needn't be suffering like Aza to identify with it. One need only be human. Everyone, at some point, knows what it's like when the mind develops a mind of its own."
—Jennifer Senior, *THE NEW YORK TIMES*

"There is tenderness and wisdom here, and a high quotient of big ideas." ***—THE WALL STREET JOURNAL***

★ "A teenage romance in which the love story is more about loving yourself than another; it is an incredibly powerful tale of the pain of mental illness, the pressures of youth and coming of age when you feel like you're coming undone."
—SHELF AWARENESS